WHEN THE MOON TURNS FULL OVER VALHALLA

Thyri locked the door of her cabin with trembling fingers. She got the bottle that Kaerglen had given her. Whiskey, he had called it. She drank deep as the sharp pain began to stab at her.

It begins ... Thyri groaned. *Do you think of me, Astrid, when the moon turns full over Valhalla? Do you remember the woman ... or the wolf?*

The whiskey didn't help. Thyri's screams mixed with the wind, chilling the blood of the ship's crew. The first mate reached her door, tried to gain entrance.

"It's locked, Captain!"

The sound of wood giving way to bone split the air. Thyri's door flew open ...

Worlds of Fantasy from Avon Books

THE CHRONICLES OF THE TWELVE KINGDOMS
by Esther M. Friesner
MUSTAPHA AND HIS WISE DOG
SPELLS OF MORTAL WEAVING
THE WITCHWOOD CRADLE

FANTASISTS ON FANTASY
edited by Robert H. Boyer and Kenneth J. Zahorski

100 GREAT FANTASY SHORT SHORT STORIES
*edited by Isaac Asimov, Terry Carr,
and Martin H. Greenberg*

READER'S GUIDE TO FANTASY
*edited by Baird Searles, Beth Meacham,
and Michael Franklin*

UNICORN & DRAGON
(trade paperback)
by Lynn Abbey

WINDMASTER'S BANE
by Tom Deitz

Coming Soon

FIRESHAPER'S DOOM
by Tom Deitz

TALKING MAN
by Terry Bisson

Wolf-Dreams

Michael D. Weaver

 AVON
PUBLISHERS OF BARD, CAMELOT, DISCUS AND FLARE BOOKS

AVON BOOKS
A division of
The Hearst Corporation
1790 Broadway
New York, New York 10019

Copyright © 1987 by Michael D. Weaver
Cover illustration copyright © 1987 by Kevin Johnson
Published by arrangement with the author
Library of Congress Catalog Card Number: 86-91005
ISBN: 0-380-75198-4

First Avon Printing: May 1987

AVON TRADEMARK REG. U.S. PAT. OFF. AND IN OTHER COUNTRIES, MARCA REGISTRADA, HECHO EN U.S.A.

Printed in the U.S.A.

K–R   10 9 8 7 6 5 4 3 2 1

for Elric

Book I: YOUTH

My name is Gerald; I'm sure of that much now.

Earlier today, I turned the key to unlock the door to this chamber I had not entered in nearly a year. I admit, I entered the darkness only after an interminable period of time during which my will waged ruthless battle with my fears of this place. On the threshold of Hell, I thought then. In my mind, I imagined all the screams of the damned echoing silently, maliciously within these walls, waves of the most terrible sound kept at bay by the fragile dam of a single beating heart. My heart.

Somehow, my will forced me across to the room's sole window, and I threw open the shutters.

Everything should have been caked with dust, encrypted as it had been for so long. But no, it was as if time had stopped here. As if, within these walls, the passage of time is measured solely by my presence. My desk—all my work—as if I had left yesterday.

And the pool—Satan's Chalice, as I have come to think of it—lay still, its surface like a gleaming sheet of polished red metal.

The sun has long since set. I have worked by candlelight for many hours now, reading all that I previously wrote. What I once thought masterfully penned now seems flawed, disjointed, a shadow of what it might be. I will borrow from it and begin here a retelling of this tale which you have but begun to read but which I, in ways I will not yet reveal, have lived. Even though this is not *my* tale.

It belongs truly to Thyri Eiriksdattir, sometimes called Blood-fang.

21: Homecoming

The homeland was cooling and the summer leaves dying, beginning to fall. She liked the smell. It promised winter and a rest from the fighting—warm fires, warm mead, warm companionship. A cold wind blew from the north, and she tightened the sash of her cloak. She looked at Astrid, who rode next to her, her gaze distant, her lips curled slightly in an unthinking, natural smile born of simple contentment, a smile at peace with its mistress.

The autumn feastings were over, their tales all grown stale as the fact of another winter grew apparent. Two days ahead lay Thorfinnson land, the family homestead. They had both left it long before, but in recent years they had wintered there, away from Ragnar's army. It was home, peppered with lazy, comfortable memories: the touch of walls touched since memory began, visions of Mother's young beauty and Father's unfilled early beard, smells of family brews and family cooking. Thyri had no more argument with it than Astrid.

They rode silently, stopping at noon to eat. They didn't speak: they rarely did when alone—they knew each other far too well. Thyri could usually tell what her cousin was thinking by watching her eyes, her smile.

A thick bank of clouds blocked the sun's cold light as the afternoon progressed. Thyri thought of winter again: not so long now. Another year of war and bloodshed had ended. In the cold, no one would fight. The sword bows to ice.

The sky cleared before the pale northern sun sank below the horizon. Streamers of delicate, fibrous light washed down from the north like a false otherworld dawn, filling the night with an eerie brilliance. The moon had already risen. The land hardly darkened, and they continued to ride. The night air was fresh, and Thyri realized how different it felt to be away from the heady smells of Ragnar's drinking hall. She retreated again into hazy, pleasant thoughts, losing time itself until her horse balked, drawing her outward.

Astrid had stopped. Thyri listened to the wood, hearing naught but a lone owl's hooting in the distance. *Men?* They had passed the last homestead near dusk, and none but the king laid claim to the stretch of land they currently crossed. It was too rocky, too treacherous for crops. Soon, the winter would make even the road impassable with neck-deep snows concealing crevices and encroaching roots. In the spring it would be worse as the forest reclaimed its own. Few traveled here. In time, Thyri guessed, there would be no road at all. Ragnar had carved it during the early years of his reign while repelling invaders from farther north. Now he had the ships to move his men in proper Viking style.

Astrid dismounted, drawing her sword. Moonlight streamed onto it, caressing strange purples and blues from runes near the hilt. The blade rose like a flame from her silver gauntlet.

Loki whinnied and Thyri leaned forward to stroke his neck. She drew her sword—a sister to her cousin's. Moving slowly, she took the reins of both mounts in her free hand and whispered happy things in their ears. Then the silence pressed in on her; even the distant owl had stopped. Wolves, she thought. The wind came from the north still—no predators in the wood there or the horses couldn't be calmed. She concentrated on the trees to the south and Astrid's progress west, up the road.

After fifty paces, Astrid paused. She retrieved a dark object from the ground and started back. Her face was grim. In her hand was a bloodied boot. She held it out to Thyri. One long red strip of flesh dangled from the top.

"He was horsed," Astrid said. "His mount panicked and turned back for home."

A thin crescent was imprinted in the boot's leather. Thyri gasped.

"Yrsa's mark!"

"My sister's work has traveled far from home," Astrid said, her eyes searching the forest to the left of the road. "It went north."

"Just one animal?"

Astrid nodded.

"Why didn't it go for his horse?"

Astrid shrugged and attached the boot to her saddle. "It dragged the rest of the man away," she said, mounting. "If it has tasted human blood, it will desire it again. We should catch it before we make camp."

They followed the trail of blood into the forest. The size of the wolf's paw prints disturbed Thyri but she said nothing; Astrid had eyes of her own. The procession through the trees themselves made her uneasy; the silence was unnatural, and she sensed something watching them, something dark and hiding from her scanning eyes. The short search ended in a pulpy mass of bone, gore, and small bits of flesh.

We should have found it still feeding, Thyri thought, eyeing the mess detachedly. Darker thoughts rose up: *We should have found it among a pack.* One wolf could hardly cast such a spell of silence over Nature.

Overhead, the clouds had returned. Tracking grew more difficult. As they turned to follow the wolf's tracks, it began to snow. A glade away and the visible trail lost, they dismounted. They still had its scent. They could continue on foot or simply wait and draw it to them. Whatever it was, it was canny. Better to meet it in the open, without branches hindering swordplay. Thyri untied a flask of ale from her saddle and paced across the glade, drinking thoughtfully.

Astrid stood by the horses, sword in hand, staring moodily into the trees. "It is close," she said, tucking a slender braid of forty-two knots behind her right ear. "It has been close all along."

Thyri took the flask from her lips, wiping her chin with the back of her gauntleted hand. She nodded absently.

Astrid touched her mount's ear. "Stay alert, Yrafax. You let us know if—"

She stopped, shifting the grip on her sword. Yrafax tensed and pawed at the hard ground. He neighed, then bucked.

Thyri looked up. Astrid's gaze followed. A white shadow in the trees fluttered and blurred, streaking toward her. She whirled away from it, her sword swinging around, tearing shallowly along its side.

Spray of blood, Thyri noted. No phantom but mortal. *It bleeds.* Ale forgotten, she crossed half the glade while the wolf landed and turned, striking at Astrid again with blinding speed. Thyri saw all in acute detail: sword point parting moist white fur, blade glinting as it sheathed itself between ribs and angled for the heart while the beast writhed into the attack, fangs dripping and eyes blazing with a fire too intense and furious to be of this world. Wolf, Astrid, drawing closer. Astrid falling back. Wolf embracing. Fangs on throat, tearing away flesh. Drops of blood, arcing slowly, relentlessly, through the air . . .

Astrid had missed its heart. Screaming, Thyri was on the wolf, driving her sword into its shoulder, spraying its blood over white fur and the ground's patchy carpet of powdery snow. It lashed out, grazing her thigh. She backed off, readying herself for a more thoughtful strike. Astrid's fall had unnerved her, spoiled her reasoning. She concentrated on the wolf. It snarled at her, its muzzle crimson. It leapt.

So huge, she thought. It's so impossibly huge. Keeping her sword steady, she threw her weight into the attack. The blade entered next to Astrid's. To reach its heart? She felt it smashing through the beast's ribs. Her boots gripped the ground, then slid for a moment before she fell with the wolf. All through the fall she watched her sword sinking into flesh, probing deeper, closer to *something* that had to be vital. Her back hit the ground—it still lived. Its hot breath struck her face. She shifted her shoulders, wrenching her blade to the side with all her strength and drenching herself in the thing's blood as she ripped its chest open.

Die, dammit! Die!

Pain flashed through her as fangs dug into her shoulder; then she wrenched her blade again, found at last the wolf's heart, and felt its weight crash lifelessly on top of her.

For a very long time, she could see nothing beyond Astrid's bloodied face and the gaping hole in her cousin's neck that had appeared so suddenly, so unbelievably fast. She cradled in her arms truly half of her life, a part of her that the best swords of the North could not have taken in fair combat.

She felt fear rising within—irrational, a terrible feeling that all her past, all her life, was a lie. How else could Astrid, who had not been *scratched* in combat in the past three years, have fallen with such lack of ceremony, with such ease? The panic gripped her, and she fought it with savage, primal fury. *A warrior cannot seriously flirt with any fear and expect to live.* Yet the wolf had killed her friend, cousin, and lover, and she could not believe it had happened. She lost herself, emptying thought, taming her churning emotions before allowing them to consume her. Grief and rage. If anyone or anything had come upon her then, she would have killed blindly, without thought. It was only when Yrafax stamped and snorted demoniacally that she became aware of more than her grief and Astrid's torn body.

She shot a fiery glance at the horse and snarled, then jerked her gaze in search of whatever had alerted him:

Where the wolf had fallen lay the bloodied corpse of a man. His chest was torn from side to side, and the rune-blades stood up in a V-shape from the wound that closed even as Thyri watched.

She laid Astrid gently on the grass, rose, and pulled the swords from the body. Its face grimaced. The man's features were gaunt and gnarled. Hauntingly pale skin sported a scraggly, two-day growth of beard.

Thyri screamed and brought Astrid's sword down across his stomach, cleaving through his spine and part of his hip. The upper torso flinched and went still.

Turning from him, she built a fire of the tent and bedding furs. She threw the halved body onto the small pyre and watched the flames enwrap it, then she lifted Astrid's body onto Yrafax and mounted her own horse. Tears still streaming down her cheeks, she set off for the road.

The night was long and full of ghosts. Astrid rode before her, draped across Yrafax's saddle. He somehow knew where to go; they reached the sacred vale just before dawn. It stretched out before her, crusted with wind-brushed snow. Staunch evergreens fringed its northern edge, some bent low and twisted from years of enduring winter gales. And below the hard ground: the dead of centuries past; ancestors whose lives had been spent laying claim to the unforgiving soil.

She spent the morning in the wood, slashing and hacking at a fallen tree, venting her grief while building a pyre for Astrid that stood to her shoulder. She made it wide and strong, driving its stakes deep into the ground. At one end she built a ramp of tilted logs. The last flurries of snow passed as the noon sun drew overhead. The clouds were breaking, and the snow on the ground dazzled in places with blinding brilliance. The horses lingered on the edge of the wood, scratching at the ground in search of clumps of still-green grass. Thyri called Yrafax to her.

He came, gazing at her with large brown eyes. She scratched his forehead. "You must follow my cousin," she said. "Keep her from harm, Yrafax."

She brought her sword around then, slashing through Yrafax's neck. Severed arteries sent streams of red across the snows. The horse's gaze remained fixed on Thyri's until his legs buckled and he collapsed, the impact raising clouds of powder that danced over him like spinning, glittering ghosts.

Harnessing herself like an ox, Thyri hauled the dead horse onto the pyre, the strain taxing her strength to its limits and igniting fiery agony in her wounds. She lay, after that, next to Astrid —resting, weeping anew. Then she placed Astrid carefully on the pyre and arranged her lover's cloak, trying in vain for a while to scratch stains of blood from the green cloth. In the field, among her ancestors, she chose a spot and dug out a wide plot a foot in depth. In late afternoon she set fire to the pyre and watched it burn.

The ashes she scattered in the grave under moonlight. Before covering them with a low mound of dirt, Thyri laid Astrid's rune-sword over the charred, flame-shattered fragments of Astrid's bones.

"Serve the gods well, my love," she whispered. She filled the grave. Standing back, she screamed wordlessly at the night, her fingers probing the swollen, throbbing holes in her shoulder.

She drew her hand away, looked at the blood, and shivered. She felt— I don't know—the dead buried in that sacred vale reaching out to her? Or her own fears animating the death of that place in her mind? The feeling, whatever it was, wasn't pleasant.

She was twenty-one that night, though she was hardly innocent or unpracticed. She had survived four campaign seasons, and she had risen to share with Astrid the command of a Viking longship.

10: Changes

Thyri's tale. It begins with the woman, but the woman begins in the girl.

The crops had taken and flourished, heralding summer. She ran through the wood, feeling the crush of soft leaves under her feet. Her nose filled with a scent of burning pork; the wind blew it from where Gyda, her mother, offered up parts of their dinner to Thor and Freyja. *Freyja to feed us, Thor to protect.* It was the way—so said her father. Thyri ran until the smell was gone and only those of the trees, the flowers, and the sun on the moss remained.

She had a spot by a bubbling stream where she liked to go alone, to dangle her bare feet in the cool current or just think. The spot was under an aging willow. A crescent of white rocks formed a bridge that went halfway across the stream, and the water directly under the willow was calm, lapping onto a sandy beach. She sat on it with her knees to her chin, flexing her toes in and out of the sand. Looking out onto the rocks, she imagined Astrid there: grinning, kicking her long legs in and out of the water; laughing and diving into the deep pool at the end of the bridge. Summers ago, they had shared that private spot. Only one other had been there, during Thyri's ninth summer—Skoll, a wild boy who had taught her how to kill birds with a sling. She counted him her friend second only to Astrid. He was dirty and lanky, with bright eyes and a way of mocking Gyda's calls that always made Thyri gag with laughter. He had taken his name from the wolf that chased the sun; Thyri guessed he had never had a real one. Two springs before, she had fared out into the wood expecting to find the boy. He'd promised to return; he didn't keep that promise then. He hadn't still.

Recent years had been lonely with Erik, her brother, still too young to satisfy Thyri's sense of companionship. She had grown in the company of many older than she—two older brothers and two older cousins. She thought nothing of the three years that

8

separated Astrid and herself, but Erik's six years and Thyri's ten were worlds apart.

Astrid had left when Thyri was seven. A tall, cloaked stranger had arrived at the homestead to talk with her father and uncle behind the closed doors of the hall. A long, fiery conversation had followed, with Thyri and Astrid pressing their ears to the outside wood; they could hear their fathers raging, but not clearly enough to pick out words. From the visitor they had heard nothing. At the end, the stranger had left with Astrid, and Thyri's father had threatened to beat her should she not cease her crying and her attempts to follow. Her tears had been tears of fury: no one would tell her where Astrid had gone. No one would tell her even why Astrid had gone. She still didn't know. But she would soon learn—with not even a snapping twig to warn her.

She felt a hand firmly in the center of her back, and suddenly she was rolling forward, sputtering and thrashing about in the shallow water. She heard light laughter and frantically swept wetly dripping clumps of hair from her eyes.

Her cousin's blond hair had grown long and silky with a thick, three-knot braid on one side. She wore a thin cloak of forest green cotton and carried a bow and quiver on one shoulder with a battle-ax on the opposite hip. She had breasts, and she had grown tall. She towered, a lean giantess awash in patchy sunlight filtered through willow leaves. Her laugh mellowed into a wide grin as she helped Thyri from the stream.

Eirik, Thyri's father, was the first to notice them. His calls brought excited shouts from his brother and their sons in the fields. Outside the hall, the family gathered around the two girls, firing questions mingled with laughs of joy. Eirik opened the doors and led them in.

Astrid set her bow and ax by the door and Egill, her father, gave her his seat at the head of the long-table for the telling of her tale. Thyri sat next to her, and Astrid took her hand beneath the table. Thyri's mother brought mead.

"I'm happy to see you, Father," Astrid said to Egill, "but I cannot stay long. You know where I've been. You sent me with Scacath, and much of what she promised has already come to pass. I have come now for Thyri. She is to follow in turn."

Thyri's nails bit into the back of her cousin's hand. Astrid did not wince; she continued to smile placidly at her father while the color fled from her uncle's cheeks.

"No," he said. "Not both of you."

"When Scacath came for me," Astrid said, "you thought her

crazed. She offered a bag of silver for me. You refused. She needed her magic." She paused, smiling sadly at her father as the disclosure brought tears unbidden into his eyes. "It's all right, Father," she continued. "She cast a spell to persuade you to part with me, but it was *meant* to be. I am happy. She told you she would teach me the ways of the warrior and that this was my Destiny. I have come to prove this. And to take Thyri that she may learn what she herself must learn. You know she desires nothing of the normal ways of women. I bring no spells for her, only myself as proof of Scacath's teaching. And another bag of silver of the same weight as the last." She reached inside her cloak and brought out a pouch that clinked as she tossed it toward Thyri's father.

Eirik looked at his brother, drained his flagon of mead, and slammed it on the table. He glared at Astrid. "Spells and silver! Odin's beard, girl! You're nearly a woman! How can you speak of wielding a sword?"

"I can and I will."

"And Thyri as well? You're mad!"

"I can prove that you are wrong."

"You can, eh? How?"

"A test of ability and prowess. You may name it, though you cannot name the sword for I have not yet begun my training with that weapon. We will wager, yes? Should I lose, Thyri and I shall stay here and do your bidding."

Eirik scowled and fell quiet. Egill leaned over and whispered in his ear.

Thyri spoke, breaking the tension: "Father, I *want* to go!"

"Silence, child!" Eirik snarled. "You Astrid, who would think yourself a Viking, do you dare to wrestle with arms your strong brother Halfdan?"

"I requested a test of ability and prowess, and you suggest a test of strength. I would dare, but I could not win without deceit and the possibility of dealing grave injury to my brother whom I dearly love. I would wish that you name another test." She smiled at Halfdan, then turned back to Thyri's father. "But if this is what you require, and you will name no other test, I will respect your choice as a cunning one."

Eirik chuckled. "You have learned to use words, girl. I will name another test. Wrestle to the ground with Halfdan if you wish to give me proof."

"To the long pin, the short pin, or just the fall? The long pin, Uncle, is another test of strength, and I would deal more harshly with my brother than I would wish. But if this is what you require, and you will not say the short pin or the fall, I will respect your choice as a cunning one."

"By Odin, girl, you begin to sound like a saga," he said wearily. "The short pin will do."

"Very well." She looked at Halfdan, her elder by four years and but a summer from adding his strength to his king's army. "Brother?"

He nodded and rose from his seat. Astrid squeezed Thyri's hand before rising, then the siblings moved to stand several paces apart in the open space between the long-table and the fire over which Gyda's hog boiled in a large iron kettle. Astrid glanced at Thyri, then looked to Halfdan.

As Thyri watched them, she grew fearful. Astrid was tall—nearly as tall as Halfdan's six feet—but her brother bore the muscles of the field on his arms and was twice the weight of his sister. Yet Thyri's fears did not reflect in Astrid's eyes. Assuming a relaxed, poised stance, she taunted Halfdan with her eyes and the sway of her hips. Halfdan tucked his beard to his chest and stalked toward her. He lunged, and Astrid stepped aside, bringing one knee up against his chest. In the same motion, she cupped his chin in her hand and swung around behind him, pivoting to land solidly on his back.

Thyri's heart raced. Astrid threw her hands over Halfdan's eyes and moved her legs so that they scissored her brother's apart, twisting his body and upsetting his balance. He fell back and Astrid swung away, still holding him by the head. Halfway through the fall, she pulled herself in, reaching across for his far armpit. By the time he hit the floor with a loud thud, she lay across his chest.

Thyri looked at Astrid, amazed, only partly believing that she did not dream. She had seen men wrestle—she didn't know girls could. Not, at least, against men. And to defeat one almost a Viking?

Astrid leapt quickly to her feet and reached down for her brother's hand. Halfdan gave it, grinned, then yanked her down to him, hugging her and burying his head in the flowing mass of her blond hair. "I shall hate to see you leave again, Sister," he whispered. "But if you must, may Thor protect and guide you."

They embraced, then rose to face the others. Astrid looked solemnly at first her father, then her uncle. "Well?" she asked.

Thyri watched Eirik's eyes as he looked to the others around the long-table and the old ones who sat in the corner next to the pot. She had never seen her father's gaze so helpless, so unsure. "My daughter will learn *that?*" he asked at last.

"That," answered Astrid, "and more."

"And the sword?"

"Eventually."

His hand went to his chest, to the iron symbol of the Thunderer's hammer on the strong chain around his neck. He fingered the pendant and looked curiously at his daughter. Thyri looked back with pleading eyes. She went to speak, but he signed her silence. Eirik stroked the pendant and stuffed it inside his tunic so that it rested on his skin.

"Then so be it," he said, looking from Thyri to Astrid. "Stay the night. We have a hog to eat."

Astrid smiled warmly.

Eirik laughed. "And take back your silver. I do not wish to sell my daughter."

"You are not selling her. It is the way. If you do not take the silver, then Scacath will not take Thyri."

"Take the silver," Egill said.

Eirik nodded grimly. "Gyda! More mead! We shall drink to rival the gods this evening!"

Astrid sat, smiled at Thyri, and took again her hand.

Late that night, Thyri led her cousin through the dark to her room behind the hall. Years before, they had shared it between them. Thyri felt this night the last she would ever spend there. Though it was dark, she pictured everything in her mind, wanting suddenly to capture forever every small detail. In fact, it was a simple room, with its soft bedding on the sleeping ledge and Thyri's white chests and her chair next to the table with the mirror of polished steel. The room's sole decoration, the miniature hammer symbol of the Thunderer that her father had forged for them long before, hung on the wall above the low entrance where it had been for as long as Thyri could remember, long before Astrid had first left.

Astrid pushed her, and she fell giddily onto the ledge. They had drunk of the mead—Thyri overly so because her father seldom allowed her the privilege. Gyda's light snoring purred from a room beyond, and Eirik's bellowing laughter occasionally reached them from the hall, where he and Egill and his sons continued to drink, their tales and songs growing both louder and longer as the night wore on.

Thyri crawled to the corner of the ledge and reached out for Astrid, only to find her sitting on the far end. Thyri rose then and groped on her table for a candle and tinderbox. The yellow light showed her cousin smiling thoughtfully, her eyes distant. Astrid's fingers fumbled with her braid, which terminated, Thyri noticed, in a large bead engraved with runes much like those she had seen drawn by the *volva*, Asta, her father's mother's aunt. Astrid undid the braid and began to reknot it.

Thyri watched her spin one, two, then three, and finally four knots before she affixed again the bead and tested its grip.

"Why did you do that?"

"Do what?"

"That—with your hair. You looked so far away. Like Asta looks when she's casting, or when she's sleeping with her eyes open—it's hard to tell."

Astrid's eyes lit up and she laughed, stroking the braid with one hand, fingering the bead with the other. "It's true that my thoughts were elsewhere, but not like Asta. The braid and the saga-bead are symbols. Each knot recalls for me a battle, either within or without myself. Each is a valuable lesson learned or a tale worth retelling. My braid is humble. I will tell you my knots at another time when they will mean more to you. Scacath's braid, I think, has as many knots as the sky has stars. She never wears her hair unbraided and I have vowed that neither will I. But you needn't do the same. Sleep now, Thyri. You will learn much more later." Astrid blew out Thyri's candle and pulled her back onto the ledge, where the two girls curled up together and slept.

Late the next afternoon, Thyri stood next to Astrid and faced Scacath across the short space of a small glade in the wood. The ground sloped gently down before her to where a lively brook wended out from the wood to touch on the edge of the glade. The sun burned into Scacath's hair, which gleamed in the way only the blackest of blacks can gleam. The woman's braid, terminating in a stone bead like Astrid's, appeared little more than a thick strand of hair from where Thyri stood. But when the sun struck it right, it scintillated, its twistings casting reflections in all directions like a gem of countless facets.

For moments Scacath merely looked at them, a knowing half-smile touching the corners of her lips. The look made Thyri nervous; she likened the smile to that her mother wore when tasking her, refusing to entertain her protestations. But the face was different: her mother's was thick, while Scacath's was thinly triangular with a sharp chin softened only by the transcendent quality of her skin—pale where the light struck, dark and shadowy where it did not. Her eyes loomed large over a pert, childlike nose. They were silvery blue and fathomless. Beneath the triangle of her face, a contrast of frailty and strength continued. She was lean, yet her breasts stood out proudly against the fabric of a green cloak held together by a round clasp engraved with runes much like those on the beads. Beneath that, she wore nothing. In those shadows, Thyri sensed terrible power.

Scacath's smile bloomed, dispelling Thyri's unease. She looked first at Astrid. "You had no difficulties then?"

Astrid laughed. "Only in giving him the silver."

"Well, we expected that." She turned to Thyri. "Welcome, little one. Do you know why you are here?"

"To become a warrior, like my brothers."

"No—not like your brothers. Your fate is both darker and grander than theirs, and for this you will need strengths and skills much greater. You will leave here such that your Thunder God would deem you a cunning and worthy opponent. Or you will leave here not at all."

To that, she could find no words. She could only look into Scacath's eyes in wonder.

10: Magic

Scacath sprang from the blood of an ancient race of the North-lands and the darker woods of the South, though it later made its home in Erin. Lugh Long-Hand of the *Tuatha de Danann* was her father; her mother was a goddess who had ridden from Southern lands in the hunt of a great stag, twenty hands at the shoulder, which she slew outside of Lugh's hall.

The huntress had stayed with Lugh for two years after Sca-cath's birth, then Lugh had raised his daughter alone until she herself had left home, taking with her much knowledge, for Lugh had great skill in all the arts known to men and gods. Because of her mother, Scacath had ever felt removed from her people. She'd desired to know her mother and to see the many things she'd imagined she could not see among the children of Danu. She went to Manannan, the son of the sea, and she gave him her body. In return, he taught her the *feth fiada*—the spell of hiding and shape-change. Scacath thanked him, transformed herself into a great raven, and flew off into the worlds.

She spent many years "observing the denizens of all worlds, observing them at work, at love, but mostly at war." She flew over the battles and duels of all, and she watched and she learned. She witnessed the battles of the Tuatha de Danann and the war between the sons of Odin and the sons of Njord—wars in which great powers had raged, tearing asunder the very fields on which they had fought. When her father's people fell to the sons of Mil, she remained free in Midgard while many others fled. And with her freedom, she witnessed the passing of her mother's race as the cult of the One God ripped Olympus from its roots on Earth.

Later, during that time when the Tuatha de Danann still con-cerned themselves with the affairs of men and they came to favor the sons of Ulster in Erin, they asked Scacath to train for them a hero. She did so, and the hero, Cu Chulainn, performed feats worthy of legend. Thyri would learn of his tale only after many years, and from the sorceress, Megan Kaerglen, not from Sca-cath.

After Cu Chulainn, when Scacath learned of Odin's hanging by his own hand on the world-tree and gaining thereby his first eighteen runes, she went to him, entering Valhalla in the guise of his raven, Memory. She stayed with the All-Father for three nights, and she gave him her body. In return, he taught her the rune that turns away missiles from one who bears it. This rune she cast upon the blade of her sword and upon the blades she forged for her students.

Thyri had grown with a love for those stories of the gods of the Northlands, but she'd always sensed qualities of the unreal within the tales. They'd added glitter to her secluded life, but they hadn't *described* it. She had never seen a giant, or a dwarf, or an elf, much less any of the Aesir with their great halls, their fiery passions, and their battles. Though she'd been told that Asta possessed magic of a sort, she had never *seen* it. Thus she'd never fully believed.

Scacath, however, showed her very early that magic was real. And Scacath's teachings made the gods real—Thyri's gods, and those of many others as well.

From the road, before taking the twisting series of paths leading to Scacath's grove, Thyri had seen the smoke of fires in the near distance, as of a hall or a small village. She never saw these from the grove, even when she fared out into the woods in the direction she thought the fires must have burned. Scacath told her that she had, in coming there, stepped sidewise away from the world in which she had grown. Only those with great power of their own could come into the grove against Scacath's wishes.

Within it, around the glade to which Thyri would go each morning for water, were many other small clearings, some grassy, others worn to the light brown of packed earth by years of use. In two such clearings were huts of a strange construction: walls and roofs of soft, resilient furs and skins laid over a sparse framework of curved branches tied tightly where they met in the center of dome-shaped roofs. Thyri hardly expected the structures to withstand the rigors of winter, and she first entertained the idea that winter might not come at all to Scacath's world. But she found soon that the seasons did indeed turn as usual, and her hut, which she shared with Astrid, wintered as well as her father's hall. Better, in fact, for here a fire could be built in a depression in the center of the earthen floor, and she could sleep as close to it as she dared.

The floor of the hut sloped down from the fire pit so that the furs that covered it would not become wet with water flowing in from the outside. The roof was capped with a cone-shaped panel of hardened furs that could be lifted with a braced pole to allow smoke from the fire to exit. Furs of marten, sable, mink, fox, and rabbit, sewn together in such a way that they provided both carpet and bedding, covered the floor. Two large chests for clothing and some smaller boxes were arranged to one side, and racks for cloaks and other things (Astrid's sword greeted Thyri from its place on one) hung about the walls of the other side. Wet things could be dried near the fire on hooks swung away from the walls.

Thyri never saw inside Scacath's hut; the students were forbidden to enter. She would idly wish later that she'd dared, but by then the fantasy could not harm her, the world of Scacath having become like a dream, as it certainly seemed to her while she learned its ways.

Between the two huts was the common, a clearing where food and drink were stored and where they ate and occasionally passed time in talk, though always with a purpose as Scacath would never converse idly. She was ever the teacher. This clearing remained grassy year-round and stayed open to the sky as well. Here, the weatherlessness that Thyri had contemplated for the entire area prevailed. Not even a breeze would blow unless Scacath wished it to fan the flames or clear the smoke of fires. When it rained or snowed, the clearing remained open to the sky, and even in the darkest weather they could see the stars above as clearly as on a moonless night. For a long while, Thyri would have little time to think about this, for before her first day had passed, Scacath began her training.

Shortly after a dinner of berries, goat's milk, and duck, two great ravens flapped into the common and lighted on Scacath's shoulders. Astrid excused herself, and Scacath smiled at each bird, stroking them in turn.

"They are called Hugin and Munin," Scacath said, "after the ravens of your Odin. They are my friends, and you will see much of them while you are here."

Thyri looked at Scacath and the ravens. She could think of nothing to say or ask, so she did not speak, only smiled as best she could. She noted that the ravens' eyes did not stray. They did not dart about after the usual fashion of birds, and she felt intelligent purpose in them. She decided then that it would be unwise to assume anything at all about Scacath and her grove.

"You say nothing," Scacath said. "Good. It means you are thinking. The way of the sword begins in the mind and in the senses. The mind must always be such to expect the unseen and the dangerous, and the senses must be sharpened so that they might tell the mind that such exist. The greatest of warriors, even gods, may be slain by a mere scratch of a thorn if the proper poison has been applied to the tip. A missile may be dodged, if one anticipates its coming. Prey, animal or human, may be tracked over almost any terrain if one knows how to perceive. Battles are won and lost in the mind and senses, not in the sword, which is but one of countless instruments capable of dealing death. It is useless in and of itself."

Scacath paused; when Thyri said nothing, she stroked the ravens again and continued: "Foremost also in the mind of the warrior must be the understanding that the concept of *friendship* may conceal an enemy. One is lucky to find in life even one true friend. Most find none at all, though they think and tell others they have many. A friend, a true friend, is one to whom you can entrust your life in any situation you might imagine with never a possibility of this trust being betrayed. Think hard on this and remember it well. A warrior is wise never to take a friend out of loneliness and expect devotion in return. A warrior should never make a pretense of friendship unless it be to attain a specific goal, and then a warrior must remember the nature of that friendship at all times and not allow herself to believe otherwise. You will build relationships on rank and loyalty to king and custom, for trust and compromise are among the ways of men. But so are wars and deceit. Lieutenants have poisoned captains while drinking in friendship. Your life is all you truly have, so you must be sure that when you entrust it to another, that trust will see it safely back into your hands."

"Is Astrid my friend?"

"Yes, little one. The bond between you is as strong as any I have seen in all my years. But even this bond may be sundered by sorcery.

"I am not telling you to trust no one, nor am I telling you to be afraid those you do trust might betray you. I am telling you to be aware and observe. I am not telling you never to love. Indeed, life is hardly worth living without love. But a warrior will never perish by the deceit of another because she will always be aware of where and how deceit might lie, and she will notice its presence before it strikes. Train yourself to see things as they are, not how you wish them to be."

Thyri did her best to take these things to heart and ponder them often. At first she felt confused, but as time passed and Scacath told her more, teaching her to watch things carefully so that when they changed she would know and be aware of the

change, her labors began to bear fruit, and she began to understand.

She had come expecting to spend her time fighting and learning to wield weapons of all sorts, but she spent most of her first
year in training thinking, watching, and trying to understand the
things Scacath told her. The tasks set for her seemed odd. Scacath
once had her sit for an entire day in the grove, asking her later to
tell of everything she observed, both within and without herself.
Another time, Scacath struck her, violently enough to bring tears
to her eyes. While Thyri rubbed her cheek, Scacath asked her to
go to the grove and return either when she could describe exactly
how she felt right after the blow or when dusk came and the smell
of fires reached her nostrils. Thyri did not return that day until
dusk; she had been unable to form her feelings into words that she
thought her teacher would accept. Scacath explained at dinner
that this was because emotions dwell more deeply inside than
words, which are truly but tools of the heart. Sometimes, when
the emotions are very strong, they are unable to make the tools do
what they require; Scacath likened it to a man trying to build a
castle with but a shovel and pick. She told Thyri to be wary of her
emotions during such times, for they could as easily harm as aid
her. Thyri thought deeply on this one, but much time passed before she felt she understood.

Such was the nature of Thyri's first year of training. When she
asked Astrid of it, Astrid would say that such had been hers as
well, but the older girl always refused to give Thyri any answers,
though she might occasionally ask questions that Thyri found
helpful. Astrid would tell her nothing about the training to come
except that, when Thyri worked with Scacath, she worked with
Hugin and Munin. When Thyri questioned this, Astrid smiled and
said no more. It was the way of the teachings that all things
should be uncovered in time—only when the student was prepared. Later, Thyri accepted this and asked of Astrid less knowledge and more companionship; this her cousin gave as freely as
she.

So the seasons passed. The leaves of the grove turned as the
sun grew colder and the days shorter. Astrid killed an elk then,
and Scacath took it into her hut from whence she would bring
portions of the animal throughout the winter. As the first frosts
came, Scacath drew runes on a piece of ground in the common
and spoke strange words over it while her students watched. A
spring bubbled up out of the ground, and Thyri no longer had to
go to the stream each morning for water. When the snows came

and the days grew shorter still, Scacath continued the training unabated, and though Thyri grew accustomed to weathering the biting winter winds, her thoughts in the day often turned to the evening when she and Astrid would lie in their hut, wrapped in furs and whispering quietly by the crackling fire.

In the spring, when the snow and ice melted, Scacath dispelled the enchanted well and Thyri had again to go to the stream for water. It pleased rather than irritated her. The wood along the path grew greener each morning and the dewy landscape, full of vibrant color and a multitude of fresh, newborn scents, excited her. The short trip made her feel very alive. The days grew longer, and as the day that marked the anniversary of Thyri's arrival approached, Scacath began to teach her the basic stances and movements of weaponless combat. After breakfast on the day itself, Scacath gave Thyri her first test.

The morning was warm and the sky clear. Thyri sat with Scacath, Hugin, Munin, and Astrid in the common. She waited, again patiently watching Scacath stroke Munin. She had learned to tell the birds apart: Hugin was slightly larger than his brother and a small patch of gray touched his feathers just above the shoulder of his right wing. Finally, Scacath looked at her carefully and said, "The time has come, little one."

Thyri smiled at her teacher but said nothing.

"Very well," Scacath chuckled. "Go to your hut and bring me your comb."

Thyri looked at her curiously. "What about the test?"

And Scacath smiled.

The path from the common to the hut showed Thyri nothing out of the ordinary: just her tracks, Astrid's tracks, and the marks of various small animals. She checked it several times, then she did the same with the other trails to the hut—the one from the stream, the ones into the grove—but she found them all as expected. Nor did she discover anything unusual in the surrounding wood. When she finally dared to approach the door and inspect it, she found small scratches in the bare skin along the frame. Birds, she thought. *Ravens.*

She went out into the wood and found a branch fallen from an aging oak and measuring two arm-lengths. Standing to the left of the door and as far as she could from the hut, she worked the branch into the opening and flung open the panel. Nothing happened, and she heard no movement from within the hut. Still, she waited several moments before approaching.

The hut's interior seemed as it should with everything as she and Astrid had left it that morning. She looked about, carefully tapping at the furs, paying special attention to those between herself and the small vanity box that held her hair things: her comb, a few wooden pins and clasps, and the leather thong with which she sometimes tied back her blond mane. The box itself sat atop her chest of clothes, and she avoided disturbing it or its perch while probing with the branch. When she had satisfied herself that nothing out of the ordinary lay among the furs, she stepped carefully onto them.

Well inside the hut's entrance, she noticed a subtle difference in the air. She felt a tingling on her skin and smelt a tangible sharpness that she felt she knew but she could not place. The sensations grew stronger nearer the box. She stooped to look at it, standing slightly to one side in order not to cast her dim shadow in the way of the diffuse light that permeated the hut through the thinner patches of the walls. She tried from several angles until she found the scratch marks she sought.

A claw had barely touched the wood of the chest, and the corners of the box on that side bore minute pits where she guessed the bird had taken hold in order to lift it. The pits were on the wrong side for opening the box—the hinged side. She searched her memories for the one that would tell her exactly where on the chest she had left the box. The exercise succeeded only marginally—she only *felt* that the box was placed improperly. Her real success came primarily through the poignant reminder that she needed to be more aware of these things in the future. She decided that it had been lifted, something placed beneath it or something done to the bottom before it had been placed almost as before.

Thyri sat back on the furs and thought. If something had been set beneath the box, she needed merely to open it very carefully and remove her comb. If the trap had been set to fire upon opening, then this was her worst approach since the trap would spring with her just where it would expect her to be. To avoid that, she could topple the box with her branch, setting off the trap in the first case, and probably even in the second. And she might not be able to get the comb if she made a mistake . . . Because she'd found the claw marks on the hinged side of the box, she decided to anticipate the first danger, but she took care and reached up from far to one side before lifting the lid, very slowly and very carefully. Nothing happened.

She stood and backed away, then approached and peered in. Her comb lay there, just on top of the thong, right where she had left it. She smiled, reached in, lifted it out quickly, and dashed out of the hut.

Scacath's luminous eyes cheated the sun's reflection as they absorbed its light, stealing it, taking it somewhere further inside her. She took Thyri's comb in her hand—a long, delicate hand with thin fingers, immune to the calluses of the sword. "Did you learn the nature of the trap?"

Thyri looked at her curiously. "No. That wasn't part of the test."

"No." Scacath grinned brightly. "It wasn't. You felt it though, didn't you?"

Thyri thought back to the sensations—the tingling and the smell. "I think so."

Scacath turned her lips to Munin and whispered. The raven flapped away, toward Thyri's hut. "You did. Munin has gone to remove the danger. You did very well, little one. You sensed the magic. We placed a rune under your box—a simple one, but you would be sore now had you disturbed it."

Astrid laughed. "Sore! My arm burned for a week!" She smiled at Thyri. "I'm proud of you, cousin. You have earned your bead and first braid without injury. When I took the test, I got the comb, but I couldn't resist tapping the box from a distance to see what would happen. My first braid will forever remind me of that mistake."

"Your path will grow more difficult now, little one," Scacath said, "but do not fear it. You have proven yourself worthy of the training. Do not forget what you have learned so far." She reached inside her cloak and brought out a rune-bead, holding it and the comb out to Thyri.

Astrid stepped forth, took a thick lock of Thyri's hair in her hands, and slowly separated three strands. While Astrid fashioned the braid, Thyri held her bead next to her cousin's and learned that the runes were the same.

"What does it mean?" Thyri asked. "The rune?"

Astrid paused. "It means blood," she said softly.

21: Ghosts

She sat on the sand, staring at the scattered snowflake patterns on the ice that lay like a veil over the surface of the pond. Everything was still, the forest around her like a cavern that swallowed all sound. Swallowed her thoughts. Her nightmares.

"I knew I'd find you here," Erik said, crashing through the underbrush.

She thought of early summer in the land of the Franks, the sun warming green, rolling hills, painting her lover bronze. Birds overhead, swimming in the clear blue. Cool grass. The reflection of a solitary cloud in a dewdrop.

"You did everything you could, Thyri," he said, squatting next to her.

Astrid wrapped in Thyri's sables on a cool autumn evening. Long legs stretched teasingly over the warm earth near the fire. Lips moving slowly, a low voice whispering secretly, passionately of tales she'd heard, things she'd dreamed. The sables sliding ever so slowly over her skin; the voice trailing off . . . a breast, beaded with sweat, shining in the firelight . . .

"She's in Valhalla," he said, putting his arm around her. "It was meant to be."

She wanted to push him away and hold him at the same time.

"Odin must have sent those wolves for her, Thyri. No mortal could have killed my cousin."

She couldn't speak, couldn't tell him.

"Are you sure she wasn't ill?" he asked.

Dumbly she shook her head. She wasn't sure of anything.

"I remember when I was little," he said, "and Father would tell that my sister and cousin were special, that they would be the mightiest of all the Vikings in the land. That they would spit in the faces of princes and break the hearts of kings. That they would love gods, Thyri. That you and Astrid would love gods." He started to cry. "I would see you both, and I'd want to be like you. Why did she have to die?"

Like a fountain in the garden of Despair, she rose. "Come, brother. You have a life to live of your own."

He stood slowly. Straight, he towered over her. As tall as Astrid, his long hair almost as light, his eyes crying for her.

And Thyri saw him laughing, hanging off the edge of her ship with his sword out, skimming the surface of the waves. He had joined her crew the past summer. His sword had followed hers into battle, and she suddenly realized that it had been but a game to him. Once, Thyri had asked Scacath to take him into training after her. Her teacher had refused without explanation. Thyri now thought that she understood why.

"She died," Thyri said, "because everything dies some time. Flowers die. Trees die. So do warriors. And gods."

As she led him back to the family hall, he told her that the king's skald had arrived that afternoon and had spoken long with Eirik and Egill. She fell silent again, wishing she could leave, disappear into the forest and never return, never see another human face. But her legs kept moving surely in the wrong direction.

Inside, the chatter of voices assaulted her like knives streaking through the air for her heart. The skald had lifted the cape of mourning from her family's shoulders. He had captivated them with tales of the king, of southern lands, of ancient prophecies and innocent love. Gyda had kept their flagons full, and her father and uncle laughed idiotically at the skald's every word, every gesture. The old ones huddled in their corner, giggling. Only the volva and Yrsa next to her remained solemn. The volva's gaze fell coldly on Thyri.

"Thyri!" Eirik said, approaching her when he noticed her presence. "Come! Sit! The royal skald himself has composed for you. It is a song fit to be sung in the hall of Odin!"

"Or the hall of his slaves," the man said, feigning modesty.

"We'll let Thyri decide! Sit, daughter." He turned to the skald. "Sing!"

Without ceremony, he began. "The Lay of Astrid and Thyri." He began with their exploits under Ragnar, blown out of proportion so that they struck Thyri's ears like empty legends. She'd heard them all before. On a few drunken nights, she'd told them all before. The ache inside of her grew.

And then the skald sang of Astrid's final battle. How a hundred hunger-crazed wolves had risen out of Niflheim and fell upon Astrid and Thyri as they'd slept. How the two of them had gained their feet, swords in hand, and laid into the wolves, killing three or four with each stroke. Then how a wolf so ferocious that he must have been spawned by Fenrir himself had dealt Astrid a mortal wound even as she'd killed him. And how Thyri then slew the rest in her rage, seven with her bare hands, three with her teeth. . .

Slowly, she forced the song, her family, her memories, and her thoughts out of her mind.

She wished that she'd had the strength to tell them about the *were*-beast, to tell them the truth.

She wanted to die.

11: Changes

In her second year with Scacath, Thyri's training began in earnest. Her teacher intensified her work with wrestling and the way of the hand-foot strike, which also involved the learning of those parts of the body most susceptible to pain. Thyri learned quickly, but the process brought her many aches and bruises. Astrid, instructed by Scacath, helped. In the evenings, she taught Thyri the ways to rub, at least in part, the soreness from the body. Again, Thyri grew quickly used to the changes in her routines; they made her feel happier, they proved her progress. She enjoyed, too, falling asleep to the rhythm of Astrid's gentle, knowledgeable fingers.

The months flew by and summer turned again to fall. Thyri learned the use of the bow and the ax, and she began to hunt with Astrid. Scacath began to show her all manner of weaponry to make her familiar with the ways these things—the spear, the crossbow, the dagger, the dirk, the staff, and many others—could be used. She only *showed* Thyri their uses; she did not teach them yet. In time, Thyri would learn to wield a great variety of weapons with skill, but her first real tasks were the bow and the ax.

And she learned the traditions Scacath had developed over her years of training others. The rune-bead and braid were most important, for they served to remind the warrior of herself and of all valuable things learned: the victories and defeats, the hows and whys. When Thyri asked why Scacath wore hers always, her teacher told her laughingly that it would take her days to rebraid it.

"Others," Scacath said, "make a ritual of braiding only before battle, remembering each trial as each braid is fixed."

The sword, Scacath told her, was the end to which all her training tended. The way of the rune-sword. Scacath showed Thyri her blade and the one she'd forged for Thyri:

It was late fall, the morning of the winter's first snowfall. Scacath unsheathed the two swords and laid them on the light powder of the glade. The morning, painted crisp and white, carved itself vividly into Thyri's memory. She wore a brown cotton shirt and trousers, the latter tucked into soft, pliant boots lined with the fur of a rabbit she had slain early the past summer—her first bow-kill. The light crushing of the powder under her boots made her more aware of all her movements, and she noticed for the first time the strange sensations she felt in her stomach when her breasts rubbed against the fabric of her shirt. Scacath, dressed the same, with the addition of her green cloak and its rune-clasp, had never seemed more elegant, more ethereal, or more darkly, primally omnipotent. Like a dream, Thyri thought. Like a dream she'd had and forgotten long before in which gods had fought gods, taking and dealing blows that could rend mountains in two. A dream she'd lost in the daylight—until now. The glade, with its sheen of early winter, sparkled in time with the cold tinkling of the icy stream. Thyri and Scacath were alone there; Astrid, Hugin, and Munin were elsewhere.

Thyri looked at the blades. Neither showed any sign, any mark, of battle. All edges were razor sharp. The hilts were identically plain, built for strength and function, not show, and they had cross guards of thick, squared metal. The flats, however, told quickly the differences between the two. Though unscathed, Scacath's had the stain of age. Runes marked it from hilt to mid-blade. Thyri's (and Astrid's, she knew, for her cousin had spent many evenings honing its edge) looked fresh and bore no runes.

"The runes. Are they magic?"

"Very," answered Scacath. "Can't you feel it?"

Thyri tried to sense the tingling and the tang. She had come to notice it more often—in the common, around the ravens, occasionally around Scacath. She could not feel it here. "No." Her answer was uncertain, but Scacath smiled.

"You are honest, and I am glad. The magics for iron have a more subtle flavor as they must have, for the metal is strong. Had you said yes, I would have known you lied. The magic can be sensed, little one, but you might train yourself to hear the footfall of a cat, or the breath of a fly, and yet never feel the magic in iron. Remember this."

Thyri looked at the unmarked sword. "This is mine?"

"Not yet. This is that toward which you work." She paused, drawing from her cloak a thin, flexible gauntlet of silver, like Astrid's. She held it out to Thyri. "Pick it up if you like, but put this on first."

Thyri took the gauntlet and fitted it on her hand. The tips of her fingers did not quite reach the ends of those of the gauntlet, and the whole thing felt loose. "It's too big."

"Of course. It is yours—for your hand two summers hence. You must become used to thinking of the gauntlet and sword as one."

"Why?"

Scacath smiled. "Because the gauntlet is fashioned for the sword. Because your sword will one day bear runes such as mine. Their magic is strong, and once you have grown accustomed to it, it cannot harm you. But even then, certain sorceries can turn the blade against the wielder. The gauntlet guards against this. Were you now to touch my sword, unused as you are to its power and without the gauntlet, possibly even with it, it would kill you."

Thyri nodded silently and reached for the hilt of the unmarked sword. She grasped it and picked it up clumsily, holding it before herself and inspecting the blade. A moment later, she set it back as it had been on the snow.

"You did not test it as a weapon," Scacath said. "Why?"

"I think," began Thyri slowly, "that I will remember this moment often between now and the day the sword becomes mine in truth. I do not wish to remember the feel of wielding it wrongly, as a child."

Scacath smiled her half-smile, took back the gauntlet, picked up the two blades, and whirled, leaving Thyri alone with her thoughts.

Thyri learned other things that year, other twists of Scacath's teaching that blended rune-magic with the way of the sword. Scacath once said that she might, if she wished, teach her students the way of the runes alone. But this she did not wish. The runes she gave were presents, symbols, not teachings, for the magic of the runes was bound to the destiny of the gods, and the destiny of the gods was the sword. "When the runes will fail, the iron will not": these are the words Scacath said to Thyri. As such, neither Thyri nor Astrid would be taught the runic ways, though it came to pass that Astrid learned much through observation alone due to a gift of magic that Wyrd had granted her at birth.

The rune-gifts of Scacath were four: the bead, mostly symbolic with a slight charm of remembrance; the clasp, a talisman of presence and restraint, attuned to the mind of the bearer who, in battle, might cast clasp and cloak aside with but a thought; the fifth rune of Odin, which sends missiles astray of their mark; and the twenty-third rune of Odin, the rune of sharpness: the sword that bears it need never be honed and will leave battle with the same edge that it held at the start. These last two gifts came, respectively, at the ends of the seventh and sixth years of training. The clasp came also at the end of the seventh—a parting gift from teacher to student.

Scacath told Thyri much of that which was to come: how she would learn more of the weaponry she might one day face, both visceral and sorcerous; how she would conquer fear and detach herself from herself so that she might use fear's energy to defeat its sources; how she would learn the sword with first two hands, then one, using in her freed hand another weapon for parrying rather than a shield for hiding behind; and how she would learn of many other methods, inferior methods, Scacath told her, which opponents might use.

As Thyri learned all this, the seasons turned and in early summer she took her second test. Scacath showed her a pale lizard but three inches long in the palm of her hand and set it loose to scamper off into the woods. An hour later, she sent Thyri and her bow out after it. For another hour, Thyri tracked it. She found it hidden in the bark of a tree, its color changed somehow to match the bark. Smiling, Thyri impaled it there with a single shot, then took it back to the common where Scacath and Astrid waited, Scacath for the lizard, and Astrid to tie the second knot in Thyri's braid.

Thyri's third year with Scacath was by far the most hectic of the first three. It was the year that Thyri learned to fight with the staff, and a year during which Scacath told her so much about so many things that she often spent long hours in the evenings lying back on her furs, calling up first one curious thing heard during the day, then another, turning them over and over in her mind and trying to patch them in with the rest of her knowledge. She felt as if she worked on a puzzle that would suddenly transform and grow into yet another picture just when she thought the first almost finished. And the new puzzle was always more complex and disjointed than the one before. Scacath told her that this was life, and it was good that she saw it thus at such an early age. So Thyri would build the pieces again into an almost-picture, only to watch them crumble while trying to fit the last few into place. So it would go on forever.

The third year was also the year she entered womanhood. During her thirteenth summer, she could feel her breasts growing and her hips widening by the day. The transformation scared her at first but by midsummer she had come to enjoy the new, sensuous feelings that accompanied the changes. And she had other things, happy things, to think about then: she would shortly gain her sword, and her growing body, as she accustomed herself to its feel, would be much more powerful, more suited to the demands of strength and fluidity that the sword training would require. And she would look also at Astrid and see how strong and beautiful her cousin had become, and she would think that soon she too would be thus. The cold nights of that winter played the backdrop for Thyri's first flirtations with passion. She and Astrid began to add the sharing of their bodies to the sharing of their thoughts and hearts.

When spring turned again to the grove, Thyri began to spend many hours thinking of her next test. She did not ask the others. She knew they would not answer. But she thought on it just the same. It came on a cool morning, defiant of the bright pastels of the season's flowers and the verdant green legacy of the spring rains. An overcast sky of patchy gray hung motionlessly over the grove, threatening a storm that would not come until late that afternoon. Over a breakfast of goose eggs and goat's milk, Scacath explained the task.

"Today, little one," she began, "you must go to the place where the stream issues from its underground course. It is a cavern, dark and fraught with danger. In the back, you will find an object that you must return to me. You will know what it is when you see it. Bring it back, and you will have your third braid and your sword."

"How far must I journey?"

"Maybe a day there and back, maybe a lifetime." And Scacath smiled.

Thyri went to her hut and fashioned a torch from a thick piece of wood, a torn shirt, and the stub of a candle. After securing the wadded, waxed shirt to the wood with a length of copper chain from a necklace, she set about transforming another old shirt into a pack into which she placed her tinderbox, some dried pork from the cache in the common, and a hook with a long piece of twine. The last she added as an afterthought; she seldom fished, but she would be traveling along the bank of the stream.

She put on long pants and her boots and her green cloak, fastening it with a plain bronze clasp. She attached her hand-ax and a short dagger to her belt, slung the pack over one shoulder, her quiver and bow over the other, picked up her staff, and left the hut. At first she started for the common; she could hear Astrid's light laughter there. But she hesitated after a few steps, paused, and turned confidently toward the glade and the stream.

Picking her way along the bank, she had often to stop and cut away patches of the thick growth that flourished near the water. Her bow would snag, but she resisted the temptation to cast the weapon aside; she could regret that action later in the day. Before noon, the forest thinned and the ground grew hilly. These were new sights for Thyri, and she had to push herself to keep moving. It helped when she thought of the reward for success.

She reached the cavern early in the afternoon. The closer she got, the stranger it smelled. A thick, odious musk lingered in the heavy air. Huge paw prints marked the ground all around the cavern's mouth, which was four times as wide as it needed be to provide an exit for the stream. Two sizes of prints—two bears. So much for simple traps, Thyri thought. And it was summer; the pair probably had cubs. As if in answer to her thoughts, a high, light squealing issued from the cavern's mouth, and a lower grunt followed.

Thyri knew bears, or, more properly, she knew of them. She had never seen one, but she could construct a picture of one from the size of the tracks and droppings, and she could imagine their enormous fangs and claws. She and Astrid had once come across the mutilated carcass of a doe, the victim of a hunting bear who had mysteriously been drawn away to leave its prey half-devoured. Scacath had told them that few bears ate meat, but there were some who, once having tasted blood, made a habit of it. Thyri wondered if these bears were such animals, and if, indeed, one of them might have been responsible for the doe. She sat for long moments trying to separate the smells of the individual animals. She did her best to recall the scents around the slaughtered doe, but the effort rewarded her not.

She wondered if she should wait for them to leave, then decided against it. Listening carefully to the sounds from the cavern, she learned that only two of the animals were home—one big one and a little one, presumably a mother and her cub. If she waited, the father could very well return and she would have more bears to face than she cared to think about. The thoughts made fear real to her for the first time. She had never felt so alone, and though Scacath had often said things that Thyri had felt in her stomach, her teacher had always awed her more than anything else. This was different—no matter what Scacath said or did, Thyri felt she could trust her. The bears were real, and if she was caught by them inside their cavern, they would surely do their best to kill her. She became aware of her age. She had turned thirteen the past winter. If she did not succeed, she would never turn fourteen.

But she couldn't turn back. She knew this and felt it so deeply that the very thought of forsaking her sword, the meaning of her future, for a fear of fang and claw, however sharp, sickened her. Throughout the past year, Scacath had stressed the importance of containing her fear and she realized now that she must do this to pass the test. In essence, defeating fear *was* the test. A part of her stepped back then, watching, learning, and calculating, while the rest of her being trembled.

The stream issued from the cavern's mouth against its left ledge. Thyri saw no possibility, at least from the outside, of reaching the back of the cavern along any path across from the bears. She had to go straight back.

The water was cold, though she knew this even before she dipped a curious hand into the current. On the hottest days of summer, the stream by the glade was not a place to linger long in bathing. The waters near the surface were pleasant enough, but the cold briskness below made feet and legs numb, and traversing the stream by walking along the bottom was dangerous not because of any particular threat of drop-offs or sharpened rocks, but because of the cold—a cold that attacked the nerves, creating sensations that lied to the brain.

Thyri didn't waste time worrying about freezing. She didn't plan on staying in the water any longer than she needed to reach a point deep enough in the cavern to avoid the bears. She got as close as she could while still keeping some undergrowth before her, then she took off her bow and quiver, her pack, her cape, and the rest of her clothing. Gathering several short but solid bits of branch and bark, she fashioned a float from her pack. After satisfying herself that it would work, she made a bundle from her shirt and secured the torch and tinderbox within. She tied it with the length of twine, then tied the pack to the float. She checked the structure once again in the water, making sure it still worked; she had no desire to be caught in the darkness of the cave without light and warmth. Before she entered the water, she tied her belt with her ax and dagger tightly around her naked waist.

She stayed underwater as much as she could, staving off the cold with thoughts of her alternatives: to walk boldly into the lair or to lie in wait, hoping to get clear bow-shots on each of the animals. The latter option could take days. As she entered the cavern, she began to wish that she'd made a harness to drag the float along behind her, freeing the hand she was using to guide it. As she stroked deeper and deeper into the darkness, her thoughts were of warm winter evenings with Astrid, and fears of losing her torch by snagging it on a ledge or, worse, by a curious swat of a bear paw. Or by an unseen foe attacking from below, forcing her to use both hands, freeing the float to the whims of the current that would push it back into the gray daylight without her.

The cold was numbing. She clambered out of the stream at the point where she first, while gasping for breath, smelt a lessening in the musk that pervaded the area around the lair. Trembling, she pulled the float from the water into the darkness. Clasping it to her breast, she staggered away, first finding a wall, then following it. The ground under her bare feet was soft, as of a silt laid by the stream over the cavern's rocky floor. For that she was thankful; her blind groping brought her toes against enough sharp things as it was. She wondered if the bears had noticed the man-smell invading their domain.

After several minutes of following the wall, she realized that a coldness close to that of the water had enveloped her. Unless she soon got warm, she would die as the cold worked its way into her heart. She found a niche in the wall, collapsed into it, and forced her trembling hands to part the bindings of the pack. Her heart raced as she drew out the torch; it was damp in spite of her precautions. She laid it on her lap and groped for the warmth of the tinderbox. The little clay vessel sent fire into her numb fingers when she touched it. She uncapped it, finding the embers still red and hot. After several frantic moments, she managed to set the shirt she had waxed alight. It sputtered uncertainly at first, then blazed as the wax took hold of the wood and the flames boiled the moisture away. Thyri planted the torch in the silt and warmed each part of her body with its heat, heedless of the poppings that sent bits of fiery cloth and wood against her skin. She almost welcomed the burns.

She would have liked to linger there longer, but she soon took up the torch and continued on. The light would not last forever, and she knew neither how much deeper she needed to delve, nor whether she had, in following the wall, taken a turn away from the main passage that led to her goal. If such were the case, she would have to backtrack and start over again, possibly having to face the bears. For now she pressed on. In the cavern along the stream, she saw many beautiful sights—things that glittered with all the colors of the rainbow. They hung from the ceilings and rose from the floors. Some met, creating columns of grandeur fit for the halls of the gods. Perhaps, she thought, some god *did* dwell here. Perhaps this was the road to Niflheim. The glittering pillars would give way to fanged beasts of dark rock, and the rivers of Muspellheim would cross the stream, and she would pass their fires to reach the great gates where Loki's son, Garm, lay chained, awaiting the end of all things.

At the end, she reached a chamber past which she could not fare. The stream poured from the far wall and but a handspan separated its surface from the rock above it. By the opening, on a low pedestal of the rainbow-stuff, rested a thin, silver gauntlet and the sword that Scacath had shown Thyri six seasons past.

Thyri took the gauntlet and pulled it onto her hand. It reached to her mid-forearm and glittered in the torchlight along with the rainbow-stuff. She smiled—it fit now. She took the sword by its hilt and, with it in her right hand and the torch in her left, turned back to seek the daylight.

Legend might have it that Thyri slew the bears as she left: that she, unversed, wielded her new weapon with the skill and grace of one who had studied its art many years. That this day she became a warrior. This did not happen. She left the cavern as she had entered it, with the tinderbox secured on the float. She did, however, hold the sword above water as she swam, not wanting to tarnish the blade.

21:Changes

"You should at least learn the making of a stew!"

Gyda stood, hands on her ample hips, glaring at Thyri. Thyri glared back at her mother, saying nothing. She ached—her heart ached, her body ached, her shoulder throbbed. She didn't care—the last few weeks had buried her pain much deeper.

"You chose that life," Gyda said, throwing her hands up and returning to her work. "I have lost two sons, a nephew, and now a niece. You think we don't mourn with you? You think we don't feel some fear when you, Halfdan, and Erik leave here with swords strapped to your sides and blood and plunder burning inside you?"

Gyda went to her, bending to one knee and placing her hand on her daughter's arm. "Why, Odin, do you pain us so? I ask it of him every day. And every night I sleep without reply." She looked pleadingly into Thyri's eyes. "Put away your sword, Eiriksdattir. Marry. Bear me grandchildren."

Thyri sat, shoulders hunched, staring blankly at nothing. Gyda sighed, rose and brushed off her skirt.

"You are my impotent son," she said distantly. "Unable even to sow our seed among those people whose lands you rape."

Only Erik's company had been bearable, perhaps because she saw in him an innocence that she'd lost. But her love for her brother could not lift the shadows from her heart. He'd known Astrid too well. He could not cease his speculations on the reasons for Astrid's fall: a sickness that she had concealed from Thyri, the snagging of her blade on the root of a nearby tree, the failing light, the snow. . .

Thyri could only nod and shrug dumbly at each successive explanation. But the ache Erik's words brought her burned fiercely, and she desired only to run from it.

Then there was Yrsa, Astrid's sister. Yrsa was not like them. She was shy, mousy, and skilled with her hands, spending most of her time alone fashioning cloaks, shirts, and boots for sale and trade with the spring merchants. To Gyda, she was the daughter that Thyri had never been; Yrsa's mother had withered and died shortly after her third childbirth. When not sewing leather, Yrsa's only interests were Asta and the mysteries of the runes. Thyri saw little of her, and for that she was thankful. Neither Yrsa nor the volva had eyed her kindly since she'd brought word of Astrid's death.

She found herself mourning anew for Astrid each day, each moment. She couldn't get it to make sense. Astrid was Valkyrie; she wouldn't be coming back. The entire world had changed, darkened, in the space of one fatal moment.

She rose unsteadily, going to the door of the hall. She opened it, heedless of the icy winds gusting in. The first hint of moonrise tainted the horizon, and she slammed the door shut. Somehow, she could still feel the moon outside, rising . . .

She ran to her room and huddled on the ledge. Her mother yelled something after her but the words lost to the rolling thunder in her head. Her shoulder began to throb terribly.

"No!"

The scream issued from her unbidden. Her door opened, her mother's frame filling the space.

Agony gripped her, tearing at her every nerve. Bile rose to her throat, and vomit spilled out onto the bedding and the floor. She heard Gyda's voice again, then her vision went red.

She killed her mother in a blind, dispossessed rage on her way out of Egill's hall. It was her first taste of human blood.

Over three nights of the full moon, Thyri roamed the country-side, feeding.

Her house was in turmoil. Yrsa found Gyda in time to look from the hall and see the white wolf bounding away across the snow. Of Eirik: his wife's death turned his heart black and folded into itself. His face fell devoid of expression. He did not speak. He did not even weep.

Egill, however, listened to Yrsa and Asta with growing horror as they told him the lore of the *were* and the dark runes that served it. Loki's spite—his warping of a light elven lady into a malevolent, vampiric beast in the image of Fenrir. She had denied him his pleasure. Aelgifu was her name and dark was her Destiny. She had loved a mortal prince whom she tore near unto death as they lay together under a rising moon. From there she ran, and she took her own life the next morning when the beast left her.

Her lover, however, had survived. This unknown prince had spread the curse. In Asta's eyes, that curse had found Thyri.

Halfdan was sent for. Egill raged through those days, stomping about the hall with his father's war-ax gripped tightly in his fist. On the first day he battered Erik senseless, smashing his nose and cracking several ribs when the boy refused to join in the hunt for his sister. Eirik was abed. Asta and Yrsa stayed locked in the old one's chamber, casting and recasting their family's fortunes among a house of whispers but for Egill's furious railings.

Halfdan arrived on the third day and he and Egill set off immediately into the wood with bow, sword, and ax. They did not find her until after moonrise. She saw them and ran. They tracked her too well, boxing her in among boulders and rocks. They rained arrows upon her, putting three in her side before their quivers were spent. Then Egill sent Halfdan against her.

Thyri killed her cousin, part of her full of ecstatic fire at the taste of his blood, another part loathing and screaming out to some god, any god, for mercy. Then she killed Egill, who had forced Halfdan's death, rending him as she had her mother.

By day she cowered in a small cove that looked out over the sacred vale of her ancestors. She would cry out her pain to Astrid and be answered by naught but silence. She would look from her cave's mouth and see the sun warming the ground over Astrid's rune-sword. She would think of that blade and how easy it would be to unearth it and bury it in her breast, spilling her own blood over Astrid's ashes. But she was too weak for that crossing into the field in daylight. And when night fell, so came the hunger, leaving her no time to think of the oblivion waiting buried for her in the earth.

After the third night, when she slew her uncle and cousin, Thyri stayed in the cave for two days. That second night, after the setting of the moon, she crept out and went slowly across to Astrid's low mound.

Her fingers clawed at the frozen earth which fell away in unwilling clumps until she grasped that which she sought. She drew out the sword and planted it point first in the soil before her. The light of the stars caressed it as she wiped away the dirt. The wetness on her cheeks streaked with brown as her tears caught cloudy dust from the air. The blade clean, she drew it slowly from the ground. She gripped the cold iron and set its point to the flesh just below her left breast. She closed her eyes, breathing deeply.

"Thyri."

She looked up.

Astrid stood before her, ablaze in silver armor. A winged steed pawed at the frozen ground behind her, tossing its head. He looked at her and she recognized his gaze. *Yrafax,* she thought. Her eyes filled with new tears, and all the pain, all the horror of the past month leapt into her mind. She tightened her grip on the rune-sword. "I will join you now, my cousin."

"No, my love. Do not do this thing." Astrid's words were like music, her voice no longer of Midgard. "You must live for both of us. You must love for both of us now."

"But it is not right! I have become as your slayer! I have tasted the blood of our kin!" Sobbing wracked her body. The point of the sword pierced her skin. She hardly felt it, such was the pain in her heart.

"You are strong, Cousin. You will learn restraint. You must leave Hordaland. Go far from here and begin another life. Your sword will see you through. And when the moon sets upon you, be one with the wolves. Don't fight your Destiny. Prey will come easily; you needn't kill men for food."

"Don't leave me, Astrid! I cannot—" Her words failed in her sorrow. She knew she asked the impossible.

"I serve the All Father now, Cousin." She stepped forward and lifted Thyri from her knees. She smoothed the tangled hair from Thyri's face and kissed her gently. "Do not fear, Thyri. Your day will come to enter Valhalla. But that day lies ahead, not here."

She pulled Thyri's head from her breast and brushed away her tears. "Take my sword. I no longer have need of it. Perhaps with it in your hand, you will feel me near." She parted from Thyri and went to her horse. "Farewell, little one."

Astrid and her steed faded away with a mist that descended on the field, then went as suddenly as it came. Thyri stood there, naked under the stars but for the blade jutting out from her clenched fist. Along it, starlight danced. The dead of the field called again to her but she hardly heard them. She turned slowly and started east, toward her home.

13: Departures

"Hello, little one," Hugin said. "We have waited these three years for you. Astrid has reached her final year, and Scacath must take her beyond that which is our ability to teach."

Thyri tried to smile. It was the day after her third test. Scacath had told her to follow the ravens to the glade. They had reached it before her, and when she'd arrived she'd found not two birds but two young men, generously muscled and black as night. One stood as tall as Astrid; the other was shorter. Both wore nothing but scant breechcloths of green cotton and belted scabbards for their swords. Their heads were bald, and ivory white teeth shone from their mouths as they laughed at Thyri's astonishment. She'd known immediately that they were the ravens; their eyes hadn't changed. The big one was Hugin, the smaller, Munin. Mind and Memory.

"By your eyes, your cousin never told you of us. That shows her strength better than ever her sword arm might. We know how close you are."

"She told me," Thyri said, "that you trained her. But she told me not how. I might have guessed had I had the time."

"But you hadn't."

Memories of the past three years rushed into her mind—all the things she'd learned and wondered upon. "No," she agreed. "I hadn't."

Astrid spent a week that fall at Egill's hall and brought back news from the world of men. Erik was now a strapping youth of ten summers and helping his father work the smithy. It was then that Thyri asked her teacher to take him next. "He shall be trained," Scacath replied, "after the fashion of the Vikings, and he shall reach Valhalla by virtue of that teaching, not mine."

Ragnar of Hordaland had a daughter named Gyda who was born on the same day, some say the same moment, as Thyri. The princess had grown very beautiful and powerful. An entourage of men from the Kingdom of Vestfold had come to Hordaland that summer. Their king and leader, Harald, son of Halfdan called "the Black," had led the entourage. From what Astrid knew, the king was but a boy, perhaps no older than she, but all said that he possessed that air of a great leader and warrior, and Asta had told her that his mother had dreamed a great prophecy of his Destiny —of a thorn driving itself into a tree as great as Yggdrasil, drawing blood from it that covered the trunk but left the upper branches white as snow. He had come to Hordaland seeking Gyda, who he had heard was the fairest of all maidens in Norway.

He had stayed at the hall of Ragnar for two weeks during which he could constantly be found at Gyda's side. After those two weeks had passed, he'd proposed marriage to the princess. It is said that she laughed and replied, "To think that I should marry such a petty kingling as you!" He bore the insult with grace, and he did not strike her. He'd left, vowing to conquer for her a kingdom worthy for her to rule as queen.

Neither Thyri or Astrid knew the princess, but the story rooted within each of them a dislike for the girl and her capricious ways. They discussed the portent of Gyda's act for the homeland, and they wondered whether Ragnar would have them fight against the armies of Harald, whom they thought terminally stupid for his fascination with Gyda. The talk was prophetic, and it came to pass that the only lasting enemy of their years together under the banner of Hordaland was the southern kingdom of Vestfold.

The following summer, Thyri took her first test with her blade, and Astrid gained the fifth rune of Odin for hers. Scacath gave Astrid her rune-clasp on the day she left.

The glade lost half its light for Thyri when her cousin walked away. They had endured the preceding weeks well, laughing often and talking of the great things they would do together once Thyri's training was complete. That training intensified after Astrid's departure, and Thyri hardened her heart and welcomed it with renewed vigor.

That fall, when the sword training extended beyond stances and strokes and began to batter her body, Munin offered to aid Thyri in tending her wounds. She refused his offer and retired to tend to herself, thinking of Astrid's hands and wondering where her cousin slept that night.

Eventually, Thyri accepted the friendship of the ravens if only to fill some of the emptiness left by Astrid. She accepted Munin's in particular. It happened on a day the following spring when the sky was bright, the breeze soft, and the pastels of the flowers against the ubiquitous green were laughing at her solemnity. Her dark thoughts of the past winter were forced to the back of her mind to dwell with her first glimpse of Scacath, Skoll's laughing eyes, and other early experiences that were part of her and yet part of another—a child, not *herself*. Memories, she had found, could be cast aside, at least temporarily.

They had taken rest under the shade of an oak on the rim of the glade next to the swift stream that bled from the earth through the cave of the rainbow-stuff and the bears. Hugin changed form —a nearly instantaneous phenomenon with but a faint aura of magic shrouding his figure just before and just after the change. He flew off to seek his mistress.

A large welt high on Thyri's left arm oozed redly where the flat of Munin's blade had pierced her guard. With a dirk, she could have parried the blow without training. As it was, she had used her sword two-handed. She was quickly learning the limitations of that technique even though her wrist was not yet strong enough for a one-handed style.

Munin inspected the wound and applied a salve to it, bandaging it with strips of cotton that Thyri wore so often that she felt them almost a part of her normal clothing. After tying the bandage, Munin's hands fell on Thyri's breasts. She sighed. When she did not pull away, he bent over and kissed her lightly. He lifted her up and pulled her shirt over her head.

They began slowly, and Thyri accepted the new sensations with hesitation. His touch was light, but not as light as Astrid's. But she liked it, even though she wasn't sure that she wanted to. His caress was insistent, clouding her thoughts. She gave in to the waves of pleasure that followed. She felt the aches of her body melting away, much as they had when she'd lain with Astrid.

Munin freed her hips and legs from the loose leather skirt she wore. She found her hand moving under his breechcloth, discovering that uniqueness of man that she had seen but never felt.

Neither spoke until Munin rolled on top of her. She gasped at the sudden feel of his weight. "It will hurt at first," he whispered. "I will be gentle."

"Don't," she gasped. "I want to know how it really feels."

So Munin drove himself deep within her. She screamed, and that moment was the first time she managed to fully forget how lonely she was without Astrid.

Thyri sought Munin's company from time to time during her last years with Scacath. The teacher was aware of it as she had been aware of Thyri and Astrid and even of Astrid and Hugin (of which Thyri learned only through a later admission of Astrid's).

Scacath would speak little of these things, but she made it clear that, in the arena of love, their bodies were their own. In the arena of battle, of course, things were quite different.

So Thyri went to Munin as she felt the need for comfort, and Munin was always there to fill the need. She came to love him in her way, though no one could ever completely fill the spaces in Thyri's heart that her several partings with Astrid left behind. And Thyri knew that when she left Scacath, she would return to Astrid, thus leaving Munin. He belonged to Scacath body and soul.

The seasons turned, and the following winter Thyri was tasked with the letters of the dead empire of the Romans, the onetime rulers of all the lands to the south of the world of the Vikings. She studied scrolls and books in the evenings next to her fire as Astrid had in years past, though her cousin's studying had had little meaning then. She found in the script a comfort, as if it added not another complication to her puzzle of the world, but the promise of a thread that might aid in holding the pieces together.

So passed Thyri's last years in training. Scacath cast the rune of sharpness on her sword so that she might spend less time in the evening on it and more in thought and study. This gift came at the end of her fifth year—one year early. She asked Scacath of this; her teacher told her only that traditions were meant to be broken.

Thyri took her final test and earned her seventh braid in a battle to first blood with Scacath. The teacher won, but Thyri lasted a full minute before catching a thrust in her left shoulder. She knew she had done well to fend off Scacath's attacks for so long. While Scacath inscribed the fifth rune of Odin on her blade, Thyri bade farewell to the ravens.

At parting, Scacath smiled her half-smile and handed Thyri her rune-clasp. "Farewell, little one. You are leaving with but a fraction more than that with which you came, though you may not think so now. You came here with your heart, and you leave here with your heart.

"The world of men will bring you pain, and though I cannot be there to guide you, I hope that I have given you the tools with which you might bear it well. I took you from loyalty to home and crown, and to that I now return you."

Scacath said these words in the glade where Thyri had met her seven years before. The sky was bright, and a light breeze blew from the north, calling Thyri to the road. When Scacath finished, the ravens took their places on her shoulders, and she turned. As she walked away, her form grew hazy, and by the time she reached the far end of the glade, she was as transparent as the still surface of wine in a goblet. Thyri could see through her to the trees beyond. And above the branches, she saw thin wisps of smoke, as of the cooking fires of a hall or a small village. Into the trees Scacath stepped, then she was gone.

21: Homecoming

Thyri was naked but for Astrid's sword that final day she returned to the family hall. Her hair was laced with ice and separate strands chinked against each other like light, ethereal armor when she moved. Her feet were numb, then burning, as she stamped on the floor of the hall and slowly, agonizingly, approached the fire.

All the old ones but Asta huddled in the corners, staring at her, whispering. She paid them no heed. Not a glance to even acknowledge that she knew where she was. There were no other sounds but those of the winds outside and a high keening that came from beyond the hall, from Asta's chamber.

When she was warm she turned for her room, sword before her, her hair dripping a wet trail behind. Her things lay in disarray over the cot, nothing important missing but her own blade. On top of the heap was an old, worn scroll. She took it up and unrolled it, her eyes scanning words they had first read five years before, in her sixth year with Scacath. Hugin had brought it to her from the world of men. The script was Latin:

Dearest Cousin,

Many times have I tried to write you, but always things have come in the way. Sometimes it has been a task assigned me by the king, sometimes the need to practice all the things I have learned (much of which you will know by now). And sometimes it is my loneliness for you, which runs so deep that I cannot draw on the words to speak it, much less work laboriously with this quill to write them in this strange tongue. Perhaps it is best, for now you will have had time to learn this writing, and you will not need Scacath or the ravens to read my words to you. I write to you, not to them, though I miss them as well.

Among Ragnar's men I am thought of highly for my skills, though it was not so at first. I earned my ninth braid after being here but a week. The king took me in, for Scacath had informed him of my coming and convinced him of my skill long before (perhaps by her magic? There is a rune she uses that persuades. I could never figure it out; its magic is much too refined for my clumsy talent). But Ragnar took me into his hall and gave me a room by the hall of the women, not, he said, because I belonged there, but that there I might avail myself of the baths and not be required to use the stream with the rest of his warriors. At first I thought this unnecessary, as well you might be thinking as you read this, but I assure you that a woman has enough problems gaining the respect of a male warrior without adding the allure of her body to his already-wrong thinking.

The hall is huge! We could fit five of ours into but the main room of this one, and Ragnar has another larger still for the small army he barracks between here and his fields, though most of the warriors are often absent—to their homes or to battles where they carve their way to Valhalla. In my two years, I have already fought and killed so often that, without the aid of the braid and the bead, I would have lost track long ago.

In the hall, I often have to match the arrogant gaze of Gyda. I still do not like her. A young boy, not even of ten summers, once came upon her by accident as she bathed with her maidens in the river. She made Ragnar kill him and send his head in a sack back to his father. I am not to question my king, but that hardly seems a wise way to rule. Ragnar is a good man, as strong and brave as any of his warriors, but his daughter is his weakness. I have thought idly of slaying her, but I think she knows of my disdain as she no longer stays long in any room into which I enter.

I have heard that Harald of Vestfold has just begun his campaign for her heart, though I have not had occasion to face his forces in battle. I think that it will not be so for long. I don't think that Ragnar will sail openly against Harald, but I can easily imagine him sending his warriors to the aid of those kingdoms against which Harald turns his strength. He does not wish to lose his daughter. If he were wise, he'd send her to Harald bound and gagged. The girl knows no humility.

As for me, I have fought against marauders from the North, mostly homeless men whose fathers' halls came into the hands of older brothers. All they seek is land, and for that they cannot be blamed. But when they seek it in the realm of our king, they show their lack of inspiration. They would do better to fare into the lands of the Saxons or the Franks, where they would not be facing Viking blades.

And I have fought the Danes at sea as well, though it makes no sense that they would come north into our waters while there is such plunder to be had in the South (I know, for I have been there as well!). It would seem that we Norse have not a direction, but only a lust for battle. I have seen men reach *beserk* fury and die with laughter on their lips, welcoming the call of Valhalla. Thus it is, though I think, perhaps out of ignorance and inexperience, that it need not be thus. We are of strong blood; you cannot imagine it but must see it in the faces of our foes to the South. And we are many too. I have seen the sea covered with our sails, while each ship is bound for a place different from the next. Were all to sail together, we could crush the legions of Surt! But this, for reasons beyond me, we do not do. Instead, we fight each other as well as the rest of the world.

It is not a bad life, and it births such tales as you never hear men tell except at the drunken feasts that follow the slaughter of an enemy host. Still, I often imagine you and I at the front of an army that would cause the Thunderer to pause, but though the men will accept me as a warrior, the problems confronting a leader are great and varied, and I do not think myself equal to the task. At least not yet.

Perhaps Harald of Vestfold is a leader who might unite the Vikings. But he is yet young, and his unity may come too late. The strength we have is now, and misuse now may make it impotent twenty years hence. At any rate, I should soon find myself on the battlefield with him, my sword against his, and not by his side. In the end, it doesn't matter. The ways of the warrior, all the ways of the warrior, lead to Valhalla—to serve Odin until Ragnarok.

My braids are twenty-one now. I will not tell them here, but will wait until we are again together, and make each a story for a separate night when, our passions spent, I will carry you into the realm of dreams with my words.

I miss you Thyri, little one, and await your arrival at Ragnar's hall with such longing that you cannot imagine. I know that you must have labored long to read this (as I have in writing it!), and I do not wish you should spend your evenings fashioning a reply in a language you do not yet know well enough to use. Your coming here one year hence will serve as your reply.

Astrid

After reading the scroll, Thyri stared at it, her dripping hair smearing the ink and destroying the delicate parchment she had taken care to preserve for so long.

"Father's dead."

She turned, crumpling the parchment in her hand.

Erik stood in the doorway. His hazel eyes were blank, empty of emotion. "He came here yesterday and took up your sword. I watched him. He gripped the hilt and would not let go until the sorcery killed him. I have the blade hidden. I will get it for you if you wish."

She wanted to smile at him—at his bravery, at his failure to condemn her. She cried instead. "Take it, Erik Eirikson. Fashion for yourself a gauntlet of silver and bear my sword into battle. Perhaps then you shall remember your sister as a warrior and not as—"

The words caught in her throat. Through swimming tears she surveyed her possessions arrayed before her. Asta's keening grew more intense, more malevolent.

"The volva tries to purge the evil from our blood," Erik said. "She and Yrsa have not stepped from her room for two days. They work magic to slay you."

"May they succeed." Thyri picked up a leather shift and pulled it over her head, then sat to pull on her boots. She gathered together her belongings in silence. Clasping her cloak, she stepped past her brother, out of the hall that was now his, and into the snows.

For two nights she prowled the shoreline in search of a seaworthy craft for one. She settled on a fishing skiff with a single mast and locks for eight oars. She wrapped Astrid's sword in oilskin, stocked the small boat with food and drink, and set sail. She followed the Valkyrie's belt star—the one that whirls from one end of the sky to the other over the course of a night. Thyri didn't know where it would lead her. She didn't know what she would do if the winds died. She didn't really care.

Book II: THE ISLAND

I proceed with some misgivings. Ten times as many words might be written to bring me to this point, and many things which I have mentioned only in passing could be discussed here at great length. But then, when I think on it, little might be gained, and much lost. The Twilight is of central importance, and its roots lie in Astrid's death.

I apologize to my reader if the haste with which I have told this tale thus far has created confusion. Many of the characters I have presented must seem little more than names, and though several are important, particularly Gyda of Hordaland, Harald of Vestfold, and Thyri's brother Erik, I will not ask that they be committed now to memory. Their importance will become apparent in due course. My only excuse is that I have tried to cover twenty-one years of a woman's life in this space, and those years were far from ordinary. I pledge here to proceed in greater detail.

Other volumes, I suppose, could be written of the exploits of Thyri and Astrid during the four years they were together after Thyri left Scacath's grove. For the most part, they were happy during this time, but they did little more than live and love from one battle to the next. Astrid gained, over time, a moderate degree of competence in the runic ways. I wonder yet if that might not have been what slew her. Perhaps, confronted with an unnatural foe, her thoughts turned for a moment to consider her sorceries. And in that moment she would have lost the advantage of her sword. It would, ironically, be then that the runes began to fail the iron. Astrid need not have died, and Thyri need not have felt the fangs of the wolf. Without her curse, Thyri would not have come to affect the lives of so many men and gods alike, and Lif and Lifthrasir might now be molding the ashes of Midgard to their liking, perhaps making the same mistakes as we who came before.

I will mention now that I do not profess to understand the majority of that which Thyri learned under Scacath. I am no mean swordsman, and I have lived my life on the strength of my sword and my wits, but the techniques of Scacath get caught in my imagination. And they were not taught to be thought on; they were taught to be practiced with repetition so exacting that one would hardly imagine the end result to be a free, flowing, and impossibly powerful style. I am able, then, only to write *of* it. Perhaps someone, if not myself, may glean from it the essence that made it so effective.

And still my researches have not shown me why two girls from a young barbarian kingdom warranted the attention of one such as Scacath. Perhaps there is no answer. I can imagine the Norns sitting in their dark cave, weaving their tapestry of life. Perhaps near the end of their work they grew bored and wove in Thyri and Astrid to make their final days more interesting.

Lastly, here, I paint a final picture thus far only sketched: Astrid had the type of beauty that has always reminded me of spring. Her blond hair was long and silky, grown to just above her waist before she died. Her eyes were sky blue. Her face was full and round and little-girlish with that delicate Aryan symmetry that gives the Norse such presence.

Thyri stood a head shorter, and her hair was streaked with dark and reddish gold. It was thicker hair, and it splayed over her shoulders like the mane of a lioness. While Astrid was tall and gracefully lean, Thyri was a small, compact bundle of curves and muscle. Her face was more animated than Astrid's; screwed into a mask of rage, it was the face of a cornered wildcat. Full of joy, it was a face of innocence that could break the stoutest of hearts, even with the jagged, inch-long scar that ran down from the lower lid of her left eye. But that scar is another story. Her eyes were deep hazel, and the scar ran down from the one like a permanent tear.

Magic

Figures approach through the clouds. She runs. There's an eye where the moon should be. Watching—no, looking for her. Not yet. Not yet—she hides. It isn't time yet.

"Easy girl."

The figures pass overhead. The pride of Odin—the Valkyries —on winged wolves . . .

A hand on her breast, another on her brow. They are damp.

What?

"You're safe here. Be calm."

Wet all over, she shakes. Her head throbs. She opens her eyes; a white brilliance stabs through, forcing her eyelids shut. She tries to sit, but the pain knocks her back. She feels something at her lip—water. She opens her mouth and the cool liquid makes her tongue tingle. She drinks and feels the water rush down her parched throat, burning, caressing.

"Easy! You'll drown."

Water. She remembers: the boat, the ocean, the numbing cold after the storm. Relentless. *Am I dead?*

She remembers more. "The sword! Astrid's sword!" Thyri tries to sit again; the pain doesn't let her.

"Shhh."

The hand is soothing and the voice almost purrs. "It is here. Safe. Try to rest."

She rests. She wanders back into the clouds. She looks up at the eye. It still can't see her. It still isn't time.

"I found you among the rocks," she said. Her body was lean and firm, rippling supplely in a black cotton shift as she sat on a stool next to Thyri's cot. Her skin was pale olive, and she had dark eyes and full, friendly lips. Thyri judged her about twenty-five. For a moment, Thyri almost believed she was with Scacath.

Her long black hair was pulled back over slightly large, delicate ears, then fell freely down her back. Thyri sat and her vision blurred as the blood rushed from her head. She blinked; her eyes

51

fixed on a small mole decorating the slender line of the woman's neck. Her mouth filled with saliva and she felt a dark, hungry stirring within her.

No!

She smacked the side of her head with her fist. She opened her eyes again. The woman shimmered, then grew solid. She smiled. Candlelight ignited black, playful flames in her eyes.

Thyri looked around. They were in a small earthen hut with clay jars and pale green plants cluttering shelves lining the walls. Skins covered the floor and braziers burned in the four corners, perfuming the air with enticing incense. Another heady aroma came from a larger pot warming over a gentle fire by the door.

"You are not Norse," Thyri said, looking back to the woman.

"No. I'm not."

"You speak my language well."

Her awareness grew. A long stream of sunlight cut through a slat in the hut's door to lose itself in the candlelight. A fireplace, its embers cold and gray, was cut into the opposite wall. From outside: the bleating of a goat, the occasional cluck of a chicken, the mating call of a grouse in the far distance. The dull roar of the sea nearby, pounding against a cliff. Invigorating, moisture-laden air. There were no sounds of men. The hut faced west—were it the morning sun beyond the door, the birds of the morning would have been singing out their greetings to the day.

The woman smiled. "Thank you. I try to learn all that I come across. The mysteries require it. I could not have healed you otherwise."

"You are a witch?"

"I have been called that."

Mystery in those black eyes, Thyri thought. *Mystery and dark, knowing mirth.* "I was dying?"

"You were not well."

She looked longingly at the pot. "Where am I?"

Light laughter. Shadows deep as moonless black dancing in those mysterious eyes. "You're hungry, aren't you? Not surprising." She got up and ladled a bowl of stew from the caldron and handed it to Thyri. "You are on Kaerglen Isle," she said. "It's just off the coast of Erin. The name can't mean much to you. We're a very petty kingdom." She paused. "Kaerglen is the name of the ruling family. My name is Meg."

Forcing her hands to steady themselves, Thyri tipped the bowl to her lips. Small, fresh chunks of rabbit meat and little onions stung and tantalized her tongue.

Days, she thought. She had tasted nothing for days. Licking

the spoon, she grinned at her hostess. "Thyri Eiriksdattir."

"Do you speak Irish, Thyri?"

"No."

"Then I must teach you. It will make your convalescence pass quickly."

"How long have I been here?"

"Four days."

"I should be well soon?"

Meg nodded. Thyri tried to remember the sea. She had left Norway two days after the last full moon. She had been on the sea three days before the storm hit, and she could remember three days after that. But then . . . ?

With twenty-five days between one full moon and the next, she could account for twelve. But how many lost at sea? "The moon," she asked. "How full is the moon?"

Meg laughed. "Eight days yet. You needn't worry."

"About what?"

"That the moon will call again before you can leave me. You do not want to kill me."

How did you know?

I am a witch.

The shadow eyes smiled. "I know many things," Meg said. "I tended you for four days. To heal, I entered your dreams. You're afraid, aren't you? You have not been this way long."

"No." Thyri lowered her eyes. Less than a month; it felt like forever. And suddenly something in Megan's gaze made her feel warm, loved. She felt that tang of magic, but she felt it comforting her. Healing her yet.

Megan had bewitched her.

The charm was probably in the broth that she poured down Thyri's throat until she could stomach no more. Or perhaps it was only the eyes; they have caused many other, more impressive things to come to pass.

Still eating, now on her second bowl of the stew, Thyri spoke of Astrid and how they had found the *were*-kill on a lonely Norse road. She spoke of the tracking and how the beast then set upon them. She spoke of Astrid's death and of the wolf's transformation. She spoke of her first change, when she had killed her mother, and she spoke of the trauma of the ordeal—the agony of the changes, the three days of fear and blood and hunger, the slayings of her uncle and cousin.

And she told Meg how Astrid's shade had stopped her from slaying herself and had bid her leave—to seek a life in the world apart from the Vikings. Thyri spilled her heart, hardly aware that anyone listened. Once started, she had to get it out. She had denied and lied to herself about the truth for too long. It was burning a hole in her soul.

"This Astrid was very special to you?" the sorceress asked when Thyri's words finally gave way to muffled, wracking sobs.

"We fought many years side by side. She was my cousin and—" She stopped, gazing into the shadow world in Megan's eyes. Nymphs danced there, whorls of black pleasure trailing up and down their thighs.

Lover?

Yes.

Meg drew a long bundle from among the skins at her feet. She unraveled it. A faint violet light played along the edge of the rune-blade. "This was Astrid's?"

"Yes. Do not touch it. It may kill."

Meg smiled at her obliquely. "I have touched it already. It is very strong." Her fingers traced over the runes, and Thyri wondered what powers she commanded. *She's a witch* . . .

"This is no normal weapon," Meg said. "The lore of these runes has been lost to most for many years."

The shadow gaze fell on Astrid's sword. Thyri felt a darkness rising within her, as if only those eyes kept her sane. She shook her head, casting away the tendrils of madness. "Why did you save me, Meg?"

"Why not?"

"You do not know me, but you see into my nature. I would have let me die."

"I am not you. Astrid told you to live on: heed her. The stars favor you. I tried to cast your future and learned nothing. The mark of Chaos shelters you, and that in itself hints at your Destiny. You bear a blade from the realms of Twilight, and I know of only one who brings such weapons into this world. Besides, you are Norse, you are fair, and I have little company and few friends. And your soul is not black."

"Nor is it white." Thyri squinted, noting the casual way Meg handled the weapon. "What do you know of Scacath?"

Meg tested the rune-sword in the air. "Little, but enough. Do not lose this."

Thyri smiled, watching. "When you slash from side to side, don't reverse like that. Do it like this." She traced a loopy, upside down *T* in the air with her finger. Meg tried it; Thyri advised further, but the sorceress shook her head, smiled, and handed Thyri the sword.

"I am not a warrior," Meg said. "If I must kill, I prefer subtler methods." She sat down on the edge of the cot and brushed the hair off Thyri's cheek. "You are very beautiful."

The sorcerous grip of Meg's eyes faded suddenly. Thyri looked into a face of mortality, of woman. Meg's neck taunted her, scant inches from her face. She remembered the wolf, deep inside, stirring in its dark lust when it had first looked out on her savior. And she thought also of Astrid.

She turned away.

The witch smiled distantly and rose. "Would you like more stew?"

"No. Thank you. I feel tired again. How long before I am well?"

"A few days. You must learn much in that time. I can aid you with spells, but you are too weak yet to begin. Sleep now. We'll start in the morning." Meg turned.

"Meg?"

Traces of shadow mirth again, flitting in the doorway. "Yes."

"Thank you."

Meg shrugged and left. Thyri lay back, closed her eyes, and cried herself to sleep.

She woke the next morning alone. Near silence from without: the sea was calm, only swallows called to each other in the distance. She rose and staggered to the hut's door. A morning fog was lifting, the sky overcast but still.

She stepped out. An unkempt path ran from the hut's door into a stand of wood a hundred or so yards to the south. Meg's home was built into an embankment, shielded from gales coming off the sea. The ground to either side was muddy, scattered with straw. A fenced-in garden stretched along one side of the path and several hens scratched at the ground nearby. From beyond, behind the hut, sheep bleated.

Thyri looked down at herself. She wore a short shift tied loosely at the waist—lighter clothing than she'd worn at sea. And it had a clean smell; Meg had dressed her. A breeze teased her bare thighs. She heard laughter nearby, shrugged, and started toward it through the mud that squished pleasantly between her toes.

Meg faced away from her, hands on hips, facing off a goat that had caught itself in a thick patch of the muck. The witch still laughed. She wore a shift like Thyri's and calf-high boots. One hand held a coiled rope.

Thyri trudged to her side.

"The storm you weathered at sea did not direct its fury at you alone," Meg said, still watching the goat. It gave up its struggling and sat back on its haunches with a vulgar plop. "They grazed this stretch bare long ago, and a good rain can leave the ground here like this for weeks." She waded to the goat's side and tied her rope loosely around its neck. "I could perhaps repair it"—she glanced at Thyri—"but this sort of thing has a certain primitive charm." She stood, smiling brightly and wiping a lock of hair from her face with the back of a muddy hand, streaking wet brown along on her cheek. Thyri laughed. The goat stared at them blankly.

Meg stepped back, breathed deeply, and started to pull on the rope. Thyri joined her, and together they hauled the animal out onto firmer ground. Meg untied it and it scampered away toward four sheep that grazed along the edge of the southern wood.

"Well," Meg said, eyeing the splotches along her forearms. "Shall we bathe? There is a hot spring a short way into the wood."

The spring bubbled out of a rocky outcrop into a pool ten feet across, which itself ran into a briskly cold stream. Meg fell on the grass beside it and pulled off her boots, then took them to the stream where she knelt and forced them into the current.

Thyri looked up. Swallows swooped back and forth through the treetops above. A rabbit burst through a bush, hopped toward the spring, then noticed Thyri and shot out of sight.

She sat at the edge of the spring and eased her feet into the water, brushing the mud away with long, critical strokes. The downy hair on her legs seemed lighter than usual, almost white.

The sorceress carried her dripping burden to the spring. "Peaceful, isn't it?" she said, sitting next to Thyri. "This is where I come to think."

"Isn't it lonely?"

Meg laughed. "You mean living here? By myself?" She dipped her boots next to Thyri's feet, then laid them aside on the grass. "What is loneliness, Thyri?" She rose and pulled her shift over her head. "I have a peace of a sort in my heart."

Thyri looked up. Meg's hair dangled freely around her waist. Her nipples tightened under the caress of the open air.

Thyri's senses heightened, responding to the nearness of Meg's pale flesh. The sorceress moved then, thrusting the triangle of soft black hair between her thighs into Thyri's view. She dived into the spring, leaving Thyri's senses reeling, her mind raging chaotic war with itself. She closed her eyes and saw her hands touching those lean thighs, probing their secrets. And she imagined her claws springing forth, gouging to the bone, spraying the morning red.

And then, without warning, Megan's eyes . . . a feeling of calm, peace.

You fear for nothing, little one.

A hand on her foot, tugging playfully, then forcefully, pulling her off the rocks and into the hot, steaming water.

Your body is ever your own, except when the moon comes.

She found herself floating, her hair tickling her face. Deft hands slid her shift over her head.

And even then you are lost only if you believe it so.

Thyri surfaced. Meg's playful smile fell away. Hesitantly, she reached out and traced the inner curve of Thyri's shoulder with her fingertips. She kicked forward, melting their bodies together. "Let go of your fears," she whispered. "Your curse cannot touch us here."

Later, Thyri lay back on the grass, watching the clouds break overhead, picking out shapes of eagles and bears and watching one cloud transform itself from the profile of a warrior with shield into the laughing face of an impish hill giant.

She lay where Meg had placed her, her head in the center of a circle of squat, gray, undressed stones. She could still feel the wetness of her hair behind her ears. The tang of sorcery filled her sixth sense—Meg's spell, to teach her Irish.

The sorceress sat before a small incense brazier behind Thyri's head. Flowers and shallow bowls of oily liquids were set around her. She hummed softly, occasionally touching damp fingers to Thyri's forehead. In her lap was a small harp. She built her hum into melodious song and her fingers danced lightly on the harp's strings. The music gripped Thyri, possessing her until the sky grew dreamlike and the ground under her giving, as if made of down rather than earth. Meg's song had no words, but it spoke of bright truths: of happiness shared among men; of the warrior with raised, open palm and friendly eyes.

Of moving lips. Of lips moving.

The perception of a mouth.

The pictures grew. Red, moving lips. Sentences returned: *She had moving, speaking, lips. She lips that moved and spoke had . . . Lips moving had she (waving tongue and voice in her throat —she spoke) The woman spoke . . .*

Vision grayed, the lips fading to crimson-limned shadows, the last sentence echoing: *The woman spoke, spoke, woman spoke, spoke, man spoke, woman spoke . . .*

The thought-language wasn't Norse. Not any language. *I have no tongue,* she thought. The lips were solid again and they smiled. *Move to her ear! Speak softly of the beauty of sunrise in no tongue, in every tongue.*

Language is given, only speech changes.

The lips grew, grinned, and opened, swallowing her. A melody—not Norse—of a farm boy cursed with the love of a lady weaved in tragic tempo through the altar halls of the sun. She heard it; she cried. Her tears filled with honeysuckle and moonlight. They fell through her, and she dreamed.

Departures

"We are on the north side—here."

Megan pointed to a nondescript spot on the parchment map of Kaerglen Isle over which she and Thyri bent. The island was roughly pear-shaped with a short peninsula in the southwest. "In the southeast corner is Castle Kaerglen. The isle is well populated within a day's ride of it. With a good horse, you can get there in a day and half."

"Why do you live so separate from them, Meg?"

Two days had passed since Thyri had first wakened. She already felt strong; she had managed some fair sword-practice that afternoon.

"I do not enjoy their company, and they fear mine."

"Why?"

She smiled. "I'm a witch."

"But your skill can be of much use to them. Surely the king can use you?"

Thyri spoke carefully, in Irish. To her amazement, Meg's spell of the day before had worked, as if it had opened a room in her mind that craved to be filled with new words, new ideas. Meg had explained that the spell had provided a structural basis upon which they needed only add vocabulary, and this process had been aided by further sorceries. Thyri felt she already knew Irish better than Latin, and she'd spent years laboring to master *that* tongue's script under Scacath.

"The king distrusts sorcery. He has his reasons. On the peninsula, here, in the South," Meg said, pointing again to the map, "lives Pye, the wizard of the Blue Moon. He is Kaerglen's cousin —once was his adviser. Now they are bitter enemies. The wizard desires Castle Kaerglen, and one day, I think, he will take it."

"Why?"

"He is powerful, very cunning, and his soul has turned black. He has no army to speak of, only what beasts he conjures from time to time, but he has repelled every one of Kaerglen's attempts against his grove. Or his army's attempts—he rarely involves

59

himself in military matters. I've tried to offer him my aid, but he refuses it."

"Why?"

"He has advisers who tell him to distrust all mages, whatever their power or motive." Meg took the parchment map, rolled it up, and handed it to Thyri. "Take this with you. You will need to know the lay of the land six days hence."

"I will stay with you, Meg, if you wish. You saved my life."

She laughed. "Stay? While your body screams out for blood? You are a warrior, and every part of you wants to seek service for your sword. Kaerglen, though not very bright, is an honorable man. He rules with a gentle hand; it is his advisers who lead him astray. But you can aid him. You want to aid him. You also want to dangle the point of your sword before Pye and force him to tell you the nature of the Moon Mysteries. Tell you how you might be rid of your curse. His assumed title mystifies you, doesn't it?"

Thyri looked down at her hands.

"I'm sorry, Thyri. Don't think that I'm reading your mind, because I'm not. You intrigue me, and I see well the people who intrigue me. I asked the last question for another reason—a warning. Do not let him tempt you. There is no cure for the beast within you."

"No . . ."

Meg smiled at her sadly. "You can leave tonight. I will conjure a gate for you. There is an inn at Kaerglen called the Blooded Boar. In stepping through the gate, you will step through the front door of the public house. You should find the Captain of the Kaerglen Guard there—a man by the name of Cuilly. Impress him, and you will find service for your sword. It will not be easy; the sword is a man's toy here."

"So is it elsewhere, with a few exceptions." Thyri placed her hand lightly on Meg's, then ran it slowly up her arm.

Megan Elana Kaerglen. If ever I encountered one as enigmatic as Thyri, it was she. I have no proof, but I doubt Thyri would ever have seen Kaerglen's shores were it not for the sorceress. Whatever her ultimate purpose, Meg drew her here.

Wildfire

Thyri forced her way in through the crowded tavern tables. She wore her sables over a light leather jerkin, and she wore the boots she'd lined with the skin of a rabbit she'd killed long ago. Her sword swung prominently at her side. The inn was full of noise, but all of it died by the time she reached the bar. The innkeep stared at her questioningly.

"Mead," she said.

"Let me buy for the costumed whore!"

A loud, adventurous voice behind her.

Several men laughed. Thyri turned and laughed back, the torchlight casting a dark shadow in her teardrop scar. "Save it for the goats," she said.

She took her mead and paid the innkeep, then turned back to the crowd. Most in the house were soldiers. She scanned them, looking for Cuilly by Meg's description. She found him in the corner, drinking with whom she guessed were two lieutenants; he watched her like the others. She smiled coyly when their eyes met.

A large man, goaded by the others, rose and approached her. "Are you the one with the mouth?" Thyri asked.

"You have no manners, girl," he said, stopping in front of her. "I'm going to teach you a lesson."

Thyri laughed and glanced at the blade at his belt. "Won't you use your sword?" She placed a hand on the hilt of her own.

"Against a whore?" He lunged, barely managing to stop as Thyri whipped her blade from its scabbard and leveled it at his throat. He backed away slowly. The men behind him jeered.

"Draw your sword, goatherd."

The fear of what he saw in Thyri's eyes had not yet overcome his bravado. He went for his blade. As he brought it up, she smashed hers down, landing a crushing blow on his hilt. He winced in pain. He lowered himself for a lunge, but a hand fell on his shoulder from behind, and Cuilly pushed him aside.

"Who are you, woman?" he asked, glaring.

He was tall and brawny. Thyri knew the type: fairly level-headed, she could see it in his dark blue eyes. A commander by virtue of wit *and* ability. But only so much ability—he hadn't taken this wizard who afflicted his king.

"Who wants to know?"

"I am Sean Cuilly. I command these men."

"Well, then, Sean Cuilly. I am Thyri Eiriksdattir. I wish to join these men."

He laughed. "Where did you get that sword, wench? If the smith put you up to this, I'll personally flog him."

"You're not very quick-witted, are you, Sean Cuilly? Can you not see that this blade is finer than any your men bear?" She waved it in his face.

He eyed her distrustfully. "Leave, girl. I'll not have you disrupt my men."

Thyri matched his gaze and shifted into a relaxed fighting stance. "Perhaps you would like to throw me out?"

Cuilly touched the hilt of his sword, then glanced at the man he had pushed aside. He was on the floor, still wincing, nursing his hand. "She knows what she's doing, Cap'n."

Cuilly laughed after a moment and looked back at Thyri. She smiled, saluting him with her blade.

"Do you really want to live with this rabble?"

"I have some silver. I shall stay here."

"We muster at dawn each morning."

"So? I'll be there. I will enjoy teaching your rabble how to spar."

"Will you?" He laughed. "Come, let me refill your mug. You can tell me how a girl masters the sword."

They drank and talked of weaponry and war. She told him of longboat raids into Germany with Astrid. They spoke of technique and strategy, and Cuilly's respect for her grew as the night wore on. But she would speak only of battles and courage. Of her presence on Kaerglen Isle, she would say nothing.

That puzzled Cuilly. Outsiders seldom found the mist-shrouded island. The legends said that the mists could foil armadas. He had grown up believing them. The only merchant vessels that could find the isle easily were native. But now this woman with laughing eyes and a blade that looked forged in some hell pit had simply shown up out of nowhere.

And the blade was well trained. Its mistress floated in his mead-laden vision, speaking of experiences that paled anything he had seen on his island. Before the night was up he offered her the wage and barracks of a lieutenant. Even if she couldn't fight, he reasoned, she surely talked a great battle.

What else were lieutenants for?

Dawn was hazy with the light rising in bands of deep red coursed with orange rivers, teasing the paling blue overhead. Thyri breathed in the air and stomped about the training field, getting the feel of its earth into her feet. She drew her blade and tested it against the morning.

On the crest of a hill high above her she could just see a corner of the castle—the seat of the island's power. She wondered if the royal family had risen as early as she or if they lay still in their down beds, dreaming the dreams granted only those born to rule.

The practice field was skirted by barracks on two sides and the quarters of the officers on another. The side facing the castle was left open for parades and demonstrations. For the moment, the field was hers alone. She danced around it in a system of attacks and parries, imagining a formidable foe as fast as she. She imagined his sword longer than hers. She imagined his strength greater.

Men began to emerge from the barracks, yawning, rubbing sore eyes and heads while their stomachs rebelled and vented foul fumes into the air. They watched Thyri's sword-dance. Some laughed. Most watched her dully through glazed eyes, occasionally looking away when the rapid flashings of her blade grew painful.

Thyri fought on until she slew her invisible foe. She eyed the disordered ranks of the men before stamping off to lean against the officers' barracks, gathering in her sables against the cold. For a moment the men continued to watch her, then the door behind her creaked open and the field sergeants barked their charges into line.

Cuilly came out while his lieutenants marched through the ranks. He stopped next to Thyri and squinted into the morning haze.

"I will not help you," he said, rubbing the stubble on his chin. "They must see you for themselves. There are those among them who feel that strength of sword alone should make them commanders. Others are wiser. But you start at a disadvantage with them all."

She scratched idly in the dirt with the toe of her boot. "I have commanded men before, Captain."

"Yes," he said, starting away. "But it was never easy, was it?"

* * *

His small army settled, Cuilly announced with deadpan seri-
ousness his recruitment of Lieutenant Thyri Eiriksdattir. The
ranks rippled with comments and muffled laughter. Thyri sought
among them the man she had put down the night before in the
Blooded Boar. He laughed along with the rest.

Cuilly surveyed them. His command voice boomed out, loud
and strong: "Those among you who have something to say on
this—come forth and speak you minds!"

The men were for a moment taken aback. They shifted; their
captain's gaze was hard and icy. Those of uncertain conviction
began to fall silent.

"Respec'fully, Cap'n."

A short, brawny swordsman sidestepped from the sergeants'
line. His eyes were alert, his features patiently intense and scarred
by many years in his chosen profession. "Even if she's more'n
she looks," he continued, "as I heard went on at the Boar last
night, she can hardly be 'xpected to stand well in the field. Few
fancy moves is one thing. Womens got no stamina. Can't keep a
good hilt grip for more'n a minute at a time."

The sergeant drew raucous approval from his men.

The captain smiled wryly. "Well voiced, Duagan. Step farther
to the flank." He turned to the others. "Any who think the same
and are prepared to back their thoughts with blood may join this
man!"

The declaration further disrupted the assembly. When all motion had stopped, eleven men stood behind Duagan, some as
scarred and seasoned, others young and arrogant.

"Well met," Cuilly said to them. "We shall spar this morning.
He who defeats Lieutenant Eiriksdattir shall gain a week's liberty
at the brothel of his choice."

Smiles behind Duagan. Moans from the massed ranks—a few
tried to break and join the contestants; their sergeants forced them
back into line.

"I'd rather bed the lieutenant, with all due respect, sir."

A broadly grinning youth among her foes. Thyri placed him at
twenty, maybe a year more. He was tall and lanky, sporting a
disheveled blond mop. His gestures were lazy and slightly
clumsy. Her gaze fell placidly on his. He grinned, but Thyri's
unblinking pressure shortly turned his eyes.

"You may petition her first for that privilege, soldier," Cuilly
said.

"Duagan oughta be first!" someone protested.

"She ought'nt get to use that sword, Cap'n," another said.

"Switch says it glows evil. Says it's what beat 'im last night."

"What matters a woman with *any* sword," Cuilly countered, "to a week with the best port whores, paid by the king's gold?"

The men laughed heartily and Thyri broke her long silence: "Let you each choose your weapon, it matters not to me except that we are matched. I tire of this foolish chatter." She looked them over slowly. "But let each of you say now that, should you lose, you will consent to my command." She glanced at Cuilly. "Any who refuse this should be returned to the main ranks."

Cuilly appraised her anew. Of all things, he hadn't expected this. The challenge had attracted the worst, the most headstrong, hardened, and foolish of his men. Eight of the twelve had been before him to answer for incidents requiring his disciplinary hand —stolen chickens, brawls in both city and port. Duagan himself had once led a drunken band of soldiers against the crew of an English merchantman that had rested overly long in the port.

And she wanted to command them? "Well?"

Slowly, each man nodded. None refused Thyri's demand. Cuilly looked at her. *Who are you, woman? Where did you come from in truth?* "Each battle," he shouted, "to first blood or submission by mace or staff! Fall out!"

Thyri unclasped her cloak and stepped forward into the spreading circle of men. The youth who had spoken out moved to face her. She raised an eyebrow.

"Swords," he declared. "I am afraid of no blade."

Thyri shrugged, drew Astrid's sword, and closed on him. He charged. Iron clanged against iron as she met his blow. She brought her knee up sharply, into his stomach. He bent in pain.

"You are careless, young warrior." She smashed her pommel down on his sword hand and the weapon clattered to the ground.

Thyri backed off. The youth straightened painfully, glaring at her.

"Submit," she said.

He grunted. "First blood," he muttered, grasping his blade. "So said the cap'n."

A moment later he retired from the field, a long, slashing wound across his right breast, just over the nipple.

The next man fought with knives. She marked him in the same place as the last and then it became a game to her—marking each man in turn on his right breast. None declared an unedged weapon against her. As the morning wore on, the crowd began to cheer. Some of the soldiers, however, grew afraid. Whispers of sorcery surfaced anew.

Duagan was the last. He swaggered out to face her, drawing his sword in salute.

"Will you wear my mark as well, Sergeant?"

"Aye, mistress. I'll spar w' you." He looked to Cuilly, then to the awed soldiery. "But not for any whore or e'en the crown on yon hill! These eyes never seen a blade worked so well or so quickly. And eleven men afore me! Woman's got stamina more'n the lot o' you!" He grinned at Thyri. "I'll be yer right hand. Be you woman or demon, I'll die for you if ye'll have me."

She faced him, her stained blade lowering. He looked like a tough, wildly grinning bulldog. Tears rose to her eyes.

Duagan charged, swinging wide. "No tears now, woman," he grunted as he closed. "Ye'll lose all ye've gained."

She recovered and faced him again. Grinning yet, Duagan ripped away his jerkin and bared his chest. He drew a knife from his belt and put the point to his flesh, drawing it slowly up and around. He cast Thyri one last bemused look before turning on the soldiers.

"What're you staring at? Game's over—move your legs! Been slouching all morn. Ye're going so.t."

From the side, Cuilly looked on. He watched Thyri take up her cloak and clasp it; then she approached him, with Duagan, marked by his own blade, at her side. Cuilly began to wonder just what it was he'd done.

For the next few days he could hear her from dawn through dusk, shouting at them, laughing with them. Cuilly left her alone. As long as she returned them to their barracks too worn to cause trouble, he didn't mind.

It was the king who truly troubled him. The full moon approached and Pye's power would reach its height. Already, the steady sorcerous onslaught kept the king abed. If the wizard's hold did not break soon, Coryn would die, leaving the island to either the wizard or Queen Moira. Neither prospect sat well with the captain of the guard.

Since the king's cousin had retreated into his groves, Cuilly had managed nothing. When he fared into the wood, demons rose from the ground to slay his men. The wood would not burn. Those who lived to return from it came always with no news of Pye's exact whereabouts. What good then was his new lieutenant and her tamed maniacs?

Blue Moon

". . . an' that's the whole of it, mistress."

Duagan sat back and took up his flagon. Thyri sat across from him, drawing patterns in spilt mead with the point of a dagger. She drained her flagon thoughtfully.

"Among that wood," she said, "I can find him."

"An' kill him? He will not meet us with iron."

She hailed the innkeep to refill their flagons. "I do not fear death, Duagan. In many ways I desire it."

"Then we'll tell the cap'n. He'll be ready to try anything now. Moon goes full night after t'morrow."

"No. He would lead us all in. Even should we succeed, many would die. And I doubt we'd succeed. A smaller force will carry with it surprise, and that is what we will need."

Duagan grinned. "Won't none of us fail you or betray you, mistress."

Fresh mead came and Thyri paused to drink deeply. "Can't all go. Some have to stay and make noise tomorrow morning. Can't let Cuilly catch on too soon or he'll do something stupid. And fewer travel faster, more quietly."

"Ye'll not leave me behind."

"No." She smiled at him warmly. "I never thought that. You I want, and one other. Modraig—the youth. He is very good with a bow."

Duagan grinned and grunted. "Modraig it is. I'll rail at the others to keep in line while we're gone."

Thyri reflected on the past days as she supped alone that evening. She had garnered loyalty such as she'd never dreamed under Ragnar. In time, she thought, she could command them all.

The food went bland in her mouth. She'd nearly forgotten those last nights in her homeland. Amid fighting men, their swords, their boasts, and their brawling, she could almost believe all was well. It took her back to her days with Astrid. Before her curse.

I don't have time, she thought. *Unless Pye can help me, I don't have time.*

There is no cure for the beast within you.

She drained her flagon and spat. She went to her vanity box for her hair things and combed meditatively for a while before taking up her bead and starting to braid. Her knots were twenty-seven now. She did each slowly, eyes distant and reflective. And all the while she hoped that the night would, in one way or another, kill her pain.

They left an hour after nightfall, Duagan leading the way, with Modraig following and Thyri keeping rear guard. They went on horseback until far into the western forest; then they tethered their mounts and continued on foot.

Away from the steeds, Thyri stopped them and sat among shadows under a great elm, extending her senses into the land around her. She detected the calls of distant birds, smelt the passion fragrances of distant blossoms. She searched until she located what she sought: a faint but definite taint of sorcery. She rose, and led her party on.

Pye's grove was a dark, gnarled stand of oaks around which the surrounding forest was stunted and lifeless. Thyri stopped them in the last stand of healthy trees, beside a wide, lazy stream that passed along the edge of the desolation around the grove. All was silent within—no lights, nothing. The waxing moon peeped at them over the grove's top edge. Thyri forced herself to look at it. Though two days remained before its power would take charge of her form, she could already feel it calling to her, lovingly, menacingly. She sneered at it.

A thick, evil-smelling stretch of water issued from the grove and joined the wider stream at which they had stopped. It was up this that Thyri led them into the oaks, her sword out and ready. Duagan and Modraig both carried light crossbows. Thyri held a small throwing ax in her left hand. From within, a discordant singing erupted. The wizard, Thyri hoped, casting his spell against Kaerglen, unaware yet that his domain was invaded.

She tried to think of a better plan than simply seeking out the voice, but further ingenuity failed her. She had no real estimate of Pye's talents (would that Meg were here! she thought, cursing herself for failing to ask more about the wizard before leaving). She could imagine them: trees with eyes, trees whose branches would come to life and strangle anything unrecognized, alien. For this reason she had chosen the stream. Foul as it was, she doubted it held anything more than filth. Filth could not kill, and it seemed logical that the stream would be less protected than the rest of the grove. Pye's powers had to have limits, and she hoped that he would think the stench of the stream deterrent enough.

They rounded a bend and Thyri bumped into the first body. It lay across her path, strangely bent, its bloated face evilly grinning up at her in the moonlight, its stench assaulting her nostrils full force. Its feet were caught up in the roots of a tree, and Thyri halted the others. She felt carefully around the morbid obstacle. Bits of flesh fell off bone and caught in the dead man's trousers —leather like Cuilly's men wore. Eventually, Thyri found what she sought: the man's right leg was bound against the roots with heavy rope. She smiled grimly. Pye had placed his guard there— a guard with nothing sorcerous about it, a guard of fear and revulsion.

She freed the body and pushed it around behind her. It floated slowly away with the current. Farewell, my friend, she thought. *You have served the wizard long enough.*

Modraig gagged as the rotting carcass that had once been a man went past him. When he fell silent, Thyri led them forward again.

They came on no more bodies until three more windings of the stream. The bed fell away under Thyri's feet, and she started to swim, then paused. Ahead, dimly visible in the moonlight, something loglike obstructed the surface of the water. Two more decaying human bodies lay end to end along the surface.

She tested the flow of the water. It still moved, slowly but relentlessly, its source probably a spring somewhere ahead. The bodies were being held by something. Between their lengths, they nearly spanned the stream. She signaled the others to wait, then silently pulled herself out of the water onto the bank.

She stood, dripping and squinting at what looked like a human dam. Behind the two, others were packed, floating facedown with the ones in the back bobbing lazily against the others. Most looked newly dead; she was glad that, except for one of the closest two, whose open eyes stared blankly downstream, they lay in the water the way the dead should: facedown.

She was about to signal the others out when the water behind the dead men stirred and a thick, snakelike thing slithered over a body in the back and pulled it under. A moment later, several large bubbles broke the surface. Something was in the water— some pet of Pye's. The stream was probably blocked by a net that kept its food within easy reach.

Putting a finger to her lips, Thyri signaled Duagan and Modraig onto the bank. The singing increased in volume, keeping the same discordant, pulsating pace it had had before. Still unaware that we're here, she thought. She hoped.

The dark trees rose about them like sinister, silent ghouls, Thyri sensed magic everywhere now, its overpowering sensation a welcome but alarming change from the reek of the stream. A soft blue glow came from the direction of the voice. When Thyri moved, every step snapped twigs and crunched the leaves, setting her nerves on edge. Again, she signed for the others to wait, then set forth along the bank toward the lair of the thing in the water.

The trees suddenly gave way to a well-worn path that ended next to the human dam and wound away back toward the source of the light. It widened by the stream, and a short brick altar stood on the opposite side. Five decaying human heads stared out at her from niches in the altar's base. Thyri shivered. Shafts of moonlight cast shadows in the small clearing and on the stream. She didn't look up.

She went back for the others even though she'd begun to wish she'd come alone. They had gotten in so easily; she'd anticipated some sort of physical resistance. But they hadn't reached the wizard yet.

Before they gained the path, something cut the air behind them. Thyri spun and saw a dark shape sailing down through the trees at Modraig. She threw her ax and heard a satisfying thud as it bit into flesh. The thing fell to the ground, gurgling, weakly flapping leathery wings. She speared it with her sword, then freed her blade and ax and took to the path, hoping to reach Pye before encountering any more of his groves's denizens. As it was, the path went only a short distance before opening into a clearing that was the source of both the light and the singing.

The wizard sat there, his song unchanged, the blue light steady. He wore black robes, and his bald pate did not shine under the moonlight. They couldn't see his face because they were behind him. The blue light sprang from a ball of energy that hung crackling in the air before him.

She wished again that she'd come alone: she'd have put her sword to his neck, roused him from his trance and forced him to aid her. By herself, she would risk only her own life if she failed. Now she risked those of two others—not just any two, but two who had entrusted their lives to her. She hesitated only a moment before putting a hand on Duagan's shoulder. He raised an eyebrow, then bent quickly to one knee. He leveled his bow on the wizard and fired.

The bolt flew true, but before it could reach its mark, a flare shot out of the blue globe and deflected it. It veered off and fell lifelessly to the ground a short distance away. Modraig shot. A flare caught his bolt and incinerated it mid-flight.

Thyri cursed and charged. Pye's head turned slowly. She could hear crossbows hitting the ground behind her as the others followed, drawing their swords.

Pye's left hand came up and Thyri felt the air in the grove close around her and hold her back. She struggled like a wildcat, making her way slowly forward, not caring that it wouldn't be fast enough. Pye rose from the ground, still in lotus. His body turned to face them. The blue fire lit his eyes.

He raised his hand again and it began to glow bluish silver, as if absorbing the moonlight. The ball sent flares out to the hand and it sucked them in, growing brighter still until the ball was no more and there was nothing there except that hand, shining like the moon. Light streamed out and flew past Thyri. Modraig screamed. She turned her head and watched flesh peel away from his skull under the hellish onslaught.

Another bolt and Duagan died.

The light turned on Thyri. She screamed, but it didn't destroy her. The agony stripped away her reason and she lost all thought of bargaining with Pye. Power coursed through her limbs. Her blade fell from her hand as pain shot up her sword arm. Silver links on the back of her gauntlet chinked lightly as they snapped. Her bones wrenched and warped, and the beast rose from within. Pye's face went white with terror.

Thyri grinned, her vision red and her soul wracked by consuming hunger. She leapt forward—fangs bared, dripping with saliva—and tore out the wizard's throat.

And then she fought herself. The beast, this time, did not have the fullness of the moon above it. From somewhere within, she lashed out and smashed it back down into oblivion.

Moaning painfully, she forced herself up to her hands and knees. Several hours had passed. Sunlight beat down on her; the chatter of morning in the forest was ominously absent. The grass around her was smeared with a pulpy redness. She moaned again as her stomach rose up in her throat and spilt a red bile onto the ground.

Pye lay a short distance away, his body twisted, his head lying impossibly back along his shoulder. Two blackened, still-smoldering skeletons lay beyond him.

She staggered dizzily away from the carnage, finding a path opposite the one that went to the stream. It led her to a strange structure with walls formed of closely twisted yet living trees. Its ceiling was tightly woven of green branches. Braziers burned in it, giving off noxious smells. She forced herself in and toppled the braziers onto the grassy floor. Hot fat leaked out and singed the grass. But it didn't burn; it only smoked blackly, making it difficult to breathe. Thyri pinpointed the tang of magic and snatched at it before leaving.

A pouch—three small gems inside of an aqua luster she'd seen nowhere before but in the sky. She tipped them back into the pouch and reached down absently to attach it to her belt, remembering only then that she was naked. She forced herself to return to the sight of the night's slaughter.

Her shift was in tatters, torn fully along the seam of one side. Behind it lay her cloak, apparently unscathed. Her gauntlet had a thin rip along its back. One of her boots had a wide hole in its side, the other was scratched up but untorn. The leather ties of her weapons belt had snapped. Swords and crossbows lay scattered where they had fallen. She tossed the pouch next to her cloak and turned back toward Pye's hut.

Inside, she groped with one hand, pinching her nostrils shut with the other until she found a long strip of leather. She went back to her things and sat to repair her shift and belt. Finished, she cut a thinner strip, spun it until it was like a stiff, thin strand of wool, and slowly threaded the links of her gauntlet back together. At noon, she set herself on a northeast path out of Pye's grove and into the forest. Against her thigh bounced a heavy sack containing the wizard's head.

Near evening she came to a road that paralleled the northern coast of the peninsula. She trudged along it, and slept settled into bushes alongside it that night.

The next day she entered farming land and saw a few travelers who eyed her strangely as she passed. She didn't speak to them; their field-hardened faces and bent backs recalled the grim realities that had been taken from her by Scacath. She watched a willowy young girl who labored under the weight of two buckets of milk. Milk splashed as she walked, making white spots that faded slowly into the dirt. There was a desperate, unforgiving defiance in her eyes.

Thyri watched her approach and saw herself as she might have been. Without my sword that is all I am, she thought. *All I would be. Wed, probably to a brawny, simple farmer. Happily, maybe— but no, never truly happy like that: enduring such hardship for the fleeting pleasures of nightly passions and too many children.*

Laboring under her load, the girl stumbled and fell to one knee. Thyri rushed to her, steadying the buckets before helping her ease them to the ground. Those defiant eyes glared at her. Thyri lifted one of the buckets to her lips, drank deeply, and walked on.

At noon she approached a farmhouse showed the peasants Pye's head, and offered them a silver coin given her by Megan if they would feed her. It was more money than most of them had seen in one place. They fed her well, and one young man set off to inform the capital of Thyri's deed.

After eating, she set off north and stole a horse from the stable of a wealthy landowner. She ran it near unto death as she sped northward, seeking haven with the sorceress before sundown.

"I changed."

"Early." Meg poured water from a flask onto a rag to wipe the grime from Thyri's face, then lifted her head and sloshed the remainder down her throat. She set the flask aside and glanced at the bloody bundle at Thyri's belt.

"The wizard's head," Thyri said. "He attacked me with magic born of moonlight."

"His mistake."

Thyri smiled darkly, then coughed. "He had some gems in which I sensed power. In the pouch on my left side."

Meg took the pouch and opened it. She examined the contents, then leaned down and kissed Thyri's forehead. "Thank you."

"I hoped you'd be pleased."

"The beast didn't stay long?"

"Long enough to remind me how horrible it is. You cannot imagine its hungers." *And the power it promises in return* . . . "It took much from me to keep from feeding on the wizard's carcass."

"It will be back tonight."

"Yes."

"Do not stray far. You will find plenty of game in the forest and there are shepherds a few hours to the southwest. Go there if you must, but stay far away from Kaerglen. Come back here after moonset. I will care for you as best I can." Meg rose. "Rest now, Thyri. I will wake you an hour before moonrise, then leave."

You do not want to see it.
No.
In time, Thyri slipped thankfully into oblivion.

The three nights of the wolf came and went. Thyri roamed the countryside, killing and dining, all the while fighting with and hating herself and the menacing eye of the moon that glared down at her, watching, smiling. By day, she slept fitfully in the cool darkness of Meg's hut, her dreams full of blood and death.

Near the final dawn, she crept into the hut and onto the cot, the wolf feeling an agony as great as that she felt when she became it. The world began to swim, darkening before Meg's touch drew her out. The sorceress leaned over her, brushing the hair from her face and pressing a damp rag to her brow.

I can't bear it, Meg.
I know.
Last night was the worst it's ever been.
It's over now.
Only for another month. I must do something. I have to go away again.
Why?
Because I can hardly control it. I could have hurt even you had you been here for the changes. I couldn't bear that. I have to find peace with it or rid myself of it entirely.
Where can you go? There is no escape.
West. West where the sun goes.
The moon goes there too.
But the change only works at night. I can hide in the sun.
She looked at Meg, crying, "I have to try! Don't you understand? I have to!"

"Hush! I understand. Stay tonight. I'll gate you back to Kaerglen in the morning. If they won't give you a ship for killing Kaerglen's cousin, come back to me. I'll help you bring that castle down around their ears."

Thyri smiled a shaky smile. *I'll come back.*

Kaerglen

She strode onto the practice field amid murmuring silence. Activity stopped, then suddenly all rushed into line at the shouts of their commanders. Cuilly came out of his quarters and saw her. When he reached the front of the formation, she awaited him, a wild madness in her eyes, a taunting slant in the way she stood. Her hair seemed longer, reaching far down the sables on her back. And it gleamed brightly under the sun and was streaked in places with fiery red and snowy silver.

A burlap bundle, stained with washed-out blood, hung at her side. She untied its string.

"The king is well?"

"Improving. Where have you been? We found the bodies days ago."

"Long after I'd left. My men did well." She smiled and looked for them in the formation. They were together, undispersed as yet. They stood to one side, and Dearen, a veteran of ten years, appeared to have taken Duagan's place at the front. He winked at her and smiled broadly. Tears for fallen comrades shed and dried. It was the way...

No!

She drew the head from the bag and dangled it before her, clumped hair gripped twisted in her fingers. She drew her sword and held it above her.

Heedless of their commander, the Kaerglen guard broke ranks and cheered.

Later, she sat inside his quarters. The raucous noise outside had faded to a bearable level. Cuilly was tired, worn somewhat by the celebrations of the past days. He'd had to disperse the men to calm them—set them free on the city. They *did* deserve it. Before, they had merely the knowledge that the wizard was dead. Now they had his slayer back among them.

He didn't share their joy. Deep inside, he feared her who sat at his conference table. To that, he could not admit. So he blamed his age: he was thirty-five that day.

He filled two finely wrought silver goblets from a glass flask and handed one absently to Thyri before sitting across from her.

She sipped: wine, certainly imported from lush valleys of far southern lands. The taste made her wish to someday go there and smell the air, the grapes growing fat and ripe where sun and soil were much kinder than in the North.

Cuilly downed one goblet and started on another. "Where were you?"

"Lost. Wandering the woods. He cast some sorcery on me. I did not remember who I was until this morning."

"You wandered for days with that—with Pye's head?"

She shrugged. "It was a clue. I couldn't just throw it away."

He filled both their goblets anew and sat back. "I must take you to the king. He wishes to see you."

"I want a ship, Cuilly. I have to leave."

A light flickered in his eye. He no longer wanted her around. He didn't need her—not, at least, among his men. She would disrupt things. Especially since there was no foe left to fight. Deep inside, he feared for his command. But she would leave? "What?"

"I want a ship. The fighting here is over. You don't need me anymore. Kaerglen must honor my demand."

He smiled weakly. "We shall speak to the king."

Castle Kaerglen is old. Situated as it is upon the edge of precipitous cliffs that sink into a tumultuous sea, restricting approach from the south and east, it has long proved a valuable stepping-stone for military campaigns onto the mainland. The city lies to the north, at the foot of a steep slope. A gentler decline leads to the port in the west, itself protected by rocks and cliffs on either side.

A wall, ten yards high and eight thick, lies between the city and port, linking circular, slotted towers as ancient as the deepest shadows of the keep. Passage from one side to the other is conducted through two fortified gates. The guard was seldom present. The only archers vigilant in the purely defensive sections of the wall were the ghosts of those who had died defending it, or such is the story that a young woman from the city-side might have heard in dock-side haunts from sailors who didn't wish her to leave before morning.

From the libraries in the keep, this much can be gleaned:

Kaerglen was touched many times during the ancient invasions of Erin.

The central structures of the castle were built by the Fomhoire who came first. They erected the brochs of the wall, filling the spaces with earthen ramparts. The defensive gesture was needless on their part as their conquest of the mainland was complete nearly before the final stone of the keep had been set in place.

Those Fomhoire who remained on the island later fell to the dark sons of Nemedh. These new invaders augmented the central works with rooms of their own before following their predecessors onto the mainland. They left a detachment which, after a period of time, abandoned swords and maces and cleared the woods in the south and grew barley. Yet even so, they did not forget the ways of battle. Twice they held the island against successive invasions—once after the Fomhoire intensified their bid for the mainland and again when new enemies, the demonic Fir Bolg, tempted their shores. Hastily constructed ramparts about the waist of the island thwarted assaults from the north. A few score archers placed in the towers consistently held ten times their number at bay. Both tribes, in the end, decided it wise to leave the sons of Nemedh alone. By the time the magic of Erin had spawned sorcerors and witches capable of aiding their armies, Kaerglen Isle had been forgotten.

Nothing changed until the Tuatha de Danann smashed the Nemedians in a single, crushing blow. Manannan, son of Lir, lifted the sea up under the keel of *Wavesweeper* and battered the keep, drowning all within and cracking the foundation on the port side. Nuada and the other great lords washed over the island on mystical steeds shod with silver and bridled with gold, crushing all resistance. The island secured, they restored the keep and completed the wall. Most followed their predecessors on to Erin, but Manannan and his wife, Fand, came to call Kaerglen home. He augmented the ramparts and built the port wall. It is said that, in his time, the dark halls of the keep shone with a light of their own.

All things must pass. Over time, the children of Danu lost the mainland to the sons of Mil. Manannan, Fand, and the others who had stayed on Kaerglen passed into—*otherworld* is the only fit name—with their kin. Yet Manannan cast enchantments still—when the sons of Mil later tried to reach the island they found only fog. So Kaerglen remained until Coryn Kaerglen's grandfather, Coryn mac Fain, arrived four score and seven years before Thyri Bloodfang set foot on the island. His story yet reeks of legend. It happened when the links between Midgard and *other-world* remained strong:

Fand was wife to Manannan and among the fairest of all the Tuatha de Danaan. Her beauty—and her caprice—rivaled that of Edain. It is she whose heart truly illuminates Kaerglen.

Mac Fain was young, strong—a leader of that tribe in Western Erin named Connachta, a tribe that warred with itself as often as not.

It was Samhain Eve. The druidh were in their groves. Young virgins aspiring to sorcery had withdrawn into Erin's wild embrace, hoping in their passions to open gates that would bring them *otherworld* lovers, *otherworld* lords. They would dance naked under the moon, or drink arcane potions and swim in witch pools—many girls often drowned by this practice.

On this night, Fand walked the shadow paths along the edge of our world. She was a goddess with a goddess's heart. And in the way of deities before her, she saw mortal man and lusted. She appeared before Coryn mac Fain in flowing silks and the fairest flowers of *otherworld* spring in her hair.

He had wed the daughter of a neighboring chieftain. On that first night with the goddess, he abandoned his wife. Bloody war ensued. Manannan aided mac Fain's enemies and many mortals died.

And Fand grew enraged. She stole the great ship *Wavesweeper* from her husband and welcomed mac Fain and his people aboard. They fared west, and she gave unto mac Fain the island he named Kaerglen. None had touched its shores since she and Manannan had left.

Something must be said for the goddess. She stayed with the king she'd appointed, and she bore him five children before he died in 826 by the reckoning of the One God—after thirty-seven years of peaceful rule. Perhaps she indeed loved him. He, by his writings, worshiped her.

Had Thyri known this, she might have understood the island's strangeness. No man's roots in it extended past Coryn mac Fain's first step upon it. Before this, the strongest of the field and wood had ruled—the bear and the wolf. In the first ten years of his reign, the warrior from the mainland had purged those predators from his shores.

From the city, the castle is but a half-concealed edifice among the rocks above. The dark battlements are best found by running the eye along the edge of the port wall, then veering, at the end, a moon-width to the left. One might then see the kitchen tower over the crenellated, ballista-pocked battlements of the Nemedh. In good light, one can see a corner of the keep within. Little more.

The ground at the top of the slope rises first before falling to the level of the fortress. The port wall would, even without the natural barrier, block the seaward portion of the castle from eyes in the city. Thus the view of the fortress does little to breathe fear into the hearts of enemies below whose major obstacle would seem to be gaining the crest of the hill—a fleeting goal, mist-enshrouded as often as not. The only road that leads there is on the seaside of the port wall.

To there, the Kaerglen Guard followed Thyri.

Cuilly had ordered an iron housing for the mutilated head of Pye. The cask was layered by tradition of the druidh with leaves of the sacred oak. Thyri's men bore it proudly as they rode through the city.

And a crowd of common men gathered, lining the road. They cheered, and they stared and whispered. Thyri sat proudly atop a dappled mare. She'd tied her hair back but otherwise it fell free, stirring, rippling in a lightly gusting wind. Her gauntleted hand rested on the pommel of the rune-sword, and her cloak parted at the side to let the scabbarded blade swing freely.

Through the port wall, she saw the eclectic fleet that formed the core of Kaerglen's sea power. She saw vessels with Norse lines: three merchantmen and two longships. Raiders, she assumed, that had strayed into the mists that hid the island from the rest of the world. Other ships dominated the force, strange ones both like and unlike the clumsy vessels of the Franks and Frisians —the handiwork of Kaerglen's own shipcraft. Many bore doubled masts, a feature Thyri had seldom seen and one which, in her mind, caused more trouble than it was worth: for scant increases in speed and maneuverability, the captain would pay dearly in manpower and would need more than one mouth to control the crew in battle. But Thyri watched them in the bay. They held some promise; they skimmed the waves nearly with the grace of longships, and this she had never imagined in a ship not built in her homeland. Her eye fell on one of the larger ones. It had two decked cabins—she would not need to remove the captain from his stateroom to give her the privacy she desired for the journey.

Next to the road, between it and the port, were the homes and hovels of sailors and fishermen. All were out to see her. She smiled at them and waved her silvered hand. They sang out to her, but she answered none save one: a little girl broke from her mother's grasp and ran in front of Thyri's horse. "Look, mother!"

she squealed. "She has a sword!" She looked up at Thyri and tilted her head, squinting her eyes.

Thyri pulled up her horse and laughed, halting the procession. Cuilly's steed stamped restlessly next to hers.

"Is it real?" the little girl asked.

"Yes, little one," she answered, "it is real."

The girl's mother screamed for her and Thyri bade her hear with a tilt of her head. The little one paused before she turned, beamed brightly, and scampered away. She'd been no older than four or five. For the remainder of the trip, Thyri called up the days of her youth and thought how like herself the little girl had seemed. And the girl's mother, too, like her own mother—impatient, demanding, assured that a woman's place is the home and that swords belong elsewhere. She felt a bitter sorrow even before her thoughts turned to the wolf, telling her that the sword had brought her a burden greater than ever a kitchen blade might.

The crowd followed halfway up the keep road, then Cuilly turned and bade them return home. He sent his army back as well, continuing only with Thyri and Dearen, who bore the iron cask containing the wizard's head.

At the crest of the hill, the castle thrust suddenly and fully into view. It caught Thyri up—the battlements spoke of ancient might and ancient fire, ages of perseverance. It stood there, pocked by ballista and catapult, yet ominously solid. She had never seen such an edifice, so forbidding a keep, so scarred a fortress. Not even the Franks and those other Southern peoples who claimed the dead heritage of the dead empire—not even they could boast of building walls so suited to discouraging assault. They built only with wood and earth—however impressive, their works held no light to Castle Kaerglen.

Riding closer, she saw the extent of the damage—the ruination left by the coming of the Tuatha de Danann. Though patched twice over, the battlements were a jigsaw sewn by ribbons of mortar, which crisscrossed back and forth without design. Once through the unguarded gatehouse, she saw the crack that marred the port side—the wound inflicted by the battle fury of Manannan. The stone had shifted several inches along the seam of the crack, reminding Thyri of the fault lines she and Astrid had discovered in the caverns the Dane Ottar had used during his short campaign against Ragnar (but that's another story). Some god, she thought, had built the fortress; another or the same had cracked it. No man could design such a structure in stone; no human force could cause such damage.

As written, they entered through a vacant gatehouse unchallenged. A lone thrush sat perched like a silent sentinel on the ramparts left of the gate. Thyri felt uneasy. This place, more a palace for gods than a dwelling of men, cried out for the singing of metal on metal and the raw bellowing of commanders testing the vigilance of their charges standing watch on the battlements.

Yet it was undefended, its army based on the outskirts of the city. So it had been throughout the "war" with the wizard. The combatants had fought with weapons beyond the crudeness of the sword.

And she had won in a way that Scacath had never taught her.

Pye had never once left his grove. Never once sent a demon army against the capital. Thyri felt sorrow for Cuilly and his months bent to a task he could never execute. She felt sorrow for Meg, who probably could have done what she had by . . . *subtler* methods. She felt sorrow for the people of the island; they were probably as confused as she by the whole affair.

She thought again of the little girl, her innocent freedom that could only fade away, simmering slowly in a stew of ignorance and toil, waiting for the winds of time to take pity on her pain and carry her into oblivion. Even on this lost island that everywhere seemed, like Scacath's grove, to reach beyond Midgard, the lives of men proceeded unchanged. The soil kept its divinity secret, hidden from all she'd met except Pye and Meg.

But the king must have felt this, too. How could he not—he who ruled from this fortress built for gods, he who'd endured a power such as Pye's? Why on earth had he refused Meg's help?

The road into the keep, at least, showed signs of use. The occupants of the fortress still needed wares from the city and port. Thyri thought on this, realizing how popular a rule Kaerglen enjoyed, excepting the rebellion of his cousin. Merchants could, like she, come to the keep unopposed. Kaerglen did not fear his subjects. She asked Cuilly if he had ever trained his men to defend the fortress and he shook his head.

So why was it there?

Thyri shrugged off her questions and assumed that the keep was guarded in some manner, most likely as unbelievable as its actual presence.

A tethering bar, out of place in the general design, stood next to the main portal. Thyri cast her eyes about for a stable among the disused buildings littering the area between the battlements and the keep. She saw one that must once have housed horses, but it hadn't in recent years. Weeds had claimed the ground around it and the wood had rotted through in more than one place.

The three riders dismounted and tethered their steeds.

At the great wooden doors of the keep, Cuilly turned and signaled Dearen to hand Thyri the box.

A brass knocker shaped as a coiled serpent was set on the left of the double doors. Cuilly lifted it once and let it fall against the brass stop. The clang resonated deeply and Thyri listened to the echoes bouncing through the corridors within. The door swung open, revealing a slender, dark-haired woman with a delicately precise carriage. As old as Mother, Thyri thought, or as old as she would have been. But she showed little of the signs of middle age. Thyri doubted she'd gained a pound since her thirteenth birthday.

The woman stepped forward, allowing diffuse rays of sunlight to touch her face. Thyri adjusted her estimate of age more in the woman's favor. The creases beside her eyes had not fully taken root. Her skin had that dull pallor of those who seldom fare into the sun; its lack of color amplified the doughy indistinction of her features. Her eyes were a dull gray.

She flashed Thyri a formal smile, then looked to Cuilly.

He cleared his throat. "I have brought her, my queen."

The broken silence forced Thyri fully into the present, and the woman looked suddenly *too* erect, as if her poise required conscious effort while her shoulders fought to bow under the weight of years.

"Good," she said, smiling again in the manner of those both used to decorum and despising it.

Thyri smiled back. She could not fault the woman for her curtness—Thyri herself held the customs of men born of position in contempt. Through ritual and decorum, one needed never to think or feel for oneself.

The royal smile warmed a little, acknowledging Thyri's response. "You are welcome here. My husband will be pleased to speak with you, woman of the cold lands."

"Thyri Eiriksdattir, Queen Moira."

"Very well, Thyri. Come in."

She entered. Cuilly followed and began to close the door.

"Bring your man in, Captain," the queen said. "You and he can keep the wine company while Thyri speaks with Coryn. He would speak with you after, but he would first meet his cousin's slayer alone."

* * *

The castle was lit where needed by candles held in brackets set in the walls. The queen took one from its place and quickly led Thyri past the entrance into darkened halls. Cuilly stayed in the first room, which was furnished with couches and cabinets displaying the rare elixir of the South, decanted after the fashion of those wealthy peoples whose smiths fashion glass. Once away from Cuilly and Dearen, the queen began to speak. Thyri's concentration flashed between the words and her wonder at the internal architecture of the keep—and she was counting the openings passed as well.

She had never imagined such a structure in stone. She had never set foot in any but the most meager of stone buildings though she'd heard much of great works far to the south among the debris of the old empires. Vacant monuments in the scattered necropoleis of the centuries. In Castle Kaerglen she felt strength —the strength of the bones of Ymir from which Odin and his brothers had grown the mountains. She felt also strength in the spaces, in the air, the realm of Thor and the Valkyries. As she set each foot down on the stones, Thyri set it into two worlds.

And she sensed other things as Kaerglen's queen led her deep into the keep. She felt a familiar tingling rise and fall, ebb and flow. And the tang was powerful, permeating the castle. She knew not whether it came from the stones themselves or from things hidden in the spaces between them. She hadn't, since departing the glade of Scacath, felt the presence of such powers so strongly—not around Meg, not around Pye.

Along with the counting and the sensings of magic and dichotomous existence, the words of the queen came relentlessly to Thyri's ears, flowing with scarcely an interruption:

"I hope the halls are not too dark for you, though I think your eyes should soon adjust.

"We could have more light if we wished to employ one to tend the flames, but I enjoy tending them myself.

"I prefer to think this place a home, a house for the family rather than a fortress. But there is so much space beyond our quarters. All this . . .

"I think someday I'll have Coryn convert this entire wing into a chapel so that Brenden might do his work in a place that mirrors His glory. It's either that or a cathedral in the city—out of the question, I think, due to a lack of strong backs.

"Brenden wants to start a monastery in the North, but I keep telling him that this island is not like Erin and England. It is small and contained and as such can be consecrated from shore to shore to His glory.

"I think he's depressed—Brenden, that is—because in all our years here we are little further than we were before we began. But that was mostly Coryn's cousin's fault, and you killed him, didn't you?

"Oh, but I forget you are heathen. I *did* know that. Sean told me you are Norse and I know something of your ways. You worship the Wodin or something, if I remember correctly. It's a pity —we should talk deeply on this, but that's something for another time.

"Those are the children's rooms down that hall there, and beyond are a few more I keep up for reasons I can no longer explain. We have guests so seldom.

"I wonder that we don't hear Tana and Seth at play. But no, that's right—they'd be in the garden with Brenden now, learning their letters. Very important, that. Necessary for understanding His word. I think Coryn should destroy all those pagan writings he keeps in his library, but he insists on having them. And who am I to command the king?

"Down that hall are the rooms of Coryn's mother's sister and brother. They keep to themselves mostly. I really don't think they like me much, my being from the mainland.

"Just up here are our rooms. Ah, here we are."

As the queen spoke, Thyri began to understand her. The words lacked ceremony and were like the idle ramblings of one common wife to another (an extreme comparison, but valid, regardless of the occupations of the two women involved). Thyri's hostess was concerned with showing the details of her life, but these intricacies soured in Thyri's ears, both for their triviality and for the queen's zeal for the Cult of the One God. Behind the talk, Moira sought a confidante—one whom she felt she could find only in another woman (in spite of the sword at Thyri's side and the severed head of Pye in the box). To this desire, Thyri attributed the queen's sudden change of mood. Nothing else could have given rise to such an outpouring.

The king was abed, convalescing. His cheeks were bright, and his eyes had begun to shine with health—if still with lassitude as well. A matted mane of long brown hair fell from his head and spread about his shoulders and the silken pillow against which he rested. The room had yet the odor of illness and medicine; Thyri knew this before entering, for the smell permeated the outer corridor.

When Moira ushered her in, Kaerglen's gaze was fixed on that point outside the world where the seen is but a reflection of the mind of the seer and the world carries on around it as if a dream. The king did not look up at her entrance; it took Moira's voice to shatter his reflections.

"I have brought the one who killed your cousin, Coryn."

"What?" He looked at Thyri. His face was not overly creased. He was fifty-five that day. Awareness came slowly, but he smiled.

"Thank you, Moira. Leave us." He paused, allowing his wife to nod and exit. As she did, Thyri opened the lid of the box and lifted out the wizard's head.

Kaerglen grimaced, motioning her to put it back. "Yes, that was once my cousin. No more."

The room was furnished moderately, with the bed and several chairs to the side as well as a large wardrobe carved of oak and a table upon which doubled candles granted the king light for reading. Beneath the candles lay a book. Thyri squinted at the worn cover but found that no title graced it—just an ornate gilt design with no meaning to her.

The king watched her. "It is Moira's. She insisted I have it by me, as if it could protect against Pye's magics. It was quite useless. Please, have a seat." He indicated a chair by his bed.

Thyri put down the box and sat. She reached for the book, letting it fall open where it may. The script was Irish. She recognized it but could not read—Meg had not taught her written skill in the tongue. She shrugged and set the book back, looking at the king. "The lore of the One God?"

"Yes. Does it interest you?"

"I know nothing of it." She paused. "I think not—not in a direct sense, though I find its effects interesting in a way."

"I can see that I needn't try to educate you. This is good," he said, smiling more brightly. "I know nothing of it."

"The One God is not your god?"

"No."

"But he is your queen's?"

"Yes."

"And you allow that? Is this how his influence spreads? How he wars with Odin in Midgard?"

"Perhaps. Perhaps it is good." He sighed. "I do not know. I am sure of little anymore except that I love my wife and see her goodness. And the gods of my family here—Dagda, Brigid, Lugh, the Morrigan, and the rest—they have brought curses upon us, though it was through them that my grandfather came here and came to rule here. Perhaps through Moira and her god my children will be spared my pain."

"But not you. You know nothing of this god."

"No, he is not real to me. I know only the children of Danu. I have seen them, or those few that yet remain near our world. They grow wild, and the One God has driven them from the mainland and they grow bitter with hatred. They cannot fight him, so they take their pain out on my family."

"I do not understand."

The king reached out and laid a hand on Thyri's. "You cannot understand as I do because you are from the cold lands and your gods are yet strong. Mine fade, and I am given the task of helping them do so quickly so that my people do not suffer as greatly as they might."

Thyri thought of Meg and thought how the sorceress wielded powers such as Scacath had. They did not seem powers granted by fading gods. "I think you take it upon yourself. The One God and his cult can be fought. They must be fought."

"If so, you killed one of the more serious threats to his domain. Had Pye killed me, he would have taken the throne and grown armies here with which to assail Erin. Many would have died, and Kaerglen Isle would have fallen to the wrath of those who hold power in the East. And then the little magic that remains in these rocks would go away."

"Is that not what you want—to help it go away quickly?"

"Yes, but without great suffering. Pye's way, because he did not see the inevitability of our defeat, would have caused indescribable pain."

"So the pain of war is a greater evil than the pain brought by the slow passing of your gods. Wars end, but it would seem to me that forsaking the future is eternal."

"I do not forsake my future. But the Tuatha de Danann yet fade."

The king grew distant, silent.

"It is war that is eternal," Thyri said.

"Because you are a warrior, you see through your sword."

"No, I see with my eyes. I see men with my eyes, and I see war in the eyes of men."

Kaerglen smiled oddly. "And in the eyes of women. You would have sided with my cousin had you known more of the stakes of our conflict?"

"No," she said. But not, she thought, for any of the reasons he had given. It had been Meg's tasking—her desire that he have aid. If not from her then from her friend.

"Then why the disagreement?"

"Perhaps I only wish to learn the heart of the man I served."

"You still have a place in my guard. You might *become* the Guard in time."

"I am a warrior, but the wars of your island are done for me now. I have a quest of my own."

"And?"

"I must go west," she said. "I must follow the sun."

The king's eyes grew distant again. "To Bri Leith, where the Tuatha de Danann go now to dwell—but no, you will no longer find that isle in this world." Then he smiled at her. "Take any ship in my harbor. But no more than three."

"I need only one. Fully manned."

"It is yours. But not until spring, woman of the cold lands. I will not give you men to take into winter. You cannot survive a week on the seas as they are now. Any crew I give you knows that. They would kill you before straying a day from my shores."

Thyri had known this in her head, if not in her heart. It struck home then—the realization that she had to endure four, probably five, more cycles of the moon before she could begin to seek a haven. She felt Kaerglen's eyes on her and imagined he could see the beast under her skin.

But he still smiled in his way—a sad smile, one vacant of the potency to promise comfort. She lowered her eyes.

"Your quest must be urgent," he said. "The edge of your words hints at urgency as if you wished to leave tomorrow and forget the seasons. You do not appear one who would neglect such details."

"You have great insight, my king."

He laughed now. "I am not your king. But I may be a friend. Call me Coryn. Your sword has given you that right. All that I have is yours."

The loaded but necessary pledge from the saved to the savior —Thyri understood this and knew its traps. *All you have? Your island, my king?*

What she did not desire . . .

Rather she would ask him to raise the dead and purge the foul blood that burned in her veins—two things she knew were beyond him. "Just the ship. The largest of your merchantmen."

"You ask little. You will need a place to winter. Stay here. This place has more to offer than might first seem."

"I have a friend on the north end of the island. She saved *my* life. She talks like she knows you. She calls herself Meg."

He picked up the book and looked at the cover, absently tracing the faded design. "Yes, I know that name. Megan. She yet lives alone? She is still beautiful?"

"Still beautiful, but no longer alone. At least for the winter."

Kaerglen looked up, setting the book back on its table. "I see. Well, stay the night at least. I have a library. You read, if your interest in Moira's book is any indication. Greek? Latin? Your own people have no writing, no?"

"We do of a sort. I can't read it." The runes, she thought. "I read Latin."

"Then my library contains much you may find of interest. Translations from Greek: Plato, Aristotle, Euripedes—many others who wrote a millenium ago. Many wrote of the gods, the ones the empire took into itself. The ones that fell first to the power of the One God." He paused. "You are free to seek knowledge and comfort here. As you are free to come and go as you please throughout the winter."

"Thank you, Coryn. I will stay the night. I would like to see your library."

"Good. Moira!"

The door swung quickly open and the queen entered. Thyri guessed she'd heard, her ear to the door, all that had passed. "Yes?"

"We have spoken. Prepare a room for this woman for the night. And anything else she desires, perhaps a bath. Show her the library as well."

Moira nodded and beckoned for Thyri to follow her out. At the portal, Thyri turned back to smile at the king. "Thank you for the ship."

He shrugged. "Thank you for my cousin's head. Take it with you. Have Cuilly burn it."

Patrick

After taking Thyri back to the entrance hall, Moira led Cuilly in for his audience. Thyri gave Dearen the cask and asked him how fared the men. Well, he told her. He could think of little more to say, and Thyri volunteered nothing. The queen returned shortly to take Thyri to the library.

Walking again through the halls, she wondered further on the source of the magic and wondered if Meg knew. The witch *did* know Kaerglen. Kaerglen knew her, knew about her.

The library did not contain the answer—at least not in a form that she could read. The books and scrolls were arranged within three oaken cabinets, each covering a wall of its own. In the center of the room was a large desk with several candles that Moira lit for Thyri before leaving her alone. Between the candles Thyri found a neat stack of parchment and a quill pen. Looking at them, she thought of Astrid and the letter Hugin had brought to her while she was still under Scacath's wing. Burned now, in the fires of her brother's hall. Or perhaps Erik had saved it.

Many strange scripts marked the bindings of most books on the shelves. From those she recognized, she chose Aristotle's *Metaphysics*. "All men, by nature, desire to know," it began, and the ancient sage proceeded to tell her what to know.

She scanned the pages rapidly, realizing that, if the book were any indication, the gods of the dead empire were killed not from without by the Cult, but from within. She had no interest in pursuing the argument presented once she'd found this fault at its heart. She put the book back and took a survey of the empire's gods from the shelves. In this book, she spent the afternoon.

Late in the day, Moira interrupted her reading to say that dinner would be soon served and that she would send her son for Thyri when the hour came. In the few minutes left her, Thyri took up quill and parchment and wrote:

Dearest Cousin,

I make, at last, a reply. Would that you could read it. My blood burns for the past.

Thyri Moon-Cursed.

She folded the parchment and set it between the pages of the book in the section that told of Diana the Huntress—the mother of Scacath, by Astrid's reckoning. The link to Astrid was slender, imagined more than real. Yet to Thyri, those pages between which she folded the parchment bore her own sadness in their words. The note was her message back through them—to Astrid, to Scacath, to those gods who had reigned before Odin. She mourned them, those whose immortality seemed to her as fleeting as the lives of those paying homage to it. After closing the book, she set it among its brothers on the shelf and waited for Moira's son.

The boy was slender like his mother with blond hair and blue eyes that fell on Thyri with an unpleasant arrogance.

"Mother sent me," he said in the crackling voice of a young man losing his childhood.

"She told me you would come."

"Well!" he demanded. "Let's go!"

"Why do you glare at me so? You do not know me or even my name, and I do not know yours."

"I am Patrick. Mother named me after the saint. You are Thyri. See, I know your name. Mother told me. She also told me you are heathen and a warrior. You kill without His blessing."

"And this is worth your malice?"

"You are evil."

She laughed. "But your mother who tells you so much of me welcomed me into your home."

"Mother does not see things as clearly as I."

"I see." Thyri approached him, her hand on the hilt of her sword. The boy was far from becoming a man in truth; she stood taller than he by several inches. She stopped before him and laughed as he backed through the doorway. "You are prince of this island, are you not?"

"Yes."

"You would do well to think longer on my *evil*. Your *people* are heathen, as you call them. They are also peaceful. But Christian words that sting cause heathen swords to be unsheathed. Swords cannot cut words, but they can separate the heads of princes from the shoulders of would-be kings."

She smiled coyly and cupped his beardless chin in her gauntleted hand.

Patrick's glare faltered and he spun away, leading her quickly through the hall to the dining chamber.

The dinner party consisted of Moira, Patrick, the priest/tutor of the children named Brenden, a shriveled old man named Rath, and the twins Seth and Tana, aged five. The king was not present.

The meal was served by a common woman. Thyri guessed she had cooked it as well, a remarkable feat judging by the spread of the table: roast pork, beans, peas, little onions, fresh milk and butter, and pies of apples and berries. The food Thyri relished, but she enjoyed more observing those with whom she ate.

Moira played hostess as well as she could, obviously trying not to offend Thyri's beliefs while speaking often of her own.

Patrick was mostly silent and the fire had left his eyes. He lowered them each time Thyri looked his way. At least she'd caused him to pause. She decided to be wary of the prince. It was doubtful that she'd changed his thinking with so few words. More likely, he would soon fall back into his black-and-white perception of the world and, in doing so, would count her a threat to his future.

The twins and their tutor ate silently, watching her with a strange intensity, remarkable on the parts of the little ones who should have been fidgeting in their seats and slopping their food about with the abandon of the young and undisciplined. And the priest: Thyri thought he must have been trying to fit her into his own picture of the world—she from far lands who carried the sword that had slain a wizard too powerful for his god to banish. She doubted his task would be very simple. For the priest to condemn her as Patrick had, he would need also to condemn her deed. And his nature would demand that he resolve the question. *All men by nature desire to know.*

The old one also watched her throughout the meal, smiling in secretive fashion as if seeing something in her, some purpose and meaning beyond the visible and known, and wishing to tell her he knew, that he approved. Thyri smiled back graciously.

In the words, predominantly between Thyri and Moira, little of interest was said. Only one subject brought reactions Thyri did not anticipate. It surfaced partway near the end of the main course when Moira mentioned Thyri's refusal of their hospitality for the winter.

"As I told the king," Thyri said, "I have a place in the North where I wish to winter. A woman who lives there saved my life.

Her name is Meg. Your husband seemed to know her."

Patrick started then, spewing milk over the table. He looked at his mother, who turned to him suddenly, glaring. Patrick took the corner of the tablecloth to wipe his chin, and Moira turned to Thyri and smiled as if to excuse her son's manners. "No," she said. "I have never heard that name. I doubt Coryn has either."

"But he told me—"

"You must remember that he is yet very ill. When it was worst, he would rant throughout the night about all manner of strange things unknown to him. This was the wizard's doing. Brenden thinks the spells carried my husband into a world where his dreams became fact within his mind. In this world brought by his cousin, he could be made to believe anything. Including such things as this woman of whom you speak."

Thyri dropped the subject. She knew Moira had lied, but she had no idea why. She shrugged and nodded in agreement. It didn't matter—nothing would after she'd left in the spring. She had her own worries, those same worries that plagued her anytime she grew inactive or reflective. Her torments—she needed things to do with her body, with her sword, because she could rarely face her tormentor. And that tormentor was inside of her, a *part* of her. The tainted blood that ran in her veins could never in truth command her. It could only grant power to that devourer lusting from its cage beneath her will. And then when the power subsided, she had to live with destruction caused both by her and in spite of her. Better to forget, to immerse in sensation: the pleasure of a lover, the sheer synchronicity of mind and body in mortal combat. With neither present, her sense of doom could make the problems and trials of others petty.

The constant turmoil she attracted, indeed encouraged, could stem only for a time the tides of her emotions; keep them from flooding inward to smash mercilessly against the heart of the little girl she had once been, the little girl who had worshiped passion and battle in the arena of her gods, where the line dividing the light and the darkness was, if not clearly drawn, then removed from her own existence. Not that Thyri the woman was incapable of lucidly analyzing the subtle complexities of human strife (this is far from true), but she always would tend from it as a drunken man tends to sleep to escape the increasing waywardness and confusion of his mind. She would see to a point, then fail to see further, especially during the early days after Astrid's death when she had not even begun to accept her altered nature. She had no wish to see further because careful thought would force her to place herself into context and, in doing so, she would be forced to judge herself along with the problem. She had passed that judgment already, on the vale at Astrid's grave with the point of her cousin's rune-sword poised to taste the blood of her own heart. But Astrid had stopped her.

So Thyri answered and forgot those questions surrounding Megan's connections with the family of Coryn Kaerglen. She concluded that they knew Meg, some or all of them, and that her friend had, at some time, fallen from favor in Moira's and Patrick's eyes. Megan, most likely, had once been mistress to the king and later, for reasons that no longer mattered, she had been cast aside.

Thyri saw in Megan a possible replacement for Astrid. If a rift existed between the sorceress and a former lover, so much the better.

After the meal Moira showed Thyri the baths and left her there. They are sunk under the ground floor of the castle, and a window looks from them out into the garden that grows in a space at the center of the keep.

The sun was setting and so the garden was already full of dark shadows, it being dependent on light reaching over the surrounding walls. Thyri spent several moments taking in its beauty.

Strange, intricate trees whose leaves shone green even in the absence of the sun were arranged artistically around the central fountain. Flowers of red and white dotted the ends of the branches, and the fountain's waters bubbled blackly, streaked with silver where the sunlight reflected on them from metal in the keep's walls.

Thyri sensed strong sorcery in that peaceful place.

As for the baths—the sunken pool filled the room, leaving but an arm's length all around from the walls.

Steam rose from the surface of water heated by fires beneath the stones below. Towels hung on hooks by the door. She stripped and hung her cloak, clothes, and sword on one of the hooks. She tested the water with her foot, then slid into the pool. It was hot, though not overly so; she found it soothed her as bathing had never done before. Her baths were often rare—not because she felt it evil, as many claim, but because she seldom had the chance, and actually preferred a quiet pond or lonely stream. But she'd never seen baths such as these. Those in Ragnar's hall had been caulked wooden basins filled with water heated over fires. They'd been barely large enough to sit in. Here, she could swim!

She basked in the luxury until interrupted by Patrick, who entered unannounced, stripped, and dove into the pool without ceremony. He didn't even look at her. She noted his presence but said nothing and closed her eyes, a part of her mind keeping track of his location by the sounds of his movement, another part soaking with her body in the soothing warmth of the water. After a time, she felt the prince draw closer to the place where she lounged on a sunken staircase.

Silence.

A hand on her shoulder, gliding down, brushing against her breasts.

"I want to show you that I am a man, not a boy for you to laugh at."

His voice. The hand on her breast again, uncertain.

She jerked away and spun down the edge of the pool. Tossing her head to throw her hair from her eyes, she laughed. "A man thinks like a man, sees things like a man."

She placed her hands on the edge and vaulted out, turning to look down at him with water still cascading from her body. "You wouldn't know what to do with me if I let you!"

She danced away while his face turned red and his eyes burned. As he came out of the water, she relaxed against the wall, eyeing his erection. "My prince!"

He dove at her, pinning her arms against the wall. She smiled. His eyes burned with rage then. "Stop laughing at me, you heathen bitch! I'll—"

With a jerk and twist, she reversed their positions. "You'll what?" She grabbed him between the legs and squeezed. "You are nothing, little boy."

He gasped and she felt a stickiness splatter against her wrist and forearm.

She smiled. "You see? My sword is stronger than yours. Do not tempt me, Patrick. I am not your subject."

Thyᵢ. pulled him off the wall and threw him back into the pool. She bent and washed her arms at the edge before going to dry herself. Patrick watched her silently as she ran the towel over her body.

She dressed in her tunic and leggings, pulled on her boots, took her cloak and sword from their hook, and left the baths.

Magic

Moira put Thyri in one of the rooms beyond those of her children. If the queen had any knowledge of the events between Thyri and her son, she did not show it in her manner. Just as well, Thyri thought. She'd already begun to look to morning when she would leave the place.

Her room contained one of the larger beds she'd had the opportunity to sleep in. The air was musty with age and disuse, but the bedding was fresh and she collapsed on the mattress, willing the tensions from her muscles. As tendrils of sleep closed about her mind, she welcomed them, not bothering to undress, much less crawl between the sheets.

She awoke thereafter, she knew not how long, to the sound of faint scratching at her door. Patrick again, she thought wearily, rising and unsheathing her sword on the way to the door. The opening, however, revealed not the prince but the pixie-sized Princess Tana.

The little girl placed a finger to her lips and slid through the narrow opening. Thyri could read nothing in her eyes—as if she looked through a window opening upon a vista without form. The girl's hair was dark and silky, almost veil-like—like Megan's. She wore a plain white cotton nightdress.

The princess moved quickly, genuinely surprising Thyri. She reached out and touched the rune-blade before Thyri could move it away. She ran her small fingers meditatively along its bared edge. Thyri held it firmly; movement on her part could do the princess grave injury. When the girl took her hand back, Thyri quickly sheathed the sword. She backed up and sat on the edge of the bed.

Tana pointed at the sword. "With that you kill?"

"Yes."

"My cousin?"

No, Thyri thought. "Yes."

"I could feel—coldness in the metal."

"Metal is cold."

"No, not like that. I mean like—well, more than that."

Thyri eyed the princess, this girl who had touched her sor-cerous blade as if it were a toy. So young, Thyri thought—sens-ing, perhaps, things she could not put into words?

"Sometimes," the princess continued, "I see things that my brother doesn't."

"Brothers. You have two."

"No. Patrick is not really my brother. His father is not mine. My mother brought him here with her and then I was born. Me and Seth, the same night. Seth is my brother."

Thyri reflected. Kaerglen had not fathered Patrick? But he was still prince, next in line for the throne, if indeed Coryn viewed it that way. It seemed so. It reminded Thyri that she was on foreign soil; in Norway only a father's son could take the place and prop-erty of the father. Only, in fact, the firstborn. The younger ones had to find room and home of their own.

"So you see things that Seth doesn't see."

"Yes."

"And you feel things, too?"

Tana nodded.

The girl *does* have magic, Thyri thought. Coryn's blood? He certainly hadn't special defenses against Pye's attacks. Tana, however, had been raised within the confines of the castle. The magic that permeated it might have found a home in the child. That seemed possible. It also seemed possible that the princess was mad. Except for the fact that Tana had touched the sword and lived.

Thyri tried and failed to perceive the flavor of sorcery about the girl separate from that in the walls. Her failure meant nothing; she'd seldom felt the tingling *at will* around Meg, Scacath, or Astrid, and she knew all three possessed ability in the art. Mad-ness too was an elusive quality, often hidden far beneath the sur-face of the one afflicted.

"Why did you come here, little one?"

"I—" The princess paused. "I want to show you something. Ask you something."

"Ask."

"I have to show first."

Thyri moved off the bed and onto one knee, closer to the girl. "What do you have, little one?"

"Not here. You have to follow me, and we have to be very, very quiet."

She smiled and stood. Tana gave her a hand, then fumbled at

the doorknob as a child does when only one small hand is available for the task.

She led Thyri from the room and to the left, farther away from the main corridor that Thyri had taken to the king's chamber earlier that day. The candles lighting the hall ran out before they reached their destination; Thyri halted Tana long enough to detach one from its bracket. The princess would have led her into the darkness without light. Thyri's eyes were extremely sharp, and sharper still since her first change, but she had little hope of seeing in the inky blackness that prevailed in the unlit areas of Castle Kaerglen. Not without a candle, anyway.

The floor of the hall soon betrayed extensive evidence of disuse. Dust covered it in thicker and thicker blankets. At one point they came across the skeletal carcass of a dead rat. Cobwebs grew plentifully in the places where wall met ceiling. The dust on the floor was broken only by the tracks of small feet, going both ways. Tana or Seth or both, Thyri thought. No adult, not even Moira, had such small feet.

At last Tana stopped. They had come to a door, of oak like the others, but this one was bound. It stood ajar, and Tana pushed it open. After pulling Thyri in, she returned the door to the position in which they had found it. "Don't close it," she whispered. "For a long time Seth and I couldn't get in. Until Rahne gave him the key. It locks when you close it."

Thyri looked back at the door, then detached a pouch from her belt and set it on the floor in the opening. She had no desire to be trapped in the room should the door be shut on her by Patrick or any other dark agent the castle concealed. Judging by the magic that still assailed her from all directions, she couldn't discard the idea of the door shutting itself. She had seen stranger things.

The room at first appeared a bedroom much like the one given her. In addition to the bed there was a table beside it, a chest in the corner, and a wardrobe next to it. The walls looked strange; closer inspection showed them covered with disjointed chalk markings, some seemingly purposeful, others abstractions whose designs, if they existed at all, escaped Thyri completely. She sensed an increase in the level of magic in the room as a whole. And something else, vaguely familiar.

"Who's Rahne?" Thyri asked, inspecting the markings.

"Father's aunt."

One of the old ones Moira had mentioned living in the next corridor.

"Your grandmother's sister or your grandfather's sister?"

The princess didn't answer and Thyri turned finally to look at her. Tana stood, innocently reflective. She focused on Thyri. "Both," she said.

"Both? How?"

"I don't know. But it's so. She is both of their sister." She paused. "They all used to play together here."

That, Thyri thought, made the king a son of incest—if Tana could be believed at all. It was not the first she'd heard of such things in old, powerful families. She didn't suppose it would be the last. She shrugged and went back to examining the markings.

The princess gripped the tail of her shirt. "I saw a lady here once. She looked familiar, but I still don't know how because I remember her from nowhere else. I could—see through her. She was looking for something, but she went away—disappeared when she saw me. She didn't find it."

"Didn't find what?"

"The box under the bed. Seth and me, we—"

Thyri dropped to her knees and drew an object from beneath the bed with her scabbarded sword. The box was carved of walrus ivory—a strange thing in Southern lands. A silver cross lay balanced on the lid. "Was the cross here when you first found this?"

"Yes."

Thyri removed it and tossed it back into the dust under the bed. She lifted the lid. Inside lay a ring, a plain gold band streaked with silver. She took it out and almost dropped it. Her palm quivered under its weight.

Sorcery!

Never before had she felt the tingle of magic in metal, not even in her sword. She felt it in the ring. She set it carefully back in the box and closed the lid.

"The lady was beautiful and sad," the princess said. "I heard my mother once talking with Brenden. I think the woman was Megan. Then at dinner when you said her name—I had to know."

"Yes," she said softly, taking the box and hiding it inside her cloak.

"You know her?" Tana asked. "What is she like?"

What can I tell her? Thyri asked herself. "Beautiful, as you saw her. She is kind. She is—" Thyri hesitated. "Do you believe in the One God of your mother and your half brother?"

"I—I think so. I'm not sure."

Thyri smiled and touched Tana's cheek. "You have much to learn, little one. If only there were one to teach you."

"Can you?"

"No."

"Can Megan?"

"I don't know. Perhaps. Talk to the old ones. Ask them about—" Thyri recalled her conversation with Coryn. "Ask them about Dagda, and Brigid. The children of Danu." Thyri drew the princess closer, brushing her cheek. Tana pressed her face against the metal of the gauntlet. "But," Thyri continued, "be sure to ask them in secret. Away from your mother, your teacher, and Patrick."

"Seth," Tana said. "He can know, too."

"You are very close? You and your brother?"

Tana smiled dreamily. "We know things *nobody* else knows."

Thyri laughed lightly and the princess giggled along with her. "Be sure he knows that no one else is ever to find out, okay?"

"Okay."

Thyri stood, but Tana tugged at her shirt again. "Was Megan looking for the box?"

Thyri smiled and went to the door, bending to retrieve her pouch. She attached it to her belt while keeping a foot in the opening before turning back to Tana. "I think so. This was her room."

That was the other thing that Thyri had sensed behind the magic—a musty, year-worn scent of habitation. Faint, to be sure, yet distinctly Megan's. "Come," Thyri said. "We must not be missed."

She latched the door and set her sword at bedside before disrobing and sliding between the sheets. She half expected more visitors, but none came. She thought for a while that Coryn might come, then she remembered how ill in fact he remained.

The emptiness inside her almost prompted her stealing out again to seek solace in the arms of—beneath the bulk of—the king. The desire was rooted not so much in an attraction for the man—still far too weak to be of any real use—but in an urge to goad Moira to anger, even violence. Thyri resisted it; the queen could hardly be blamed for what she was. And she would more likely fall apart than grow enraged in discovering her husband with Thyri.

Not like Gyda, Thyri thought on the skirt of dream. The treacherous bitch still lived, using her poisoned body to work the warped designs of her mind. Under Ragnar, Thyri had been as impotent as Astrid against her then-princess. Next time, she thought, things would be different.

When the darkness finally welcomed her, her dreams would not let her rest. She stalked under a red sky, her paws stained red, dripping with blood—blood from the river she stalked along.

Hungry. Everything was red: the sky, the river, the horizon, her coat. Not even a wisp of white broke the splotchy crimson that covered her body. And then the river rose up against her—an amorphous creature of blood, falling upon her. Smothering, squeezing. She fought. Her fangs found bone and crushed it. The creature fell away, but the victory did nothing to sate her hunger. She stalked on.

She left the next morning at sunrise after breaking fast with Moira. The queen talked; Thyri didn't listen.

Cuilly came for her with the dappled mare; the journey through the port into the city was uninterrupted and silent. She rode past the barracks of the Guard. Dearen and the rest of her men bade her come drink with them. She told them the celebrations, for her, had ended. Her mood that morning didn't invite argument.

Meg awaited her the following night, as if expecting her return.

"He granted your wish?" the sorceress called out.

Thyri only smiled until she reached the hut. "I must stay until spring."

Here?

Yes. Thyri dismounted. "I have something you desire."

"Several things." Meg laughed.

Thyri laughed with her and dashed for the door of the hut. She whirled there and Meg crashed into her. She threw her arms around Meg and buried her hands in dark, silken hair. "Those things and more, Megan," she whispered.

Later, over dinner, Thyri gave her the ring. The sorceress touched it as if it were not real, then slid it onto her finger.

"You went to the castle," Thyri said, "but you couldn't find it?"

"No."

"Someone had placed an amulet of the One God on the box."

"Oh," Meg said.

"The One God's symbol is that powerful?"

"In some ways." Meg examined the ring, smiling crookedly. "There is an irony here. Had I this ring on my finger while I sought it, I would have found it, crucifix or no." She looked up at Thyri, smiling warmly. "You have returned to me a part of my soul. It was made for me in the forges of Andvari. It is to my magic as your right hand is to your sword."

"Andvari the dwarf crafted your ring?"

Meg smiled mysteriously. "The children of Danu and the sons of Odin do not dwell in separate universes, Thyri. Your gods dwell in Asgard, mine in your Alfheim, dwarves in Svartalfheim, and so on, as sages have spoken." The shadows consumed her eyes softly, sparkling. She turned her gaze on the ring.

Silver wisps bled from it, spiraling and twisting around Meg's hand and fingers. The wisps grew and flowed out, rising before Thyri in a sheet that suddenly transformed into a window that looked on another world, a dreamlike, dazzling snowscape of white and silver. It enveloped her and she felt it probing, delicately lighting on every part of her being. She felt a darkness slip further away. A mournful symphony of impossible beauty came teasingly to her ears—her own song of sorrow, given voice by the caress of the sorceress. Thyri laughed and cried as the music filled her, purging her misery. She became a part of it, melting into the sparkling lover around her.

And she was flying, miles above the earth. Mountains became crinkles in a mottled patchwork of green and brown. Rivers and streams were like the veins of leaves. She dived down, faster than an arrow, faster than thought. And then she flew through the peaks of a mighty range, alighting only on the highest mountaintop where she sat, satisfied, surveying the raw magnificence around her.

She stretched blissfully and yawned, then peeked out of one eye. Meg smiled, almost modestly.

And so began Thyri's winter with the sorceress. Thyri told her also of the Princess Tana but Meg showed little interest and would always grow reticent at mentions of Kaerglen's family. Whatever lay behind her past at the castle was something she didn't care to revive with words. Thyri let it lie.

The days passed. The weeks passed. The moon came again and again, relentlessly demanding of Thyri what she did not care to give. Without Meg to care for her those three days each month, she would not have lived to see the flowers of spring. If not slain by the cold or the swords of Cuilly's men who came to the Northlands to investigate wolf-kills, Thyri would have taken her own life. But none of these things came to pass, and the breaking of winter carried her southward to Port Kaerglen and her quest for the sun.

* * *

Though asked, Meg would not go with her. Whether the refusal came of sorrow—knowledge of the futility of Thyri's goal
—or from some deep bond Meg yet felt for the island of her
birth, I know not. Megan's heart, in this and all other matters,
eludes me.

Book III: SUN, MOON

Such were Thyri's first days on Kaerglen Isle, this place I now call home. I feel as if I've been here forever.

The room in which I work is warm, comfortable—quite plain in appearance, if not in nature. The walls are of unadorned stone broken but in three places: the doorway to my sleeping chambers, a fireplace, and the small window through which I may look down upon the city by day and up at the stars by night. For furnishings I have my desk, its chair, a couch, and my stacks and shelves of books and chests of parchment. In the center of my disordered haven is the pool.

It is a perfect circle, measuring thirteen hands across. Filling it, to a depth of which I am uncertain, is human blood. Some of it is mine. Some of it I obtained from—other sources. All of it I am responsible for. Satan's Chalice. In this pool I have seen all of which I have written thus far.

To see through Thyri I have but to drink and concentrate upon memories of her. From there I may direct my perspective whence I wish—to her childhood, to her years with Scacath and Astrid, and so on. A greater draught of the blood is required to see through another, and then only some are open to me at all. One of these, Bryn Kearn, was the man chosen by Coryn Kaerglen to captain Thyri's ship across the western seas.

Kearn was an odd man. He'd run from his father's farm when he was nine and had worked the sea ever since. He knew his trade. He had accepted Thyri as passenger because he *wanted* to fare west. He didn't think she would find what she sought—the sun—but he'd desired since first watching the sun set at sea to follow it, to see what lands lay beyond. The idea scared him as well, but not enough to discourage him. His crew was another matter. Thyri, however, would help; all knew she had slain the wizard Pye. In her powerful manner and foreign beauty, many would worship her. Thus they would do what she wished. Thus they wouldn't mutiny. She would keep their fear in line.

As for Kearn's seamanship, he was one of Kaerglen's best.

Beyond that, the man had his vices, and he habitually practiced them within shouting distance of his ship.

The main docks of Port Kaerglen are all reached through tangled streets that pass through that part of the port some call Morrigan's Palm. It is the heart of port commerce, and its main avenue passes straight into the Street of Smiths on the city-side. The seaside ridge of Morrigan's Palm has been, since mac Fain's day, dotted with taverns and the brothels from which most sailors take their wives. Some of these places are said to carry the curse of Manannan. I've heard that when hostile foreign vessels dock, their crews are attracted into these brothels by faerie demons and succubi, never to emerge. I suggest this in the spirit of those lusting spectral archers in the shadows of the port-wall.

The docks are splayed in front of the main row of brothels like two legs of Euclid's triangle.

The afternoon before he was set to sail, Bryn Kearn drank in a dock-side tavern and met a strange blond man with broad shoulders and hypnotic eyes. They talked. The stranger offered him powders—sorceries he said made women placid, silent, and yet when touched they would thrill and love with the passion of goddesses. Perfect in close quarters at sea, the stranger suggested, his eyes glittering in the light of the tavern's lanterns. Bryn bought the powders for three pieces of silver.

That stranger had called himself Ragnarok. His real name was Loki, and he'd intended the powders for Thyri. It was a joke that Kearn had not the knowledge to understand.

Departures

Actually, she was six and a half—seven now, but still a little girl.

Her name was Elaine, after the tragically beautiful Queen Mother. Elaine had never seen her; she'd died shortly after King Fiann's death, twenty years before. But Elaine's mother had told her many times of the tall, shadowy queen of her youth. One thing was certain in Elaine's world: she would grow beautiful as had that sad queen of long ago.

This she thought as she lay hidden within a coil of rope among gear next to the Tuathan merchantman named *Black Rabbit*. She'd been playing on the docks after helping her father unload the day's catch. Something had taken her, lifting her spirit with the fresh smell of the sea mingled with spring. She'd run from her father; she'd hidden. Then she'd danced through Morrigan's Palm to see the king's ships. While there, she'd heard and seen the northern princess coming down Shipwright's Row. That was when she'd hidden in the coiled rope behind the nets.

Thyri who had saved the king was with a man—the nice-looking kind with fancy clothes, the kind of man her father didn't trust. They were talking together. The man smiled a lot and scratched his beard. Thyri with the sword never smiled. She walked past Elaine, gazing at the ship, frowning. She looked at the pile of gear where Elaine hid. Elaine ducked before she was seen; she listened to them talk.

"Dawn," the man said nicely. "It will be as I told you before."

"Your men will be worthless. They drink tonight—they haven't even loaded. Look at that pile!"

"Those are last minute acquisitions, milady. They will be on board when you arrive. We—the entire crew will be on board when you arrive."

"Snoring like hogs."

"With respect, milady, this is last night ashore. They must—satisfy their passions for a long time. It is tradition. We will ship without incident. It has been done many times before."

The princess didn't answer. She looked at the man impatiently, then strode away.

Elaine waited in the coil of rope for the man to leave. But he didn't. He stamped around for a while, then walked toward her. She squeezed down into the bottom of the coil. *Be small!* she thought. *Be small!*

She heard him whistling. A big bluefly buzzed into the coil and around her head. She wanted to slap at it, but she bit her tongue. She was afraid. She didn't want the man to find her; it could spoil her game.

The buzzing stopped. She felt the fly walking lightly on her ear. She held her breath and flinched away. The movement sent small, sharp slivers of wood from the dock's deck into her bare legs. She winced. The sound came involuntarily from her lips.

"Well, what have we here?"

She opened an eye; he was smiling down at her.

She murmured her name.

"Elaine, is it?" He lifted her out of the coil. "You are not in a proper place for a little girl. You want to go across the Great Ocean?"

His smile and his friendliness began to calm her fears. She liked the wild adventure that lit his eyes.

"Is that where you are going? To the end of the world?" That was what her father said was there. *Sail out,* he had once said, *to the end of the world and you fall into the downy fields of Hy Brasil, where the gods dwell.*

He looked at her strangely. "Beyond," he said distantly. "I am the captain. The end of the world is mine to give. Would you like to see it, Elaine?"

See it? she thought. *All the gods in their silver palaces?* She didn't believe it, but his eyes didn't lie. She smiled shyly.

He laughed. "Yes, say your eyes. Come." He carried her up the plank to the deck of his ship.

The *Black Rabbit* set sail the next morning with Elaine sleeping the sleep of the gods inside a trunk in Bryn Kearn's cabin.

Thyri's cabin was next to Bryn's. She might have detected Elaine by the noises that came at night, but she saw, on the first evening out, the captain retire with his young aide—a boy of about thirteen, the youngest on the ship. Thyri watched them go in and close the door. It brought dark laughter to her lips. She ignored the sounds at night. It was, after all, Kearn's command. And from what she'd seen, the boy had invited his attentions.

She spent her days in dark, brooding vigilance on the foredeck, staring for hours on end at the horizon beyond the prow. At the beginning she had brief, pointless conversations with the captain on the matters of seafaring. After a time she avoided those talks—Kearn was hopelessly ignorant of true naval combat. He was a merchant.

As for Elaine, Loki's powders worked. The emotions that passed through the girl had nothing to do with her own.

So the days passed.

Changes

The storm had raged all day, pelting the ship with freezing rain and threatening to crack the hull. Bryn Kearn sniffed at the air. He scowled at the thick blankets of cloud above, even as cold northern winds whisked them away with each passing moment. He looked at his passenger, the brooding woman from the land of the reavers. Like he, she had weathered the storm while the crew had stayed relatively dry below deck. Her cloak and her hair still dripped wetly. In her way, she was beautiful, her golden mane framing a face with but one mar—the little jogging scar under her left eye. And that in itself was almost alluring. Piercing hazel eyes.

"What now?" she asked. She spoke Irish well. Excepting her dress, her manner, and her sword, he might have taken her for a native, at worst, of the mainland.

"Hoist the mainsail," he said. "Follow the storm." His first mate climbed the ladder to the prow. Kearn glanced at him briefly. "Get the men. Hoist the mast."

"Aye, Captain."

The wind blew strongly, pushing the storm ever southward while the *Black Rabbit* tacked along behind it, cutting across its wake. The reddened sun rested just above the horizon. Soon, its setting glow would color both sea and sky. The woman would always stay with Kearn on the prow until the sun's last rays had died.

The moon, full, rose behind them. The night would not be so dark.

She looked at him, the sun reflecting in her eyes and tingeing her hair red. She spoke seldom; and when she spoke now, the words were so soft that he imagined them, at first, the wind.

"I am going to my cabin, Captain. Whatever happens, do not disturb me tonight, nor allow another to do so."

She left quickly. Strange, he thought. *Whatever happens?*

He watched the sun descend into the sea—at first a double

sphere, one real, one reflected. Later a single orb, formed as the two became one—two halves of a whole.

Let the woman do what she wants, he thought. He pulled his cloak tighter as the northern wind intensified, and he thought of what he would do with his children that night.

Thyri closed her door and locked it with trembling fingers. She threw off her damp sables and wiped her brow. Her hand came away wet with perspiration. She went to her locker and got out the bottle that Kaerglen had given her. Whiskey, he'd called it. She unstoppered it and drank deeply. The liquor burned her throat, making her choke. But it calmed her. She took another, longer draught.

Odin, she thought, *I hadn't counted on this.* She dug into her locker and frowned at the small cache of dried beef and mutton at the bottom. It isn't enough, she thought. *It has to be enough!*

Bloodless.

Do you think of me, Astrid, when the moon turns full over Valhalla?

When you look into the sky tonight, Meg, when you remember the girl you nursed to health, will you remember her as the woman or the wolf?

She tipped the bottle again, and the liquor's bite felt weaker. A sharp pain stabbed at her neck.

It begins.

She tried to get up and push the locker in front of the cabin's door, but her legs wouldn't let her.

She screamed.

"Gods!" Kearn gasped.

"It's Thyri!" the mate shouted, racing to her cabin.

The scream had drowned out the wind, chilling the blood of the entire crew. Several deckhands followed closely behind the first mate. He reached her door and tried to open it. "It's locked, Captain!" He slammed into it with his shoulder.

Kearn bounded from the prow. "Wait! She said—"

The sound of wood giving way to bone split the air. Thyri's door flew open.

Kearn started through the throng of sailors before him. Another unearthly scream and the men went chaotic, many trying to back away through him. He pushed them aside, and he saw it.

It stood over the corpse of his first mate, blood dripping from its jaws and staining the snowy, bristly whiteness of its fur. It growled at him.

"Back, demon!" He stepped toward it. Foolishly. It lashed out with one great paw. The claws raked his chest. He moved reflexively for his saber, remembering too late that it rested in a locker in his stateroom. The huge wolf backed away, still growling deeply. It dragged the mate's body back into the cabin and nudged the door shut with its bloody snout.

Kearn stood there long in silence. Slowly, he became aware again of the pounding of the sea and the sting of the wind. The men stood by him, also silent. He looked down at his rent cloak, at his own blood. He turned to the nearest man: "Get boards, and nail that damned door shut."

He lay in his cabin and listened to them. The sunlight shone through the crack under his door. He had no desire to go out; even that little bit of light was too bright. After seeing the door well boarded, he'd retired to his cabin, cleaned up, bandaged his wound, and gotten very, very drunk. He had poured extra doses of Loki's powder into the little girl's mouth and left her locked up in her trunk, sleeping the sleep of sorcery. Hours before dawn, hell had broken loose in the cabin beside his—*she* was in there, throwing herself against the barrier of her crude prison and against their shared wall.

He hadn't slept much. The voices of his men hurt his head.

He listened to wood crack as the boards came away from Thyri's door.

Morosely thoughtful, he touched the bandage about his chest where she had scarred him. The scabs itched. He wanted to scratch and tear at them to make them go away, make the darkness go away—he knew well what his wounds might mean.

The entire crew would go after her with their knives now. A greater fear had replaced that of her sword. He doubted even he, their captain, could stop them. He wasn't sure he wanted to.

Thyri sat on the edge on her bed, head cradled in her hands. She listened to the sounds on the other side of the door and cried. She looked at the bloody pile of bones on the floor and felt the bile rise again and again into her mouth. The cabin already stank of vomit. She had been sick as the *were*-beast had left her, and again when she'd first surveyed her cabin.

And she was weakened. The wolf had grown hungry after devouring the man. It had tried to break free. She'd fought it. It could easily, otherwise, have torn its way to freedom. The wood around her door cracked painfully.

"Rise, little one," she said, getting up slowly.

Time to die.

She went to her trunk and donned her cloak, fixing its clasp with trembling hands. She lifted out the long bundle wrapped in oilskin. A moment later she stood, Astrid's rune-sword held tightly in whitened fingers and pointed at the door.

A final crack as the last cross-board came away. The door flew open.

She slashed through the throat of the man in front and leapt out, dodging to the side to get her back to the wall. One man lunged at her; she gutted him with one swift stroke. The others held back for a moment, spreading out. An animal rage filled their eyes. The sun glinted menacingly off long knives. Shouts of "Rape her first!" surfaced from the back.

Maybe, she thought. *I may kill half of them, but one cannot stand against fifty for long.* Not even with sword against knives. Not even with a wall to her back. *Not, anyway, after last night.*

They closed slowly, then the slaughter began. Bodies fell all around her as her sword flashed first to one side, then the other. But they were maddened, fearless; their knives found her as well. Within seconds, she bled from wounds in her belly and shoulder. She wondered briefly why she fought at all. She couldn't win, and death would cure her pain.

But she couldn't let them take her. She was a warrior.

She winced as steel found her kidney. She slashed back with berserk fury, removing her attacker's arm just below the shoulder. His blood sprayed from severed arteries, splashing her in the face, stinging her eyes. Another blade found her stomach. Suddenly, her shoulder blades wrenched. "Not now," she screamed. "Oh, Odin! Not now!"

She dropped her sword as the emerging claws broke her skin. Leather snapped, and her gauntlet slipped to the deck. Her rune-clasp unfastened at her bidding, and she stood before them, momentarily a demonic blend of naked woman and primordial beast. She could smell fear as they broke to run. She liked the smell and threw herself among them.

She'd slain seven with her sword. She killed another twelve; the rest jumped ship. Near the end, Kearn came from his stateroom, a maniacal fury in his eyes. The torn body of his aide lay at Thyri's feet. The captain charged her, and she killed him as well.

She paced the creaking deck of the desolate vessel.

Everywhere she looked, she saw corpses through her tears. She wanted to pitch them all overboard, but she couldn't bear to look at them.

She went to Kearn's stateroom and looked at herself in his mirror. Her hair was tangled and grimy with blood. The rest of her naked body looked clean, but it did not feel that way. She bore no scars—no reminders of the blades that had pierced her flesh. The wolf's body had healed itself.

She found rags, drew fresh water from Kearn's private cask, washed her hair, and scrubbed at the intangible uncleanness of her skin, rubbing her flesh raw. She felt the ship jerk beneath her, its sail filling with a brisk, southwesterly wind that sent it skimming over the waves. A wind from Valhalla, she thought. With no crew, the gods were pushing her westward. *Odin, just let me die!*

And then she smelt life—faint, but there, nearby. The smell of the captain's aide—but no, she'd just killed him, and his scent had been—different.

She searched for the source, and found it lying on top of Kearn's nightgown in an ornate mahogany trunk at the foot of the captain's bed. She looked down into a face she knew: it was the little girl from the procession to Castle Kaerglen.

Elaine lay there, still. She thought nothing; she felt nothing. She didn't wake.

Thyri stared at her. Innocence, she thought. *Innocence in this dream of blood to torture me.*

She closed the trunk, went back to look in the mirror, then smashed the mirror with her fist, heedless of the bite of the glass. She stepped from the cabin and gazed up at the full sail. Beyond it, the sun shone merrily down at her.

Thyri snarled at it.

She locked herself in her cabin and finished the bottle of whiskey Coryn Kaerglen had sent her as a parting gift. When the wolf came to her that night, she fought it—fought its rage with one of her own. She wouldn't let it out of the cabin. She forced it to eat only the dried meat in her trunk. In that, it won a small battle. It ate well over half.

The night left her barely able to move at sunrise, and she slept well into the afternoon. When she woke she heard Elaine's scratching and sobs. The powders had worn off. Thyri slowly made her way to Kearn's cabin and opened the trunk.

Elaine launched herself instinctively into Thyri's arms. She was thin, like a loose sack of small bones. Her eyes were hollow. Thyri comforted her without real compassion; her heart lay wounded, deep in the void within her.

She held the girl for a while, then pried her away. Elaine curled up on the captain's bed, weeping uncontrollably. Thyri left and locked the door. She looked at the sun. It hung low on the horizon.

The moon was already up.

Sun will set, Thyri thought. *And soon.*

So little time.

She looked at the deck. The blood had dried and cracked in places, baked dark as mud during the day. Bodies still lay about in odd, grotesque shapes.

She wandered among them, unable to believe that she was responsible for the slaughter. Slowly, she picked them up and threw them overboard. Two bodies she found without faces—men unknown, unrecognized. These she dragged into her cabin before locking herself in to await sunset.

She sat there, staring at the dead men heaped inside her door. One had a scar on his arm—he'd worked a hoist on the mainsail. His face leapt into her mind. Hard-eyed and smiling, with a bent nose, full lips, and short bristly beard. And through the stench of death now she smelt the other man's scent. She knew him too.

She wept and was ill again. She couldn't throw them out. If she did, the wolf would win.

She saw Elaine's terrified face. Fangs sinking into her neck. Her small, bloodied body enraging the beast further. Even it would not be enough.

She wanted to drink, but all the ale and whiskey left was in the other cabin. And it grew darker outside.

Perspiration poured from her. Her vision blurred. She started for the door, for the whiskey, but the beast came then and another night's battle began.

Impervious to Elaine's sporadic wailing, Thyri didn't waken for a day and another night. When she finally did rise, she got up groggily and unlocked the girl's cabin. Elaine grew quiet and backed away from her, staring, a wild terror in her eyes.

Thyri turned and set to washing what blood she could from the deck.

She spent her days gazing into the depths of the great sea. She had no desire to look up and watch the inevitable progress of the sun and the moon. They mocked her, and she could not touch them. Nature and the gods had conspired against her—to keep her alive, to torture her. The steady wind never abated, and she hated herself for not slashing the sails from the mast. She could only let the days pass, eat from the ship's stores, and drink from the kegs in Kearn's stateroom. She drank much.

They had plenty to eat. After a time, Thyri tolerated Elaine's presence in her cabin in the evenings. The little girl would watch her with dull eyes as she drank Kearn's whiskey and his wine. On those nights, Thyri would sometimes begin to talk, to tell Elaine stories of gods, elves, and giants.

Elaine never spoke. She had withdrawn deep within herself. Thyri's words came to her more or less, sometimes coherent, other times garbled music. The girl was like a shadow, her soul stolen far away. It was not surprising. She had eaten of a drug designed for wills far more powerful than her own.

Thyri would chuckle sadly as she told her stories; the ironies of the gods no longer glittered, no longer made her yearn.

When she sighted land, she did nothing. She let the ship run aground.

Wildfire

With her sword, her sables, and a pack containing the few other things she possessed, she dragged herself out of the freezing water and onto the hard, rocky beach. Elaine lay there, sputtering and coughing where Thyri had thrust her before her.

She glanced back and saw the *Black Rabbit* sinking slowly where it had hit the rocks. She coughed out a mouthful of the briny water and collapsed. When she wakened later, it was night.

She looked up at the waxing moon. So little time, she thought. The slaughter of the *Black Rabbit*'s crew burned still in her mind.

She shook Elaine. The girl moaned; her eyes fluttered. Thyri dragged her to her feet. They staggered ashore together.

Beyond the beach, a forest beckoned with its dark branches, the embrace of a foreign land. The sounds of night welcomed them, and they wandered forth into the darkness and slept that night on a bed of pine needles.

In the morning Thyri scouted. The new land was blooming, and the life around her quelled for a time her inner turmoil. In her homeland, late spring was beautiful. In the new land, its magnificence soared past the old bounds of her imagination. And most of the life was new, different from any she'd experienced.

She discovered the tracks of other men. She found a small, dry cave and moved her things into it—the last thing she wanted was confrontation. She wanted naught but to be left alone. The cave, she hoped, would hide her fires from them.

She wondered what to do with the girl. She couldn't leave her; she didn't want to keep her. She put her in the cave and told her to stay there.

Midmorning. She watched a pair of bright red birds alight on a bush of strange berries to gorge. After a time, she scared them off and ate of the berries herself until her stomach refused more. Then she picked a large handful for Elaine, who consumed them greedily.

As the sun loomed overhead, Thyri cut a sapling, settled under a shady tree, and lazily set to work on a bow. She strung it with gut from her pack. Just before dusk, she tracked and killed a buck. They ate well that evening, but when she slept she dreamt of blood.

The new dawn brought restlessness and unease. Leaving Kaerglen, Thyri had been driven by the hope that somehow she could free herself of the moon's curse. After the full moon at sea, she had returned to that same, haunted unreceptiveness she'd courted after Astrid's death. Her hope of refuge hadn't died. It had been buried under malaise and self-hatred. She awoke still thinking dully, *West—catch the sun.*

Outside the cave and watching the dawn, her awakening vitality killed that hope. To continue west would but torture and deny her yet again. The sun had grown no closer; it would continue to set. The new land had sprung out of nowhere, and if west had brought her to it, it was all west had to give.

She gazed at the land's beauty and sat. She felt the earth beneath her and smelt strange foresty scents in the air. She closed her eyes and reached out with her other senses. Yes, she thought, *grown out of nowhere, but nevertheless real.*

Throughout the morn she sat, melancholy, contemplative, seeking a reasonable course of action whilst trying to forget that the moon in two nights would again be full.

Chill winds blew that night and she added several dried branches to her cooking fire before sitting before it on her sables. She rubbed grease from the fat of the buck into the leather of her boots, and she carefully sewed new patches of fur into the lining where it had worn away and where the emerging beast had torn it.

That afternoon she had taken Elaine by the hand and led her out to see the world. She'd begun to worry; the child's silence was unnatural. As the new land teased Thyri's senses, it awakened her compassion. They had bathed in the waters of a clear forest lake, cleansing from their bodies the lingering smell of the sea. At times, Elaine had smiled.

After finishing her boots, she set to combing the tangles from her hair—combing until the blond, silver, and red strands glinted in the firelight like a silky waterfall about her shoulders. Elaine watched her distantly.

Thyri braided—thirty knots now. She looked at Elaine as she affixed her rune-bead.

"Well, little one," she said. "What am I to do with you?"

A hint of fear crept into the girl's eyes. Thyri saw it, and it wrenched at her heart. This innocence was in her hands. What would she do, she wondered, when she was not herself?

She smiled and ran her fingers through Elaine's wispy hair. Suddenly, her other hand was on Elaine's ribs, tickling. Elaine giggled just a moment, then her eyes grayed over again.

"If you talk, little one, I can help you."

Nothing.

Thyri sighed. "If you talk, I can teach you to forget."

Elaine coughed. She looked at Thyri a last time, then curled up on the ground and closed her eyes.

Thyri laid her sables over Elaine and went to the mouth of the cave, breathing in the night. She knew already that sleep would elude her. She set to the task of binding again the tear in her gauntlet.

An hour later, the chanting began. It lilted over the forest to the cave, pulsing, hypnotic in its repetition. Thyri peered out into the darkness. The cave was set in a hillside facing a short, narrow valley. Through the trees below, Thyri made out the flickerings of other fires. A pounding of drums, thrumming and resonant, added itself to the voices.

Men, she thought. Neighbors, if she chose to stay.

She'd avoided thinking of them since her discovery of the tracks; she'd merely restricted her short travels to the wilder areas of the wood, in and around the hills. Too much else had weighed on her mind. But they'd gathered this night. She could watch them. See them and learn of them without being seen.

She pulled on her boots and set out for the valley.

They sat in a huge circle—the chanters—with the drummers in a short arc beyond. Within, an old man led the group. In the center, three young men sat facing outward. They were naked, apparently oblivious to the evening chill and the beating of the chant. Streaks of yellow and black pigment marked their skin. Their eyes seemed intent on that other world, the one beyond reality.

A rite of passage, Thyri concluded.

She had climbed a tree well outside the clearing, far enough away to avoid discovery yet high enough to give her a perspective over the intervening foliage. The resulting view made her think of Scacath's ravens and what it must have been like for them to see from the top of the world.

For a moment hope flared. Hugin and Munin shape-changed through sorcery, sorcery Thyri felt certain came from Scacath. If she could only—

But that was an old, abandoned option. Suggested, considered, and abandoned during her winter with Meg. She hadn't seen the goddess since leaving her grove. She and Astrid had tried to find her there more than once, but the pathways into Scacath's world were gone. Meg had done a casting—Scacath was not in Midgard.

Don't snatch at dreams, little one.

Thyri settled against the tree's trunk and watched the ceremony below.

The people were dark-skinned. They dressed in soft brown leather, the men in shirts and leggings, the women, who sat among them rather than apart as Thyri had seen in many societies, in jackets and skirts, a very few of woven cloth patterned with flowery designs. The men wore their hair long in the middle and shaved on the sides, a styling Thyri had never seen before. She wondered if it marked a man a warrior, since the three young ones in the circle wore their hair unaffectedly, shorn at the shoulder and held away from the eyes by leather thongs.

Beyond the gathering was their village, a collection of conical structures covered with hides and bark that reminded Thyri much of the hut she had shared with Astrid during their training. To one side of the village, and she guessed behind it as well, stretched clearings in which the people farmed whatever crops the strange land yielded. On the other side ran a narrow river.

Of weaponry, Thyri noted only bows, spears, and throwing axes—no swords. That would help if it came to a fight. With Astrid's sword she would be immune to the arrows and axes. But a few good spearmen, capable of using the reach afforded by pole-arms to their advantage, could prove more dangerous than twice their number with swords. Best, she reflected, to avoid ever finding out.

She watched as the chanting grew in intensity and finally stopped. The old man ladled three bowls of something from a pot borne into the circle by a trio of maidens. He handed one each to the young men, and they took the bowls and tilted them to their lips. It was the first time Thyri had seen any of the three move. After that, the circle dispersed, and the three sat motionless again. Thyri waited awhile, then slipped from the tree and returned to her cave.

* * *

The next day she took Elaine near the village and left her there. She watched from a distance as the girl's abandonment resulted in incoherent wailing, drawing attention from the natives. An old woman, washing clothes nearby, reached Elaine first.

The woman approached cautiously. Elaine fell mute. Others came and stood around her, staring. Eventually, the old woman took Elaine's hand and took her among her people.

Thyri sighed relief and turned away. She'd gambled. Better, she'd thought, to risk the unknown hearts of the villagers than risk the girl in the wilderness alone at night. Aside from herself, there were other predators. She'd already heard the howlings in the distance. And she'd seen the tracks of bears.

She spent the day reluctantly steeling herself for the change that would come at sunset. She ate nothing—her human body's hunger seemed to wane during the days before, during, and after the transformations. Near dusk, she retreated far back into the cave and lay down, naked, on her sables.

It was less painful, or perhaps her mind had begun to block out the bone-wrenching agonies. The snowy white beast arose and entered the new night.

She roamed farther into the hills, away from the valley and its people. She thrilled to the scents and sounds of the new land; her wolfen form's senses exceeded even the perceptual acuity she possessed as a woman. She almost lost herself, then she heard them again—heard their howlings, their calls to one another. And they called to her; they sensed her. The realization of this sent chills of longing and dread along her spine, raising her fur. The *were*-wolf bounded toward them.

Woman fought desperately. Her mental anguish caused her great pain, but it finally slowed, then halted the beast. She turned it from its brethren and sought the wildest, most desolate crags to prowl. The experience filled her with fear of what might happen if she met the other wolves and lost control of herself. She'd yet to face that eventuality. She'd been the only wolf on Kaerglen during her months there.

An hour later she was stalking a doe. The droppings she'd discovered at the pool were fresh, less than an hour old. The scent grew stronger now with each step. She could already taste the warm, sweet blood, feel it staining her fur and washing down her throat.

The trail led her to a small glade, to the doe grazing, unaware. And another scent . . . She hesitated, downwind. Something was wrong, the doe grew skittish. She leapt as it moved, and her claws but grazed its flank. When she turned to attack again, another had joined the battle.

He'd fallen from an overhanging branch, right onto her prey's back. He wore only a breechcloth and streaks of paint, and his hand was a blur as he brought his axe down into the animal's skull. They wavered together, hunter and hunted in the final steps of their macabre dance, then the doe hit the earth. He landed crouched, the blooded axe still gripped tightly, his body facing Thyri.

She looked at him. He was young and muscular—one of the three, she was sure, who had sat in the center of the circle of chanters the night before. His stance was relaxed, wary. His eyes, though, and his scent, showed no fear. He watched her as she did him. She growled.

No more human flesh!

Suddenly, he smiled. He touched his ax, then ran three bloody fingers across his chest, marking himself as if wounded. He turned his back on Thyri and quickly left the glade.

She listened to his retreat until the smell of blood overpowered her and she tore into the doe.

For the rest of the night she could smell him, sometimes near, sometimes far. She did not try to track him, or at least that part of her that was woman did not. And the woman, for the night, had already won. An hour before dawn, she began to run, tracing, retracing her trail in hopes that she would lead him away from her cave. But even when she entered it just before the first rays of hard sunlight breached the horizon, she had little confidence that she'd succeeded. The wolf left, leaving her exhausted and shivering in the dark depths of dawn.

Around midmorning she forced herself to rise, dress, and strap on her belt. She reached the mouth and leaned unsteadily against the wall. The grass about the front of the cave was littered with lily white blossoms. She had not lost the young warrior the night before.

She squinted her eyes, scanning the forest from underbrush to treetop in search of him. Her efforts rewarded her not. Cautiously, she fared out and into the forest, to the lake, to wash the night from her skin. After that, she returned to the cave and slept away the remainder of the day.

* * *

When she emerged that evening a freshly slain buck lay on the carpet of white. And *he* was there; she smelt him before she saw him sitting cross-legged at the edge of the forest. She approached the buck, sniffing it, pawing it. It smelled clean, untainted. Her hunger grew ravenous, and she dined.

Finished, she eyed the warrior and growled, deeply, threateningly. He smiled as before, then retreated into the woods. That night, as she prowled, she caught no scent of him. No sign.

The next morning she found fresh blossoms and wreaths of red and yellow flowers set about the cave. There were three large basins of scented water and other containers, one full of drinking water and one of a heady, invigorating potion. She considered ignoring it all, but she knew not what that might mean to the warrior or his people—for surely he had told them of her by now. They must have sensed some connection between herself and Elaine. What if they killed the little girl?

Suddenly, she smiled at her worries and the indignation she felt at the warrior's assuming manner, whatever he meant by it. Another day she would rather have bathed in the lake; today she was exhausted. For the basins she could feel some real gratitude. She used them and slept.

She was greeted, on the last night of the wolf that moon, by another fresh deer and a semicircle of the new land's people—ten of them in all, warriors, including the one who had found her. His hair was shaved now on the sides like the others.

When she emerged the following afternoon as a woman, runeblade at her side, she followed them into their village. Thus did Thyri Bloodfang join for a time the people who called themselves *Habnakys*.

The village was arranged in a roughed series of concentric semicircles: paired northern and southern halves. The hut they offered Thyri was in the center of the south side. Facing hers, to the north, was the hut of the Habnakys chieftain.

The structure was taller than that she had lived in long before. Inside it was much the same, with basketry mats covering the floor rather than furs and skins. A charred depression in the center marked the fire pit.

The warrior entered the hut with her. He smiled, nodding as he looked around. Then he left her alone; she heard the villagers outside disperse.

* * *

That evening she emerged and found him awaiting her, squatting patiently outside her door.

She smiled and he stood.

She held her hand out at her waist, touched her skin and covered her mouth with one hand, bulging her eyes out.

He frowned.

She made little weeping noises and repeated her other gestures.

Light flickered in his eyes and he started away, motioning for her to follow.

They came to a hut on the eastern skirt of the south side. He parted the opening and Thyri looked in. An old woman with scarred hands and yellowy bright eyes looked up from where she sat skillfully working strands of straw into a mat with those aged hands. An old man sat next to her, grinning with carefree pleasure as he flicked a string around in the face of a very young little boy. The boy giggled and snatched clumsily at the string.

Other children—five in all—roamed free in the hut. The older ones looked up at the intrusion. Elaine was among them. She looked at Thyri blankly.

Thyri smiled tearfully at her, then turned to the warrior and nodded.

They left.

She spent the night alone.

In the morning, an array of offerings lay about the entrance of her hut: cakes of meal; bowls of young, tender roots; legs and sides of deer and elk—far more than she could hope to eat in a month, never mind the morning. And the warrior sat there among it all.

She motioned him into her hut.

He looked into her eyes nervously. "Thyri," he said, then something else in his curious, lilting tongue.

She imitated his words and he frowned. She pointed to herself. "Thyri." She pointed at him.

"Akan," he said with a broad grin.

"Akan," she said thoughtfully. She picked up a finely wrought bow, one of the many gifts she'd received. She looked at him inquisitively, and he gave her its name. She repeated it and continued on with other things, working into the alien language.

She saw Elaine that evening with the old woman. Their eyes met; Elaine smiled. Some of the villagers commented softly but Thyri could not understand their words. The old woman kept

Elaine among the other children. She was yet withdrawn, but the children were friendly to her and Thyri felt for the first time a deep satisfaction for something she'd brought about. Elaine might have been scarred, but she would live. And for two terrible nights at sea, she had been the sole target of the wolf's lust for hot blood. Thyri had stopped it.

Akan

For a week, Akan came to her each morning and stayed until dusk. He was the one she'd first met; the tribe seemed happy to let him handle her for a time. And she noticed something of a fear of him among the others. She began to assimilate his teaching at a rate almost as remarkable as her conquest of Irish. Megan's spell, Thyri decided, had been far more powerful than the sorceress had ever intimated.

Akan arrived one afternoon after Thyri had spent the morning bathing in the lake and enjoying a time of solitude alone in the forest. She was naked, stretched out dreamily on her sables, not thinking of Astrid, of Meg, her curse, or anything else in particular. He entered, she rose, and he started to leave.

"Akan," she said.

He paused, keeping his eyes averted.

"Akan, come here."

He approached her, still looking away. She took his hand and lay it on her breast.

"What is your word for this?" she asked, smiling playfully.

He looked into her eyes, and she saw his surprise and shock.

"What is it?" she asked, more seriously. "What have you in your hand?"

"Thyri," he stammered, then he said those other words of his greeting.

She repeated the phrase, making it a question.

Akan took his hand away and began to wave both in the air. He said the words again, then, for lack of other words, he waved his hands above him. And suddenly she realized.

She locked eyes on his.

"No," she said firmly. "No, Akan, I am not *akiya toyn*." What did it mean literally? she wondered. Sorceress? God? Goddess? *Wolf-goddess?*

"I am woman." She took his hand and placed it again on her

breast, pressing it firmly this time, looking at him. "What is your word for this?"

He told her.

She reached beneath his breechcloth. "And this?"

Akan told her. He tried feebly to back away; she said again that she was a woman. She pulled him down to the sables and kissed him. "And this?" she asked. He told her the word nervously. "Is it bad magic," she said, "to kiss akiya toyn?"

"Yes, Thyri."

"I am not she," she stated. She kissed him again, roughly. This time he didn't resist.

Thyri grew capable of holding longer and longer conversations in the Habnakys tongue as the weeks passed. Akan remained her most constant companion, but the elders of the village began to take greater interest after the first time she unsheathed her runeblade and attempted to show them its function. The tribe knew nothing of swords or swordsmanship. They knew nothing, in fact, of metals. For Thyri this was exasperating—she knew well the techniques of forging iron, but she knew little of the methods of extracting it from the earth. Without that knowledge, the rest of her skills were useless.

Elaine, during this time, had a new mother and father. They were old and wrinkled, and they talked funny. They laughed with her and let her play with other children who talked as funny as they did. She was happy. She began to wonder why she couldn't understand what anybody said to her. She knew she was in Port Kaerglen no longer. The princess Thyri with the sword who saved the king was with her though.

Elaine wondered how they got there.

Any who might have doubted Thyri's divinity lost that doubt during a festival held a week before the next full moon. It celebrated a successful planting season, and the tribe's hunters had killed three bears, eight deer, and scores of wild fowl for the occasion.

It began solemnly, in the hut of the chieftain, a warrior named Tokaisin. Thyri felt a sense of honor in her presence there. Though they'd welcomed her and obviously thought her of supernatural origin, she had yet to spend more than brief moments in the presence of the chief—then only when summoned, and then only to stand while he watched her silently. She knew she interested him; she guessed he preferred to await a time when they could communicate on the dignified level of speech. He no doubt knew much of her already; Akan was his son.

They sat on finely woven mats of native straw. Thyri's place was to the left of Tokaisin; Akan's was to his right. The rest of the village elders, fifteen in all, sat with them in a circle. From a pouch of soft leather, Tokaisin produced a long wooden tube with a receptacle in one end. Into the receptacle he pressed a small wad of dried vegetation, then he placed the other end of the tube to his lips and set fire to the plant fiber. He breathed in, drawing smoke into his lungs through the tube, which he then passed to Thyri.

"Welcome," he said, "Thyri akiya toyn."

She took the tube and placed it to her lips as he'd done. She breathed in, and the smoke entered her throat as if attacking, trying to choke her. Mentally, she fought the desire to cough, then slowly she breathed out. Withdrawing the tube from her lips, she managed a smile. She looked at Tokaisin. "I am honored, *haiki sen.*" She handed the tube to the next elder in the circle.

After Akan breathed in the plant fiber, Tokaisin declared the festival begun. It consisted of feasting and gaming, and it lasted for days. At least, Thyri thought as it began, she knew how to react. *If only they knew the brewing of ales and meads . . .*

There were dances and songs and contests of all sorts. On the first day there was an archery competition. Domahandi, a tall warrior of thirty summers by Thyri's reckoning, put three out of five arrows into a sapling at fifty paces. Before honoring him, Tokaisin insisted that Thyri try.

Laughingly, she tested the bow they had given her and the one she'd made when she had first arrived in the new land. She chose her own. As hastily constructed as it was, its feel was familiar, and the Habnakys bows were too short for her tastes. But she'd hardly fashioned a competition weapon. She strung it, however, and obliged the chieftain. Even with the oddly feathered Habnakys arrows, she hit the thin trunk four times out of five.

In the martial tournament the following day, she defeated eleven others, including Akan, and, at the end, Tokaisin himself.

At the end of that day she cursed their pride. No degree of insistence could now make them see her as less than their goddess. They had no women warriors at all, much less one a match for the best of their men. And she wasn't sure anymore that she wanted to convince them otherwise. She knew too little of their customs. She did not wish to damage the warriors' pride by showing she was a normal woman. Assuming, of course, she could show that in any way at all.

At least of all the things Thyri Bloodfang was ever named—

kin-slayer, demon, murderess, and more—*akiya toyn* was by far the most pleasant. It caused her problems, but she lived with it for a time.

After she'd convinced Akan that she did not need food enough to feed an army, her meals had diminished to portions she could accept.

Around half of one side of her hut she had arranged the many other gifts given her: weapons, small wood carvings of people and wolves, a collection of beaded leather bands she had taken to wearing on her brow after the fashion of some of the women. And clothes—they had given her many soft doeskin jackets and skirts, even a few shirts after she'd indicated to Akan that she desired them. At first Akan had laughed; shirts were apparently for men.

He sat across from her now. He had entered moments before and words had not yet been spoken. Thyri smiled at him and he returned the smile warmly. Sweat glistened on his coppery skin; the sun that day had been hot. She gazed at him, admiring the tone of his muscles, his smooth, hairless chest, his inky black hair, and the innocent playfulness in his eyes.

"Tonight," she said, "I will change."

"That is your way," he said, "Thyri akiya toyn."

"Akan, please—I am not she."

"You came to me in my dream-life."

She looked at him and sighed. That night when they'd faced each other across the fallen doe, he had been on a dream-quest, under the power of mystical herbs given him by the tribe's lore-master. It had been a test of manhood: to meet his demon and defeat it. Thyri—akiya toyn—had been that demon. He had subdued her with kindness, but he'd subdued her just the same. Other Habnakys warriors whispered enviously when he passed by. Most of them had defeated less tangible monsters.

Thyri had heard of such practices from Scacath. Rites of passage, ways capable of bearing good fruit. In interfering, Thyri felt that she'd somehow cheated the young warrior.

"She will come," Akan continued. "It is said. She will come and her hair will glow like the burning sun and her skin like snow under the moon. She is like the earth and air and the warriors of the stars. She is one with the wolves and the land. And she is like wildfire—the toyn from which no enemy can escape. We are like you, akiya toyn, we are free. We are few, but we are free. We are honored to be your children. I—I am honored to love with you."

"Is that what *toyn* means, Akan? Wildfire?"

"Wildfire, yes." He flexed his muscles. "Fury to make the

Great Bear cry out in fear. *Akiya* means she who is mother, lover, life; she who is the dawn and the spring."

"That is a very pretty name, Akan." Her eyes watered. *If only it were so.*

"It is you. Thyri—akiya toyn. Who else might have your pale beauty? Who else might run with the wolves and be one with the earth? Who else might defeat our mightiest in battle?"

"I—" She paused, losing her thoughts as emotion welled up within her.

"Go now, Akan," she said. "Leave me. You must not be here when the sun sets."

"That is your way." Smiling still, he rose and left.

When she emerged from her hut, they awaited her—all the warriors of the village. She growled at them. She feigned charges. She fought the beast inside her with all her will—she could kill them, devour them, she realized, and they would probably let her. And that she could not allow. They were like children —they worshiped her, trusted her. Snarling, she bounded away into the forest. And the warriors, as best they could, followed, making a game of it—a test. They tracked her, and she would lose them only to later encounter them, out of breath, their faces grinning, their eyes joyous.

And she couldn't bear it. Midway through the night, she began to run. Westward ever, toward the sunset horizon and away from the Habnakys at such speed that they could not hope to match her, over terrain it would take them days to pass. The beast within her thrilled at her flight and took over. Such was her mood that she let it. And in a valley far from the eastern shores of the new land she met the pack.

Its hunt-master was called Gowrraag—he-who-fangs-the-wind. Seven hands he stood at the shoulder to Thyri's six. He had slain Klaawooor, the buck who'd killed his father, the father also of eight of the pack's seventeen adults. Gowrraag was young, strong, and proud, and he had never known defeat. When Thyri burst into his pack, fangs bared, white fur turned brown and splotchy gray by her journey, he challenged her, the other wolves growling and cowering behind him.

She faced him—all wolf, the woman long fled to dark corners within. Yet her awareness remained, and she watched in horror as she leapt and sank her fangs into his neck. Before landing, she twisted, tearing flesh from bone. Gowrraag turned on her, not yet aware of the fatal wound. Thyri leapt from his path. He landed, spun, then fell. Thus did Thyri come to lead the family-that-lives-by-the-fast-water-and-cares-for-the-deer.

Near dawn, she claimed the den of Gowrraag as her own. After the change, for the first time since the moon had claimed her, her body felt strong, stronger even than normal. And despite the fears and sorrows within her, she felt strangely at peace. During the day, the pack still recognized her. They looked to her for direction. They looked to her in fear and in simple, unaffected devotion.

After the third night of that moon, she stayed with them. She fashioned another bow; she led the hunt as woman. She learned to speak in growls and howlings—it was a simple tongue, without the abstract ideas and terms that make men so full of self-importance—and so potentially evil.

The hunt, for the fortnight she stayed, was good. But as the moon began to wax Thyri grew fearful, afraid that she would lose herself entirely to the beast. And she had left her sword with the Habnakys. She began to feel its pull.

There was a great howling on that eve of her parting from the family-that-lives-by-the-fast-water-and-cares-for-the-deer. Thyri howled with them, sang a paean to Odin, and promised she would return.

That which the wolf had traveled in a fraction of night took Thyri two days and part of another to cover on foot.

There were mysterious signs in the land. Confused flights of birds heading west. On the morning of her third day, as she drew close to coastal lands, she saw black plumes of smoke dotting the expansive horizon.

She grew afraid—for Elaine, for Akan. She found herself listening for the beating of hooves on the earth, then remembered seeing no horses at all in the new land. She waited the afternoon in the foothills overlooking the coastal valleys. The distant fires before her stretched out toward the north, where the valleys rose up sharply into dark, craggy mountains.

She noted the position of each fire while awaiting nightfall to cover her approach.

No sentries hailed her on the fringes of the Habnakys domain. Chirping insects reigned in the valley air.

Thyri smelt the village before she reached it; half of the huts had burned. Bodies, spears and arrows sprouting from necks and chests, littered the streets. Death, pungently more than a day old, filled the air.

She ran for her hut; it was intact, unscathed, but only luckily so. The attack had come from the north and there was the damage; the Habnakys had apparently turned the attackers outside the hut of Tokaisin. Thyri could not see the haiki among the dead in view.

She paused, cursing herself, realizing what pain life without her rune-blade would cause her. Not that she'd had much recent need for it, but its ways were as much a part of her as the air she breathed.

She threw open the entrance flap of her hut. The interior was neat and clean, scarcely changed from the day she'd left. Except for Akan's body in its center. He lay faceup, his expression frozen midway between ecstasy and terror. His open eyes stared at her. Insects swarmed over his face and neck, entering and exiting his mouth and a small red hole they had dug in the side of his left eye. No other wound marked his skin.

Thyri understood too clearly what had happened: across from Akan, half in, half out of its scabbard and glowing softly in the ambient light of the hut, lay Thyri's sword. Akan had come to take it, and it had killed him.

Her vision swam—went red. She threw her head back and howled, her voice cracking, tortured. She could have been a demon then, screaming at the sky, staining the new land forever with the memory of her curse and her grief, unleashing terror in the hearts of all living things that heard that horrible sound. Pain stabbed through her chest, and she began to shake. Her lament softened and swelled and then was answered, her brothers and sisters in the wood mourning with her from afar. And as suddenly as she began, she stopped. The silence caved in on her, resonating through the hollow black caverns of her soul.

She stood naked over the cold body of her lover and cried, the beast finally giving way to the woman. And, after a time in that haunted domain of man, she grew aware of her nakedness. She took first her gauntlet, pulling it on, flexing her fingers before her eyes and feeling all the while that they belonged to a woman not herself. She donned the soft doeskin garb of the Habnakys. The leather caressed her skin, its sensuous feel drawing her further into herself and intensifying her dark humor. She gathered up the rest of her things and left the hut. Moments later she started a small fire by rubbing dried bits of wood together as Akan had once showed her. She threw the hot brands onto the matting inside the hut, then sat before it, watching it burn until the supporting poles collapsed and naught remained but smoldering ash.

Later, in the forest, they came to her—the wolves she had run with and more. They arrived throughout that night, and the next morning her pack numbered three score and five. She led them north.

Wooorg—he-who-was-born-under-thunder-and-rain—found Pohati first. She was slight and young, no more than thirteen. She was Habnakys—her coal black hair nearly able to melt her into the shadows. Fire filled her eyes and her small fingers gripped the hilt of a knife chipped of dark rock. Wooorg cornered her and held her at bay. He would have killed her had Thyri not stopped him.

"Do not fear, little one," Thyri said to her. "I am an unfaithful friend, but still a friend. We will not harm you."

The girl's face, which might have been beautiful were it not covered with grime and twisted by fear and rage, betrayed scant recognition at first: snarling, she looked at Thyri; then her almond eyes softened, filled with tears, and she dropped her knife.

"It is you," she said. "Tokaisin said you would return to us. Many did not believe him. I—did not believe."

"You are Pohati, daughter-of-autumn?" Thyri remembered her; she possessed a great deal of presence for one so young. Even warriors would shy from her at times.

The girl nodded.

"Tokaisin—where is he?"

Pohati's tears welled anew and Thyri went to her and took her in her arms, resting her head on her breast and stroking her hair in silence, taking the girl's sorrow into herself.

"He died the same night," Pohati said, "though his bravery saved us all. He killed many of them. They were *Arakoy*—a raiding party. Tokaisin feared an army would descend upon us next. He led us to a haven east of here, by the great water. We did not know he was dying. He breathed his last promising your return, akiya toyn."

"What brought you here?"

Pohati drew her head from Thyri's breast, looked up into her eyes, and smiled. "I am *amazi* now. I am swift and strong. I am a warrior. Like you, akiya toyn."

Odin, no, Thyri thought. *Is this how they have paid for my treachery? Have they made their children and women warriors now? To send them out to die?*

"We can make them pay, can't we, Thyri akiya toyn? We can kill them like they killed my brother, my mother, and my sister."

Thyri nodded. She recalled what knowledge she had from Akan of other tribes. "The Arakoy," she said, "are not sister-tribe

to the Habnakys. They are from far." She waved, indicating the
northern mountains.

"Yes."

"Why do they come?"

Pohati shrugged. "The lore-master says they have not done so
in two lifetimes. But he says that our land gives more than theirs.
That is perhaps why."

Thyri wished again she had been in the village for the battle.
In so many ways could the tragedy have been averted. Akan,
Tokaisin, all the others—none of them need have died. "Who is
haiki now?"

"Tokaisin said you are."

Thyri released Pohati and turned to the pack. She crouched
and purred to them, her voice gravelly and deep.

*Wooorg, Growaaag, Awwwwrgawoow. Take five scouts each
and go north under the mountain shadows. Observe what the
two-legs do there. Find out where they are, and how many are at
each place. Tell the families there that we shall make blood with
the two-legs soon and that they may join us as they wish. Tell
them to make safe their cubs. Stay with them, but send a scout
with news to me each night. Go.*

Pohati watched the three great hunt-masters go among the
pack, choosing their scouts. Moments later, they were gone.
"Who are they, Thyri, that you make speech with them? Are they
of this land?"

Thyri nodded. "They are friends. And they are amazi now.
Like you, little one."

Duguru

Wolves can think. They have a shallow awareness and they have speech quite effective in expressing ordinary desires and thoughts. Those of keener intelligence know of the ways of man and avoid his domains. They became hunt-masters and care for their packs, and thus they reach a harmony with the land and their own. This leadership and protection is the purpose they perceive, and toward this end do they consider their actions.

Thyri could enhance that purpose with something more; she added hate for the invaders from the north. She added love for her. She made them like shadows of men, fiercely loyal warriors to die for her.

For the wolves, the communion was rapture.

Wrrgr came upon the two-legs and approached cautiously. They were not of his land; the smell around their encampment was *wrong*. He watched them until he heard Growaaag's howling in the distance, then he turned to the east.

Growaaag was hunt-master, Wrrgr his finest hunter. When the pack had stalked the demon-who-had-slain-Weegaar's-cubs, Growaaag had cornered the huge buck, and Wrrgr had brought it down. Wrrgr had been ready to challenge Growaaag for the right to lead the pack when akiya toyn had disrupted the normal order of things. Now, Growaaag's howls charged from afar that he, Wrrgr, should care for the family while Growaaag went north to carry out akiya toyn's will. A moon before, Wrrgr would have had to slay Growaaag to gain that privilege.

A new order had indeed arisen. The gods had come to lead the families once more. Akiya toyn, and another as well. Another whose presence told Wrrgr that life, in many ways, was changing.

Thyri silenced Pohati's increasingly eager chatter as the pack parted for the huge brown male who came barreling in from the west. Wrrgr stopped before them, panting, his yellow eyes full of fear and insensible glee.

"*Two-legs,*" he grunted at end.

"*How many?*"

"*Half as many as the suns between the bright moons.*"

"*What do they now?*"

He pulled his lips back in a leathery grin. "*Sleep.*"

Thyri touched Pohati's shoulder. "He has found warriors. Twelve, thirteen of them."

Pohati tensed under Thyri's hand. "We must kill them."

Thyri laughed dryly. "We do not know they are the murderers yet." She turned to the pack. "*Come,*" she growled. "*The hunt has begun.*"

She ran next to Wrrgr, Pohati following, struggling to maintain their grueling pace. When Wrrgr finally slowed to indicate that they neared the camp, Thyri fanned out the pack, sending arms of wolves to embrace the Arakoy. They closed the circle slowly, Pohati pressing tightly against Thyri's arm, her stone knife absorbing the night at the end of her other fist.

The glow of a small fire in the distance began to grow with each step.

Prying Pohati's fingers from her cloak, Thyri unslung her bow and peered into the wood before them. Pohati followed her gaze and saw only blackness while Thyri notched an arrow and sent it whooshing softly ahead. A few paces on, Thyri paused and pointed up. Wedged among branches above was the limp body of a man. A small ax dangled from a thong at his wrist. An arrow jutted from his throat, just below the chin.

Next to Pohati, a short bow lay across the top of a bush; she fingered it for a moment, then Thyri led her on. Wrrgr stopped then; the women continued alone.

They stopped at a ridge that looked onto a clearing through a short stand of trees. The tents centered on a fire. One man huddled over it. His hair was tied back in a bunch, revealing thin, sallow cheeks. Streaks of ochre curved along his jaw. Perspiration on his face and body cast orange reflections from the fire.

"He looks ill," Thyri whispered.

"He is Arakoy," Pohati spat. "Our land rejects him."

"But not his friends," Thyri offered sourly. "They sleep—do you not hear their snores?" She lifted her head and let out a strained, mournful howl.

Kill the sleepers!

Hell erupted from the wood. The families fell on the tents,

trapping those within. Claws tore at matting and flesh. Thyri was among them, stalking slowly toward the warrior who sat transfixed, in mute horror, the attack only just registering on his brain. Pohati stood stiffly on the ridge, listening to the screams with her knife clenched tightly in her fist. She tried to push herself into the fray, part of her lusting for its release, another part still a child and cowering behind and from the fierce sorcery of Thyri's sword. By the time she forced a foot forward, the battle was won.

Thyri held the point of her sword before the man's eyes. The fear there was uninhibited; his trousers clung to his leg where a wetness seeped down from his groin. He babbled rapidly, the words familiar to Thyri's ears but their structure foreign. Once, Thyri realized, the Arakoy and Habnakys had spoken the same tongue. She slowed him with a snarl and twitch of the end of her blade.

"How many?" she asked.

He stared at her, terrified.

"How many *are you?*"

"Hu-hundred. Four or five."

"Camped further west?"

He nodded nervously. "And south."

"Why are you here?"

The warrior swallowed hard. Thyri's blade flashed, cutting deep into his cheek.

"The *haiki nagara*," the man screamed. "He comes."

She turned to Pohati.

"The chief of chieftains," Pohati said blankly. "They are of the old days when enemy tribes from the west fled from the burning sun. A haiki nagara unites all children of the land. He gains the allegiance of each haiki. Or he kills him."

Thyri looked into the warrior's eyes. "How many are you? Under this haiki nagara?"

"Like the stars in the night," he said, his lips quivering into a weak grin.

"And when does your warlord come?"

"Soon," he said. "Very soon."

He fainted shortly after that. When he wakened, Thyri forced him at sword point toward the Habnakys haven in the east.

Duguru was the Arakoy's name. As Thyri prodded him through the rest of the night, his thoughts dwelt mostly on matters surrounding his personal survival. He felt himself in the clutches of demons, for wolves did not do what they had done in his camp that night. But be she demon or no, Duguru had no desire to oppose Thyri. His haiki nagara, for the moment, was very far away.

The Habnakys haven was a long grassy depression fenced into the side of a wooded hill by rock outcroppings on two sides. A cave at the foot provided access to an underground stream. The mouth of the depression flared inward, making the position easily defensible.

They arrived near dawn. Two warriors on watch woke the survivors, who struggled out of bedrolls to line the sides of the haven as Thyri entered. She pushed her captive before her still.

The Habnakys had been halved and but three score warriors remained, along with a handful of young women and boys whose fire—if not whose skill—matched that of their elders. A hollow ache filled Thyri as she entered the small camp; they should have hated her, these children she had abandoned to flame and arrow. Pohati went among them, telling them how they had captured Duguru. She told them how akiya toyn commanded the wolves.

In the faint moonlight, Thyri saw Elaine clinging to the skirt of the old man. The other children gathered at his feet. The old woman was not there; Thyri learned later that she'd died over the body of a little boy. And then the Arakoy had murdered the child.

At dawn, the tribe sang a song to Thyri of love and the sound of rain against stone. Before seeking the solitude of sleep, the families sang another song to her of other things: of her legend, of the fury of her namesake, of her beauty and her terrible wrath.

Within that joyous camp, surrounded by the Habnakys and her brothers and sisters of the wood, Thyri almost began to believe them. Though she had known nothing of the prophecy before arriving in the new land, her skills, the sorceries in her blade, and now her communion with the wolves had made her into the image of the Habnakys goddess. And wherein, she wondered, lay the difference?

Wildfire—you grow mad, little one.

Later that day she wakened Duguru and set the point of her sword against his chest. He told her more of the tribes called Arakoy and of Aralak haiki nagara.

The Arakoy peopled the forests and plains of the northlands, beyond the snows of *Hagara Kohn*—the teeth of the Great Bear. During Duguru's childhood, the tribes had warred with themselves, until came Aralak. He was a giant, standing a head again as tall as any of his warriors. He fought with a great battle-spear —blessed, Duguru swore, by the Earth Mother herself. Aralak was her servant and her herald. It was she, Duguru claimed, who had directed the warlord's attention southward.

In his fear, he grew incoherent then. Thyri had to await his recovery before continuing her questioning. His raiding party, she learned at end, consisted of scouts. Aralak planned to follow later, before the end of summer, with a full-scale invasion.

Thyri let the warrior live. Around his information she developed her strategy. First, she would stop the raiders from returning home.

That evening came scouts from the North with news of survivors and another splinter of the Arakoy raiders. The survivors belonged to the *Konanci*—a sister-tribe to the Habnakys. Thyri sent warriors to rally the surviving Konanci around their northernmost village, then she ordered death for the Arakoy scouts in the Konanci lands; Domahandi led two score warriors and two dozen wolves against them. He rejoined Thyri two days later, successful, his arrows having tasted the blood of men for the first time.

She sent Wrrgr and his family north into Hagara Kohn to spy on any Arakoy there. Scouts in the West had discovered the main mass of the Arakoy raiders; she sent another family there to watch over the foreigners and keep her informed of their movements.

The Habnakys survivors she led slowly north. She wanted to block any retreat the raiders might be depending on. She was counting then, without reservation, on Konanci loyalty to her cause.

And she sent emissaries to other sister-tribe warlords, the haiki to the south and west, whose people spoke tongues akin to the Habnakys'. She sent word from akiya toyn—this she hoped would be enough. She could think of no other method of threat or persuasion that might gain their allegiance in so short a period of time. She sent emissaries also to the more distant families. They, she knew, would come.

Sentinel

The moon, high overhead, lit Wrrgr's night like a lover leading him to paradise. The ancient one's howling danced through the trees, and fireflies flashed along the sides of the trail as he raced to answer the call.

The journey was rapture, its end Woraag Grag: one of seven legendary sons of *Worrr*, the Great One. *Grag*—"of the blood" in the Habnakys tongue.

Two score other hunt-masters sat transfixed with Wrrgr, though all eyes were filled with the ancient one alone. No growl, no howl broke the silence of the night. He spoke into their hearts with a speech beyond words.

He had come as had akiya toyn. He had summoned them to tell them one thing: she wasn't to know.

Al'kani

"Teach us to ride, and them to carry us," Pohati said suddenly.

Thyri wiped the stringy strands of hair from her eyes. They sat in the shade of a great conifer, their bodies still pouring sweat onto the bed of soft brown needles.

On the northward trek they moved only in the morning. Many of the Habnakys were old or frail, unable to walk further. Thyri had been teaching Pohati single combat with war-axes since noon. The girl learned quickly, but she was careless—too quick to strike, too vulnerable to feints. She was a natural fighter with long, agile legs and strong hands, but Thyri feared her youthful zeal would cost her in battle. She was too young to understand what was at stake. But Thyri couldn't bring herself to tame the young amazi: she wouldn't understand. She would think her cruel. Her spirit shone like the evening star, and Thyri needed that light to keep her own spirits high. And, she reasoned, they would all most likely be dead by winter, skilled and unskilled alike. Better for Pohati to die a fiery youth than a broken foot soldier.

"Too heavy," Thyri said finally.

"I'm not. At least for the big gray ones. But there are others, smaller than I. The wolves can carry us quickly behind the Arakoy. We can slay more before they arrive."

"Those are deadly missions for men. Only the wolves can attack swiftly enough, then retreat in time to survive. And with riders they would be less agile." She spoke of her plans to terrorize the invaders as they passed through Hagara Kohn. She hoped also to garrison archers along the last leagues of whatever pass Aralak might choose. But for that she needed more men.

Pohati smiled weakly, lifting the wet leather of her shirt away from her breasts and flapping it, bringing cooler air in against her skin.

"Your idea, little one," Thyri said thoughtfully, "is still good. After the scouts, we'll have an invasion to meet. If we ever get enough men I want to fight a retreating battle. We can kill them, then fall away before them like ghosts. That's why I have so

139

many warriors spending all their days cutting arrows. To do that best we need to be in many places. But we are weak then, one group unable to let another know how it fares. The wolves can travel swiftly, but they cannot bear messages as I am the only one who understands them."

Pohati smiled. "The wolves could bear children to bear the messages."

Thyri returned the smile. "You are rested now? We will see who can ride and who can bear another time. Today I am teaching you something else."

She snatched up her ax and yanked Pohati to her feet.

So went things early that afternoon.

When Al'kani, the eldest of Konanci lore-masters, entered the camp, ushered by three warriors, Thyri and Pohati were at rest again. Pohati had a shallow cut along her upper arm from which blood trickled freely.

Al'kani walked erect like a young warrior. The wrinkles on his face, however, told the truth. His grin was gapped, and it linked the lines around his mouth to the lines of alert, steady eyes. Behind him were three Konanci warriors. Thyri rose and belted on her sword. The meeting was brief. Al'kani had with him the sons of dead haiki. They wished vengeance on the Arakoy. They wished to join forces with akiya toyn.

The lore-master did all the talking. His tone was lilting, peppered with the lazy, insensible humor of the aged who live on the brink of death. Or so it sounded. His eyes shone at Thyri as if he spoke of the greatest of jokes. The two boys stood silently, staring with dumb grins and starry eyes, as if her mere presence had charmed them.

Still boys, she thought. *They look out into dreams—my reputation does not aid me.* She smiled slightly at Al'kani. "If you come to join me against the North, lore-master, you are welcome. I do, indeed, ask the aid of all Habnakys sister-tribes."

"You are haiki nagara nòw?" he asked, his grin driving the wrinkles further into his cheeks.

"No," she said. "Just a warrior like all my people."

"Not aikya toyn?"

A flare of anger dimmed Thyri's eyes. She felt the heat of the sun on her hair and heard the buzzing of flies as silence rippled through the camp, awaiting her reply. "I am who I am. These valleys face a threat from the North—a haiki nagara among the Arakoy. You have seen what a *scouting* party has done, lore-master. I wish the peace of these lands to return. And I lead this tribe because they have chosen me and because I can do it. If you can show me how this is not true, then do so." She growled lowly. Seven wolves bounded from the wood and gathered around her. One of them nuzzled up to Pohati, licking the blood from her arm.

Al'kani watched the wolves without losing his humor. "I cannot show you that," he said.

Thyri laughed. "Join us, lore-master. We shall dine soon."

He nodded to her, his eyes still insane with mirth.

They had camped along the banks of a river that ran from the mountains in the North. The evening was cool and pleasant as hunters brought in two deer and women with nets reaped three baskets full of fish from the river before the evening fires were started. Small groups of children danced in circles around rocks and trees as the horizon began to glow red and the call to dinner rang out.

Thyri sat next to Pohati in the great circle's place of honor. Al'kani sat to Thyri's other side. His young haiki sat beside him, still silent, watching passively and occasionally swatting away insects that lighted on parts of their bodies still wet from a swim before dinner. The Habnakys elders and warriors arrayed beyond spent much time talking of battle, arguing over bravery and the better ways to defeat an Arakoy. The latter debate grew heated and hilarious, lasting through the meal. Some preferred staring the enemy dead in the eye and insulting his war paint. Most liked the idea of hiding behind a bush and whooping like a female moose during mating season.

Not far away, leashed by ropes tied to deep-driven stakes, was Duguru. He was the object of thrown bones. They hurt him, but he salvaged and gnawed on them in between attacks. Thyri felt a sadness for him, the way she would for a hog that knew somehow it was to be slaughtered. Such hogs, she had observed in her youth, would often carry out their days as usual and go placidly to their deaths, nothing revealed of their pain but a certain pleading in the depths of their eyes. She had seen it often as a child. But her family had needed to eat then. The necessity here was one of leadership, stance. Duguru was the enemy, and war, after all, was war.

She made it a point to smile detachedly when any warrior or elder looked her way during the talk. Her thoughts were elsewhere: on the coming battle, her lack of strategies for it, and the fear that whatever she might come up with just wouldn't be enough.

And she thought also of Elaine—laughing, dancing, eating with the other children now as if she had grown up with them and never set foot on the *Black Rabbit*. Something in the girl had finally given, letting her life shine out again. As she ate, Thyri could hear her painfully struggling to talk with her friends. Elaine would try new words, make new sentences, and those around her would listen raptly and giggle when her attempts entered into linguistic absurdities. Elaine would giggle with them and try again.

There was much Thyri could teach her now. Much she could tell her . . . To what end? To tell her that her new life was a lie? It was not. To tell her how she had arrived among the Habnakys? Better left forgotten.

And remember, Thyri, that you were part of her nightmare.

Pohati's hand fell on her shoulder.

"You grew distant," the girl whispered. "Al'kani has suggested we celebrate this night with the mists of life. You, as haiki, must answer him yes. We are deep into Konanci lands. They are the children of the Great Eagle and we must partake of his *kouga.*"

Thyri glanced at the lore-master. He held a long smoking tube out to her. She smiled and nodded. The dried plant fiber was already pushed into the bowllike receptacle. Thyri took it and lit it with a brand Pohati handed to her.

The smoke rushed into her mouth, her lungs, with a different taste, a different feel, from the time before. She felt her scalp tingle and a warmth spreading through her torso from below her stomach. She exhaled and smiled oddly, handing the pipe back to Al'kani.

She turned to Pohati. The girl's face looked bright, almost made of crystal. "This is strange," Thyri whispered.

"It can be," Pohati said with glittering purple rainbows lying on her hair where the setting sun hit. "It is kouga, the mist of life. With it we may share ourselves with the spirits of the land. Tonight with the Great Eagle. Can you feel him?"

Thyri breathed in deeply. The warmth flooded through her body, then shot up her spine and exploded inside her head. Pohati grew hazy and solid again. "I feel something," Thyri said.

"It is he. He tests you. You are the daughter of his brother."

"His brother named Eirik?"

Pohati wavered. "I do not understand."

A breeze of discord whooshed through her abdomen. "I am not sure, little one, that I like this."

Pohati squeezed Thyri's hand and raised an eyebrow. She

turned to her right to receive the smoking tube. It had passed fully around the great circle.

Pohati inhaled the smoke, tightening her short vest. She shivered and leaned closer to Thyri. "It is not to like, akiya toyn. It is to feel."

Around the circle, several warriors sat now with chins against chests. Thyri looked at Al'kani. The wrinkled lore-master grinned brightly. Thyri counted the blank slots in his teeth. One, two, three . . . two, thr—

The boy haiki behind him smiled at her, opened his mouth wide, and croaked hoarsely. He smiled again. The boy behind him sighed and fell sideways with a dull thud. The thud rolled like thunder and boomed.

Pohati bobbed and flopped limply against Thyri's side. The young amazi's face swam around in her lap.

"There are further testings, akiya toyn," Al'kani said through his grin. "You should not pretend at what you are not."

The last pursed lip of sun parted with the horizon and sucked away the sunset, a tide of darkness claiming all, shutting out even the moon and stars . . .

. . . the ground turned black, flat, and suddenly cracked at her feet. The earth rumbled and a cliff rose up, scant inches before her face.

Silence.

. . . three, four—

The rumble, low. Distant splashing, like the sea on the shore.

. . . seven, nine, si—

. . . and the river of blood crested the cliff, descending lazily onto her head. It lifted her and smashed her back into its jaws. She felt the claws breaking through her skin.

"You are not a warrior, Eiriksdattir akiya toyn."

The voice—again, speaking the same again. "Eiriksdattir has lost herself." Laughing, leering. It came from above, without. But it came also from within; she grasped at strands of light and for her sword—her hand clutched it.

. . . sdattir, lost . . .

. . . eight, nine te—ten.

Desperately, she fought against the current and pulled herself panting from the river. She sneered at the black wasteland before her.

"What am I, then?"

"You are this!"

The beast exploded from its dark, hidden cage. Its fury overwhelmed her and let her sleep . . .

Moaning, something slapping at her leg. She grunted and rolled. Pohati, almond eyes yet glazed. Lips pursed in dreamy pleasure. Beyond her, the warriors crawling around, dazed.

"No blood," Pohati said. "No blood—like he wasn't really here."

Thyri shook her head. Her senses opened. Something behind her croaked. Her face lay against clothing—with a scent familiar but vague. A scent smelt only in another time, among others. She tried to place it in vain.

Something on Kaerglen.

Through Elaine's eyes I watched the beast take Thyri and fly at Al'kani. Before she struck, he and his warriors blinked from existence, leaving behind only that which they wore. And, in the boys' places, three large toads.

The wolf left her a moment later.

It was again surely Loki. Again being careless. Or perhaps the trickster was weakened in the new land—a land whose people thought Thyri a goddess. If she did truly defeat him then, the questions of Faith's power grow deeper and more complex.

Unless Loki had merely been testing her.

The event caused, by the words of those who had witnessed it, Thyri's legend to grow. They proclaimed her *akiya nagara,* a title which she stubbornly refused, and they sent heralds further west and south.

Time passed, and Thyri founded a permanent camp under the shadow of Hagara Kohn. A few days after she solidified her position, the Arakoy raiders tried to get back through to the mountains. They had dwindled to three hundred, yet a formidable force and nearly equal in numbers to those able warriors Thyri had at hand at the time. But she had also the wolves.

She met them on a field, when she could have laid traps and finished them with little danger. But her warriors needed experience. Rune-blade in hand, she fought at the head of a wedge of twenty archers. The fifth rune of Odin deflected Arakoy fire and protected the wedge, and no spear could breach the whirling death that was Thyri's sword. Warriors of the families protected her flanks while Konanci archers lay concealed in the surrounding wood, raining arrows among the Arakoy. And then the might of the pack attacked from the rear.

Three hundred Arakoy died that day.

Togarin

They surveyed the wolves, the great grays of Hagara Kohn. Pohati wiped the sweat from her forehead and looked at Thyri, smiling, a little nervous.

Thyri raised an eyebrow, turned, and started back through the small throng of restless, excited children. "Don't worry, little one," she called over her shoulder, "they know what you want them to do."

For a while, Pohati watched Thyri recede. Neither of them had expected her to test her wolf-riding idea alone, but Thyri's life had become one of constant interruption, this morning by Togarin, a newly arrived haiki from among the peaks.

One of the little boys grabbed hold of her hand, and she tried to cast off the nervousness that seemed to grip her more tightly each moment she remained silent. Forcing a sigh, she turned to the children. "Right," she said. "Who wants to be first?"

In the sea of small eyes and hands, excitement began to fade. The wolves watched her silently. Pohati felt her control of the situation rapidly slipping away, and she reasoned that no choice was left her but to boldly step forth, grab one of the animals about the neck, hop on, and hold on for her life. But as she started forward, the wolves grew restless. She eyed them. She could have sworn that they'd all been gray a moment before. But one of the beasts in the back looked dark, almost black, and he moved toward her, the others parting to make way for him.

As he drew closer, Pohati decided that it must have been a trick of the light; the wolf was indeed gray like the others. Up close, what struck her most were his eyes—deep blue. She could almost believe they were laughing at her. The wolf reached her, then walked past, stopping before a boy a year younger than Pohati named Kuorok. The wolf licked the boy's hand, then nudged him with his muzzle.

Uncertainly, Kuorok saddled the wolf. He tucked his feet up and, a moment later, he was in the middle of the pack, still mounted, smiling at Pohati and the other children.

"Look," he said proudly. "Nothing to it."

Pohati sighed. The other wolves were moving among the children now, choosing their riders. The largest approached her, gazing at her with sad eyes, as if he had witnessed her failure of leadership, had understood, and wished to console her. She smiled at him graciously, patted him on the head, and climbed onto his back.

As Thyri came upon the fringes of the camp, she realized for the first time just how much it had grown over the past weeks. She truly had an army now. And the tribes still trickled to her command as her word continued to spread. In a way, she was glad that the influx had tapered off. She'd grown tired of demonstrating her skills, and she hoped she wouldn't need to with Togarin.

All activity came to halt as she walked among these people she'd adopted as her own. She did her best to smile at them and not look too preoccupied, though her mind constantly turned on the confrontation ahead.

At first she'd planned to form a war council, bringing together the haiki and the best warriors of each tribe to discuss tactics. But she'd found quickly that more dissension arose from the meetings than anything else. Those who would agree to follow her would rarely agree to anything else. Their pride demanded rivalry between them. Only their faith in Thyri's divinity and the threat of the Arakoy invasion held them together. Thyri thought it wise to keep internal bickering over petty matters to a minimum. So she had quartered them separately and had begun to choose as best she could the most defensible sites for each haiki according to the tactics he proposed. She prayed that Pohati and the other children would succeed with the wolves: establishing a fast, dependable method of communication took on a greater importance as the days passed. In weaker moments, she wished for horses, but none in the new land seemed to know of the beasts she described.

She found it difficult to shake off a sense of impending doom; she had revealed to no one the exact details of the reports the wolves had brought her: Aralak had turned his forces finally into the mountains, forces so vast the wolves could not tell numbers, only such things as "like the sea" and "like the mouthfuls in a river." But the families had bought her a little time. After discovering scouting warriors mutilated by wolves, Aralak was proceeding more cautiously, trying to keep his men safe in larger groups.

To her advantage and smug satisfaction, Aralak had no idea of what awaited him: none of his scouts had gotten far enough to see anything and live to tell of it. Facing the wolves, the Arakoy might now believe that the land itself had turned against their warlord. Only in this did she begin to think she might yet emerge victorious.

Domahandi intercepted her as she neared her destination. Since his victorious confrontation with the Arakoy scouts, he had become a trusted, if somewhat distant, adviser.

"What do we know about this haiki?" she asked him. She hadn't forgotten her encounter with Al'kani; it had made her somewhat more cautious during her introductions with the leaders who had since come to her.

"Haiki and lore-master," Domahandi said, trying to match the rhythm of his pace to hers. "His people are few, but their knowledge may greatly aid us. They are children of Hagara Kohn. The haiki is also *shaimn*. Very wise."

Entering her command hut, Thyri breathed a short prayer to Odin before turning her full attention on Togarin.

He smiled at her. He seemed quite young to have been called wise by Domahandi; perhaps it felt odd because only the ancient in Hordaland were ever said to possess wisdom. "Welcome, haiki," she said, seating herself across from him. Domahandi took his place behind her.

"Welcome, akiya toyn," Togarin returned. "I have heard of you. It will be an honor to stand at your side against the marauders from the North. Too often in the past, my people have had to face them alone."

"These are not marauders," she said. "This is an army like you have never seen, commanded by a haiki nagara."

He shrugged. "It is fortunate, then, that you are uniting the South to stand against this haiki nagara and his army."

"You will aid me then?"

He burst into laughter. "Would you rather I challenged your right to command me?"

"No," she said, laughing with him. She looked to Domahandi. "Have some food brought," she said. "We have much to discuss with this man."

Habnakys women laid a feast before them. Thyri ate ravenously, but Togarin ate little. Thyri wondered if he would have eaten anything at all if he'd felt it wise ro refuse the hospitality of her table. Over the meal, she learned much: Togarin's people had lived for generations under threat of Arakoy wanderers, and they had repelled bands of the foreigners more than once during his lifetime. It seemed the Northern lands indeed were arid, less desirable than the fertile lands of the Southern valleys. Togarin knew how the Arakoy fought, but he warned her that he had little to offer in stopping a flood of the Northerners.

After eating, Thyri lifted one of the mats from the floor and scratched at the hard earth underneath with a throwing ax, trying, as best she could, to map out the mountains and Aralak's position among them.

Togarin watched her, rubbing his chin, then he sat down next to her, took the ax, and began to make corrections and fill in details she'd left out. As he worked, he began to smile mysteriously. "The path the haiki nagara has taken runs like a river," he said. "Through here, here, and here."

"Then perhaps we can ambush him," Thyri said, eyeing how Togarin had carved a trail all the way to the lip of the Southern valleys.

He nodded. "We should not let him reach open terrain. His people fight well there."

"So do ours. Still, we can never match him in numbers." She sat back, brushing her hair away from her eyes. "But we can't hide our whole army among the peaks either. If we go in, he'll discover us, and if he breaks through, we'll have no hope of stopping him."

Togarin still leaned over the map. His smile hadn't faded. He moved the ax back among the first tall peaks. "There is a place here. *Hagara Bod*—the Great Bear's heart. Huge caverns where we could hide five times your army and more."

"Perfect."

"Perhaps he will let you inside for a time."

"He?"

Togarin raised an eyebrow. "It is his heart. Most who have entered have never returned."

"Have you?"

"Yes, but I am not an army."

"Perhaps there is no danger. Perhaps it is only legend."

"Oh, yes, it is legend. It is also real. You must ask him before you lead your people there." He sat back on his haunches, still smiling. "Otherwise, he might swallow you all."

When she saw Thyri returning, Pohati laughed and raced on wolfback to greet her. The other wolves followed, some retaining their riders, others not, as many children, already covered with scrapes and bruises from the day's work, fell to the ground. Pohati herself bled from a gash on her thigh from when she'd lost her balance and landed on a sharp rock.

"You were right, little one!" Thyri exclaimed as Pohati leapt to the ground.

Thyri bent to speak with the wolf. When she stood, she looked again at Pohati. "He says he has enjoyed the day greatly. His name is Daargesin."

Pohati mimicked the half-growl. "Daargesin. Thank you, akiya toyn."

And then the other children swamped Thyri, all wanting to know the names of their wolves. Thyri went among them, and she gave names to them all. Lastly, she reached Kuorok. While Thyri spoke with his wolf, he looked on proudly. "I already know," he said.

Thyri rose. "You do? Well, then, tell me."

"His name is Woraag Grag."

"Good," Thyri said. "You are very perceptive. You will make a fine warrior, Kuorok." She looked to Pohati. "I want you to take over here, little one. The time has come for me to go ahead, into the mountains, and see where we might face the army when it arrives. I will speak with the other haiki, and make them aware of my plans. Togarin and I leave in the morning."

Pohati's smile fell away.

"Do not worry," Thyri told her. "I'll be back." She waved her hand out over the wolves and the children. "You are now a commander, Pohati. You have work to do, as do I." Briefly, Thyri gripped Pohati's shoulder, then she turned back for the camp.

Homecoming

It took Thyri and Togarin a day to get to Hagara Bod. On the journey, Thyri did her best to enjoy the beauty of the foothills while Togarin spent his time telling her the names of the plants and animals they saw, their uses and their dangers. She asked him once of the nature of Hagara Bod, but he changed the subject.

They entered the peaks in late afternoon, and just before dusk Togarin announced that they'd reached their destination. Thyri had guessed as much several minutes before he'd spoken: dark shadows dotted the mountainsides around them like so many hollow, vacant eyes.

The half-moon peeked out from behind the clouds above; Thyri stared at it, somberly reminding herself that scouting reports predicted Aralak's arriving in the valley in which she stood during the next full moon. No later, even with the wolves slowing him down.

"We should camp here," Togarin said. "There is a pool behind there," he said, indicating rocks ahead, "if you desire to swim before sleeping."

"What about Hagara Bod?"

"You do not wish to await the morning?"

"Why? Is a cavern not just as dark during the day as at night?" He shrugged. "As you wish."

"What should I do?"

"Go inside and ask his permission to bring your people here."

"Where do I enter?"

"Anywhere."

Thyri looked around, suddenly thrilled by the danger that seemed to lurk in every crevice, every shadow. She took a torch from her pack, lit it, and started for the nearest opening in the rocks. Halfway there, she paused and turned to look back at Togarin. "If I don't return," she said, "you must stop the haiki nagara."

She turned her back on him before he could reply.

* * *

Fifty paces into the darkness, she lost her torch. She hadn't dropped it; it had simply disappeared from her grasp. She started to speak, but the space before her mouth swallowed her words and her ears heard nothing but a low throbbing ahead in the distance. She stumbled toward it, feeling her way along the wall of the passageway.

She rounded a turn and met her mother, a shimmering ghost with sad eyes and a torn, bleeding throat. Gyda held a hand out toward her; crying, Thyri reached for it, but her fingers clutched at empty air, and the ghost faded. Another turn, and Astrid lay before her on her pyre, her lips curled into a empty smile, her skin tinged blue by the cold wind, crystals of ice glittering in her hair. She closed her eyes shut, but Astrid remained there, silently blocking her path.

"Why!" she screamed, her words, echoing this time, caving in on her. "Why?"

She fell to her knees, and the world swam about her. On a dark, misty plain she sat. Featureless, nothing as far as she could see, then the ground before her shuddered and the beast rose up, a tower stretching up to the clouds.

"Why do you bring your pains inside of me, pale one?" boomed the sky.

"My warriors," she said. "We desire your shelter under the next full moon."

"Warriors? Why?"

"Because you are our only hope. These are your mountains, are they not? Do you not feel the danger invading you from the North?"

"I feel it. But why should I aid you?"

"His words crashed down upon her, battering her into the hard soil, clouding her mind. She felt the beast rising within herself, and she fought desperately to contain it. "Akiya toyn," she spat through clenched teeth. "I am akiya toyn."

"What lies at the heart of war, akiya toyn?"

She felt as if a mountain rested on her back. She couldn't move, couldn't breathe. *"Peace,"* she croaked, then blackness gripped her mind, and her thoughts fell away into the void.

Togarin pulled himself out of the water and let the cool winds dry his skin. He listened to the night, wondering how she fared. Well, he hoped. He had no desire to take her place before Aralak. He half thought that he'd go off among the peaks and live his years out alone instead. With the deaths of thousands on his conscience.

He looked up at the stars, losing himself in the black depths between them. When his skin had fully dried, he trudged away from the pool for his clothing.

Next to them, next to his pack, she lay sleeping soundly. He smiled, and wondered what it was she had seen in the caverns. During his own initial encounter with Hagara Bod, he'd thought he'd died. Only to find himself waking the next morning, refreshed, naked under the sun.

Thyri lay before him now, her skin shining softly under the moonlight. Her sword and other belongings lay scattered on the ground next to her.

Togarin covered her with her cloak, settled on a blanket next to her, and fell asleep.

"What did you see?"

Still shaking her head, she sat up, squinting against the dazzling brightness of the morning sun. She blinked her eyes and saw Togarin there, solid, real. He asked her again what had happened and she told him.

At end, he sat, thoughtfully distant.

"Does that mean we will be safe here?"

"You are sure you asked of him what you wanted?"

"Yes."

"Then we will be safe here. Had he refused, you would not now be alive."

They made it back to the camp that evening, and Thyri got on with modifying her strategies to include the caverns. However weird the experience had been, she grew increasingly sure that she needed the advantage of ambush to stand a chance at all.

Her outlook on the coming battle began to improve as the days passed. A few days after Hagara Bod, a small army of children and wolves terrorized the camp, the children screaming with delight and, most important, staying mounted. Pohati assured her that they could not only ride, but that a few of them could also wield short bows, adding a new dimension to her original idea.

Pohati's council with Thyri remained constant in other areas. She made herself interested in Thyri's concerns over the overall defenses. At her suggestion, the task of fashioning arrows was given to the women, thus freeing warriors for training that many sorely needed.

Under the sun, Thyri met with her haiki and her warriors, making sure that all kept busy. Under the moon, she rested in her hut, Pohati at her side. So the days passed.

Aralak

Aralak's eyes fluttered. He could sense the old man over him, watching, ready to act should something go wrong at the end of the dream-walk. The old man's face was scarred by antiquity and a lifetime of seeking the *other* paths. But his eyes, piercing steely needles, could lay bare a man's soul. Aralak smiled and his body responded. He was haiki nagara; he feared no one. But if he were to fear, he would fear the old man. Non Sai, eldest lore-master of the Arakoy nation.

Non Sai's eyes softened, a twisted smile touching at his lips. "Well, young friend?"

The visions, their majesties, their terrors, their death. "As before. Men in shiny coats that turn our spears. Cities of gold far to the south burning. I heard the screams of children, smelt the stench of death. But it felt so far away this time."

"In time, it could be near or far or never at all. She has chosen you to see that it is never so."

"I must unite the land and take those cities into our nation. And then what? How long until the pale ones threaten our people? Do I build serpents to carry our warriors over the sea to them, serpents as they use in the dream? Those serpents are of wood, I am sure of it. I could draw them, show them to the woods-masters. But they are so huge, and the art is so strange."

"Your dream-walks will show you the way. You are chosen."

"Yes," Aralak said, sitting up, his brow tense, casting deep furrows across his forehead. "Chosen, but by whom now? The Earth Mother has not joined in my walk since we entered these cursed mountains. And now her children, the wolves, have turned upon us. We are entering the realms of other gods, Non Sai. We will lose our power."

"No! You must carry it with you." Non Sai's eyes darkened. "She is strong and she is proud. She will help you banish these other gods from men's minds. The battle is never easy, but it can be won. You must keep her close. You must have faith!"

Aralak looked up. Non Sai's worn face was a shadowy yellow

154

mask in the tent's firelight. "It is dark. My walk was long."

"Longer than most. A mist has risen, blinding the eye of the moon. It cannot see us, even with its lid opened full. It is a good sign."

"It is only the moon, old friend. Some lore I can accept, but I have seen too much to think that the moon concerns itself with my conquests. It has glared at me often enough while I've killed. And done nothing."

Non Sai rose, his withered limbs waving, his gnarled fingers clenched in fury. "It was your birth-dream," he seethed. "To war with the moon. I saw it myself. You would do well to beware of it. To walk with caution along its paths."

"If I feared the moon, old man, and hid myself away from its sight, I would not have united the tribes. We would not be here!"

Aralak rose, suddenly filling the tent with his bulk. Non Sai before him stood firm, dwarfed though his ire yet raged. "Do not cast me aside, haiki nagara. You do not understand the forces you face."

"And you, old man, do not understand that I would not *be* who I am if I trembled before your constant intimations of doom!"

The lore-master smiled. "That's it! Draw your strength from within. I warn you not to make you tremble but to make you wary. Be wary of the moon. Be wary of her light and those who thrive under it. And keep the Earth Mother close to your heart. Without her you are nothing." He sat, indicating a blackened leg of deer resting on a mat by the fire. "Eat. Enforce your strength."

Aralak snarled and snatched up the leg. He sank his teeth into it, stripping a huge chunk of meat from tendon and bone. The greasy fat dripped, smearing his chin and the broad expanse of his chest.

Inside, he seethed. Though the mountains had turned against him, he would not be denied. Some enemy, some sorcery had fallen upon the wolf packs. When he found its source, he would crush it. He had faced sorcery before and emerged victorious. He was haiki nagara. He would spill the blood of an army of demons and tear teeth from the jaws of the Northern Bear before his dream-song was over.

Later, he stood outside his tent and leaned on the great spear from which dangled the tail feathers of the eagle king he had slain as a youth. The spear was as thick as his wrist; only *his* hand could encircle it. In battle it never left his hands. Its original tip had long since dulled; both ends were now sharpened like stakes.

He could not remember the count of those whose blood had stained its wood.

The weapon was hardly a spear at all, though Aralak thought of it as such. In use and appearance, it most resembled a battle staff, a weapon Thyri had mastered before ever wielding a rune-sword. Aralak knew how to use it. The technique was new to the Arakoy yet many warriors had fashioned such staffs under the direction of their warlord. Aralak himself was shown the staff and the methods of its use by the Earth Mother, in a dream long past. Her training had not been unlike Scacath's. But it was faster—more primal, more furious.

He felt the feathers resting on the back of his hand. They did not move; no breeze had arisen to disturb them or the blankets of mist over his camp that hid him from the full, open eye of the moon. He spat—the mists had covered them each night but one since entering the mountains. It was the way of Hagara Kohn. The moon had nothing to do with it.

Around him, hidden from view, his men told stories and laughed; they had gathered together in small groups, eating and resting from the day's travels. But their laughter sounded clipped, strained. He could feel it. The wolves had touched shadowy places within them, unfettering their imaginations and fears. He would drive them hard the next day. Drive the fear of wolves from their hearts and replace it with a fear of himself. He yearned to breathe free of Hagara Kohn, to embrace fairer, more hospitable lands.

So he stood there in silence as the mist laid its burden on his hair and skin until he glistened darkly like a statue in the fountain of night. He leapt forward only when a scream disrupted the uneasy tranquility.

Some of his warriors yelped out of surprise, others held their tongues, hoping that silence would hide them from the unseen foe. They moved little; the scream had frozen them in place.

Aralak stalked forward, his spear ready and his eyes darting about, trying to pierce the white blindness. He stopped, sensing Non Sai at his side. They advanced together and found, after ten paces, the body of a sentry. Blood covered its chest, eerily stained pink by reflections in the mist.

"Wolves?" Aralak whispered.

"No pack could have infiltrated so deeply without alerting—" Non Sai paused, looking down at the torn body.

"Wolf or demon," Aralak grunted.

"Shhh!"

Aralak froze. He had heard it too: a footfall as undetectable as the sighing of grass to lesser ears. His eyes scanned the mist. For a moment he saw other eyes—red, piercing holes in the wall of white. They stabbed into him, then they were gone.

"She has challenged you, haiki nagara."

Aralak squinted at the lore-master. "Who?"

"The moon. I should have sensed her before."

"She ran from me."

"She challenged you. She possesses great sorcery."

"Can you battle her?"

"I will try. But at dawn, after the moon has set. Double the perimeter guard. That should keep her from returning."

"She appeared in the center of our camp, Non Sai."

"No. If you look, you will see her tracks. She passed among our warriors like a ghost. Double the guard, then she will not return. She has all the time in the world to choose her moment to strike."

"And what have we, old man?"

Non Sai placed a hand on Aralak's shoulder. "We have tomorrow, my friend."

Wildfire

She breathed in the morning air, not quite believing that it could smell so sweet, so rich. The change had seemed little more than a twinge; she had felt no pain. She had not whimpered in agony. She was not now curled up in the corner of a dark cave or the dark cabin of a ship, pouring with sweat, her thoughts pacing dark corridors of self-denial that led to an oblivion barred only by an unstable acceptance of Astrid's desire that she carry on. On this morning during the height of the moon, Thyri did not wish to die.

Pohati slept still. She lay among the furs, smiling; Thyri wondered briefly at what. Stooping to wash in a basin of rainwater, she shrugged and thought back to the night. She remembered little, and that like snatches of dream. She remembered a harmony, a song full of beauty and horror and light. But the horror in the song was still music. It could not torture her. It caressed her. It embraced her like her destiny; she had run and slept that night in the arms of the land. Its song still filled her, holding her close.

She remembered seeing him. Like a cornered bear he was—confident, yet ready to strike out in the only way he knew how. A clumsy way. She had danced with him. He had not danced back. She could have killed him; she'd had the chance. Instead, she'd laughed.

She splashed clean water from another basin onto her skin, leaving the air to dry her body. She tingled all over. She'd never felt so insanely happy, as if all the world were reaching out to her, telling her it would right itself in the end. She didn't think about it—she let the sensations flow.

She stepped out and greeted the mountains; she'd moved her army within two hour's march of Hagara Bod. The air was fresh, vital with late summer. She breathed in deeply, then returned to lounge lazily next to Pohati. The girl rolled and stirred, rubbing the sleep from her eyes.

"Akiya toyn, it is like the warmth of the Great Bear's heart to find you in the morning."

"And the song of the stream to find you, little one," Thyri said, completing the customary ritual. "You slept well?"

Pohati stretched, yawned, then smiled sadly. "I was worried for you, Thyri. Once I slept, I slept well."

"And I too."

Pohati's smile grew confused.

"I slept," Thyri said. "I dreamed." She smiled warmly and fell silent. They lay back, losing their bodies in the softness of the furs.

At first Pohati was aware only of a chill in the air. She had fallen again into the pleasantness of hazy dream. But the chill felt wrong. As she grew aware, a sharp breath seethed through Thyri's lips, as if she'd been hit or stabbed. Thyri's eyes were closed, but they moved frantically, making the lids ripple.

Pohati shook her, and she screamed. Her eyes still did not open. Pohati looked at her and shivered; the air in the room was very cold. Thyri's skin was streaked with sweat.

Covering Thyri with a thin blanket of furs, Pohati dashed from the hut in search of help—from a lore-master, from anyone.

The river of blood passed under a gateway of mutilated men caulked with raw, oozing flesh. Arms reached out to her from the writhing structure, pleading for aid and clutching at her; their fingernails were fine sheets of steel, the edges honed as sharp as Bloodfang. They cut her; she passed them and continued on.

And the eyes that watched her from the shore. They were pools of madness, mirrors of black tortures and maggot-infested infants with hollow, vacant, dead eyes. And then the riverbanks moved. They rose out of the water, and a sudden gap marked the space between the sea and an endless expanse of blood that reached to the horizon. With a crash louder than thunder, the gap closed, sending whirlpools streaking across the sea's surface. One neared her. She dodged, then dug her claws into the riverbed, riding out the hellish turbulence.

The banks fell again. Blood covered her, filling her eyes and mouth. She desperately held fast. She tried to cough and blood flooded into her lungs. Her eyesight went gray.

Snakes, she thought as her lungs spasmed, crying out for air but receiving only more blood. Snakes in the Great Ocean—or two coils of Jormungard himself.

But you stand on a riverbed, there are no riverbeds in the sea. Her lungs cleared and she could breathe. The riverbanks were as before—tangled morasses of roots and snake beds.

Playing with my mind, she thought. *Trying to make me afraid. Trying to kill me.*

An eye rose from the river. Its pupil was gold and it burned into her like liquid fire.

You have no mind, it said.

I have no mind, she replied. She stalked on.

Eternity passed.

"Who are you," she asked.

"I am yourself," it said. "I am the shadow within you."

"You are the woman."

It laughed. "I am far darker than she."

It rolled away, melting into the multitudes along the banks. Then the banks faded again.

Around her—colors. Bloodred to orange on her left, shades dark, unsettling, and alien to her right. The blood grew thick, like quicksand. Painfully, she pressed on.

The current lessened, and the river ran dry. She walked on polished ruby, her paws clacking heavily, throwing discord into the symphony of stars above her. She defied them to match her tune. Her ruby highway stretched on to infinity.

Cracked, Gjall, the horn of eternity. It lay where the yellow met the green, yards from Heimdall's outstretched fingers.

She loomed over the dead god. He looked so small. In the distance, Fenrir called to her.

Cracked, she thought. *But it never sounded.*

The Plain of Vigred shifted, and the Rainbow Bridge fell away. *It never sounded! It is not time!*

Colors swirled about her. She smelt it—the scent of sorcery! *Get out of my mind!*

A huge beast rose before her. Its head was of a wolf, fangs dripping, scorching the dry grass where it fell. Wings sprouted from its huge shoulders. Great wings, leathery like a bat's with veins as thick as tree trunks—they battered at her, but she refused to fight them . . . The beast faded.

A pale red sun lit the veldt.

Get out of my mind!

Out of my!

My mind!

Out!

"Out!"

She collapsed and felt hard ground tear across her cheek. She tasted dirt, then sunlight attacked her brain.

Pohati stood for a moment, limned in the doorway by a setting sun. "Thyri!" She reached her side, lifting her from the floor.

"We thought you were dying, akiya toyn. We could do nothing."

A face, strained and confused, appeared next to Pohati's. It belonged to Kon, eldest of the Konanci lore-masters. "Nothing," it repeated. "You dreamed-walked, akiya toyn."

She moved. Her nerves screamed, but she felt her body return. The knuckles of her right hand were white, cramped. She gripped the hilt of her sword; somehow she had risen from the furs and found it. And clung to it. Slowly, she released her grasp. The sword fell to the earth.

Pohati bent to retrieve it.

"Pohati, no!"

The young amazi looked at her.

"Akan," Thyri forced from her lips. "It killed him. Don't—touch." She felt her vision dimming. The effort of speech had tapped her meager reserves of strength.

"Found me," she murmured as Pohati and Kon carried her back to her bed of furs. "Found death."

"Go, Kon." Pohati eyed him levelly.

"I am lore-master," he said. "I cannot go."

"You cannot stay. You could not aid her in her need. You could not even see danger in Al'kani. She rests deeply now. She no longer needs the aid you cannot give."

Her words were cold. She'd spent the day in fear and despair. By the time she had found Kon and returned to the hut, the chill inside could have challenged the might of *Wookaela*—the winter wind. Thyri herself had poured constantly with sweat. Kon could work no magic in the hut; his chants froze; his spells dissipated along with the misty breath that bore them. And it had grown colder such that none could stay inside. Only when Thyri had yelled out had they entered and then, as if it had never been, the freezing air was gone.

But it had taken all day. The lore-master had been useless.

"I cannot go," he repeated.

"Get out!" She glared. "When the sun sets she will be healed. We do not need you. We do not want you here!"

Kon looked at Pohati. Her fists were clenched, but her eyes held back the fury of the lightning. He shrank before her anger. Turning to exit the hut, he was vaguely aware of a softening of those eyes as Pohati knelt down and laid a concerned hand on the yellow-haired, white-skinned she-wolf. Then he was out in the clean evening air, though the day's memories would haunt him for many nights to come.

Duguru

Duguru moaned and rubbed at the rawness of his wrist and hand. Blood oozed from scrapes along his thumb and knuckles, but his hand was finally free.

Night had fallen. Those in the village had gathered together in the center—the women and children, chattering and playing. He could hear them not far away. Making arrows to kill his people. The white witch was already in the mountains.

He looked down at his bound foot. He glanced at his sleeping guard. The young Habnakys warrior snored lightly.

Bones and filth littered the area around Duguru's stake. Full of fear, he took up the jawbone of a deer and began to saw through the leather binding his ankle, all the while watching his guard warily. It seemed like forever, but his foot finally came free.

His guard hadn't wakened. For a moment, Duguru hesitated. He could have killed the guard, gained his revenge.

But the guard might have screamed, attracting others. No, into the night.

He turned for the forest, west—then he would turn north. Everywhere around him he imagined wolves. Howling near—far. He began to run. The forest loomed menacingly about him.

Wolves, he heard them closer.

To the north, he thought. *Must warn Aralak.*

Snarling, right in front of him. He screeched to a halt.

Dark green and shadows. He peered cautiously, trying to calm his racing heart. One step forward—a deep growl from nowhere, everywhere.

Duguru screamed and sprang to his left. The ground gave way underneath him and he fell free for a moment, then sharpened stakes pierced his neck and torso. His scream still on his lips, he died.

Wooorg loped from the bushes and looked down into the pit. The two-leg, eyes to the sky, still twitched, still slid slowly down the stakes. The wolf howled and turned back into the wood.

162

Aralak

In the beginning there was no Earth. The Bear sat with the Wolf and the Eagle and long did they debate. They were all proud and could decide nothing. Then the Bear suggested they cast the ancient spell of time-power at the same time, in the same place. The result would be part of all of them. They would let it decide.

So they gathered in the emptiness and performed the casting. Great and terrible powers poured from each of them. Their sounds—the Bear's roar, the Wolf's howl, and the Eagle's scream—split the sky like the Ground Thunder. And in that rift there grew a light, and it gave off warmth. Brighter it grew, then brighter still until none of the three could stare into it any longer. They named it Sun.

The three released the last of their powers and scattered them like silver snow across the sky. Thus were born the stars. The Bear, Wolf, and Eagle agreed to leave Sun and fare out among the stars, there to await Sun's own creations, untainted by any meddling they might have engaged in if they'd stayed. So they left Sun before he was aware of them, and Sun was alone.

Long did he gaze into the splash of stars around him. He called to them with his own brilliance, but try as he might he could not reach them. So he gathered himself into himself and created Moon. But Moon turned out cold and envious. And Moon was like and unlike unto Sun. It was she-who-is-like-he. She/He defied Sun, and Sun banished her to darkness, starting the cycle that tortures her, opening her eye wide so that she can see the world's magnificence only to close it again, repeating her pain.

Thus did Sun leave her. He tried again, and he created the Earth Mother. She was beautiful, and her beauty shown out from within. Trees, mountains, springs dotted her brow. Her love bore her the children who play in her hair: birds, fish, all creatures of earth, air, and water. She created the Arakoy.

Moon has always loomed over her, hating her, torturing her with seasons. Moon brings the lightning that brings the wildfire that rages in the Earth Mother's hair. At night she/he whispers terrible secrets to the Earth Mother when Sun cannot hear.

Aralak had learned the details of the Arakoy lore before he was five. The Earth Mother had come to him first when he was thirteen to prepare him for his dream-walk. She had told him she needed him. She had told him also that the moon would try to kill him. This he had never told Non Sai. The life-dream seen at Aralak's birth was fuel enough for the lore-master's sense of doom.

Privately, Aralak felt little importance in omens and prophecies. He had defied many in uniting the Arakoy, and he could almost believe the Earth Mother's fear of the moon an illusion—a fear of her own. For was she not, in reality, a woman? She sought in their dream-walks a comfort not in his reverence but in his arms. Were those actions not like those of mortal women? What law denied her the ways of mortals? And if her fears were like those of mortals—unfounded, as often as not—they could be defeated by his strength.

As it neared dusk that day and he gazed down into Non Sai's pale features, he felt only anger. The lore-master lay, overcome, breathing uneasily. Earlier that afternoon he had nearly died. He had told Aralak no more of the spell he was casting than he had the night before. Aralak did not know what he had found, nor did he know what had defeated him. He'd only heard Non Sai's howl of agony. The old man had not wakened since.

For a moment, the lore-master's eyelids fluttered. But the eyes they revealed looked through Aralak, past him. And in those eyes the haiki nagara saw confusion and hopelessness. Gone was the fire, the ominous danger at the core of Non Sai's spirit.

Aralak cursed, set his jaw, and waved a clenched fist to the wind. Demoness, he thought, or goddess—*I will crush you!*

He stepped out of Non Sai's hut and its smell of stale air and age. Around him, the shadows grew. He stood with his back to the sunrise and watched the open eye of the moon peek over the craggy horizon. In the distance, a howling began.

That night he led the perimeter guard in a chasing of phantoms. The howling had grown, reaching the camp from all directions. He sent out units to find the wolves; his men either returned with no news or were found later, mutilated, their throats ripped out. Or so it was with most. It puzzled Aralak. Two of the dead had been shot by arrows. And these among those obviously slain by fang.

Who was he fighting?

Who could do battle beside the untamed beasts of the land?

By midnight he had lost five bands of warriors, a total of three score men. His men's fears grew more real. Reports—or rumors —had surfaced of a great white beast running within a pack of grays. On the back of one of those grays rode a *fofaarl*—a changeling demoness who walked among men wreaking destruction. She with the bow?

Aralak changed tactics then, ordering a spear-and-bow formation around the entire camp. It seemed to work; the howling continued, but the wolves and their unnatural leaders did not dare the defenses. It was little more than he had done the night before, and he grew more angry. Those of his men whose hearts had begun to fail, those who let their imaginations and fears run wild, he put to death. Their heads were carried through the camp with his unspoken message: *Fear me, not the enemy. Over it, you can prevail.* The example fostered a change of heart among the remaining warriors.

But problems yet remained, problems Aralak intended to solve or avoid while still in Hagara Kohn. The most pressing was the rumor of fofaarl in the enemy camp. If the Earth Mother could not enter the mountains, neither could her dark children. Near dawn, he discovered the rumor's source. A survivor of one of the lost patrols had made it back to the camp. Instead of reporting to Aralak, he had hidden, terrified. His fellows had protected him and kept his return secret for a time. But they had told others of what he'd said he'd seen.

· The warrior's name was Totka. Aralak first slew those who had given him sanctuary. Totka then died slowly, after telling Aralak all he wanted to hear.

And then the sun cracked the horizon and the howling ended. Suddenly the dawn was deathly silent.

He marched his forces without compassion that day; in a few more, he hoped to be rid of the curse of Hagara Kohn forever.

Progress was good. He camped, according to old scout reports, between two peaks whose gateway marked a straight line into the foothills and the most fertile of valleys. Once in that terrain, wolves or no wolves, his warriors would be invincible.

He had met with his commanders en route and discussed arrangements for the details of the watch. Six strong warriors had died on the road that day; the rest neared exhaustion. They could not afford another chaotic night. The perimeter defenses were made tight, watch assignments were given, and silence was ordered in the encampment to quell rumor and encourage sleep.

Outside of his rage, Aralak may have felt doom. Things weren't right. Things hadn't been right; he'd yet no word from his advance scouts. This was not the way to fight a war. But he was being toyed with, and that thought—the realization that his enemy was somewhere out there laughing—consumed all others. For a while though, all seemed well. He was nearly asleep, then the howling began.

He listened to it, shrugged it off. It intensified. It began to pound in his ears. He thought he heard disorder in the camp, but he wasn't sure—the howling buried other sounds, chased out other thoughts. He rose and went among his men, bellowing like the thunder of Mjolnir. His face grew dark and the powerful muscles and tendons in his neck swelled. He stood under the moon, naked but for the thin wrap of leather about his waist, thrashing out with words but still more beast than man. The Arakoy cowered before him. He stormed through them, howling over the wolves and waving his great spear about until all of his men—all in that vast encampment were in their bedrolls or back at their posts. And then he focused his rage on the darkness about him, challenging the wolves, defying them and overwhelming their war cry with his own. Only when the pain in his lungs grew so great that even he could not ignore it, did he stop. Then he sought out his lore-master, storming into the heavy air of his tent.

"Old man. In the name of the Earth Mother! Wake!"

The boy's, the young warrior's—no, the war chief's face hovered over him, swimming in the mist. Heavy hands shook and picked him up.

Red rivers of blood.

"Non Sai, old friend! You must cast a spell of silence! The men must sleep!"

Eyes of ancient dead bearing into timeless evil—go home.

"Non Sai!"

"Kneel to her," the lore-master said. His word/thoughts echoed.

Kneel to her.

She is power.

"Old man!"

The hands smashed him down; the face swam away. He tasted blood in his mouth. *Water of life*, he thought, then returned to the darkness.

Sentinel

The white wolf padded softly through the trees until she could see the line of Arakoy through the mist. All stared out, looking for her, blind eyes passing over her position and scanning on, faces masked by fear and fatigue. Aralak's angry bellowing rang distantly behind them, demanding their vigilance.

A spearman leaned on his weapon, his eyes shutting against his will, his mind unable to shake off the tentacles of warm, forbidden sleep.

They would be worthless the following morning when Aralak would march them mercilessly into the valley flanked by Hagara Bod. Her army slept there, awaiting the battle.

She crept away to rejoin the pack that hid in a glade a short distance away. She reached it and mounted a rock to look over them: six score wolves, Pohati, Kuorok, and several other wolf-riders. Pohati yawned; another of the children lay curled up on a bed of moss, watched over by her mount.

The night burned inside of her still, but her forces felt the weight of sleep as did the Arakoy. They had done well; they had spread death and terror among Aralak's terrified, exhausted, and unprepared warriors. She had begun the attacks in earnest shortly after midnight. By then the families had exhausted the variety of their laments.

A patchy mist had risen, complicating the terrain and providing her pockets of invaluable cover from which she would spearhead a tightly formed group of fifty of the largest, fiercest grays in her command, followed by Pohati and Kuorok, who had grown amazingly adept with the Habnakys short bow. They would choose weak points in the Arakoy defenses and strike, Thyri and the first rank of grays punching a hole aided by the children who would flank out and concentrate fire on preset targets, then taunt the adjacent defenders. Those foolish enough to pursue them had fallen to other wolves who had lain in wait.

It had been easy to avoid direct confrontation with Aralak; his roars had preceded him wherever he went. She had been free to strike like lightning, wreak havoc, and punch her way out again at a point where the children and an auxilliary command under Daargesin would be ready to give their aid.

She had lost only a handful of hunters, and the children had never really been in danger; they had had orders to avoid close confrontations once the initial surprise of each encounter had worn away. Only once had any of them been in threat of serious harm, when a lost Arakoy patrol of ten warriors had come upon Kuorok and another child from behind. Kuorok's mount, however, had killed them all; Thyri had seen the carnage afterward, unable to understand how Woraag Grag had done what he did quickly enough; or as viciously as he'd done it: two of the Arakoy had fallen with little more than skin still attaching their heads to their bodies. Ever since, Thyri had paid closer attention to the huge gray, but she'd noticed nothing out of the ordinary. She'd grown determined, however, to satisfy her curiosity before the night was done.

She leapt from her rock into the pack. She would send them to rest, but first she desired a last inspection of Woraag Grag. She stopped before him, and Kuorok backed away instinctively when she directed her gaze briefly in his direction. Woraag Grag watched her passively.

"It has been a good night," she growled, locking her eyes into the blue depths of the wolf's.

"Many two-legs dead, hunt-mistress of hunt-masters," he agreed.

She couldn't see it, but she could sense it now: something deep inside him denying her, laughing at her. She growled again, lowly, wordlessly, then leapt back onto her rock and ordered all back to Hagara Bod. She watched them slowly depart, something inside her seething, responding primally to animal threat, as if Woraag Grag's mere presence now defied her will, her leadership, her control of things.

While she quietly raged, Kuorok and his mount gained the point of the pack and led it off into the night.

Pohati nudged Daargesin to Kuorok's side and rode there next to him. Exhausted, grimly aware of the realities of the night, the children remained silent, Pohati trying to shrug off the echoing screams of the dying, those men who had fallen by her bow.

As they neared Hagara Bod, Woraag Grag stopped suddenly,

his nose held high, attentive. Without warning, he started off north.

Pohati looked frantically after Kuorok; the boy didn't even offer her a parting glance. Woraag Grag began to run. Quickly, Pohati turned to the nearest child and ordered him to lead the others back to the caverns, then set off after Kuorok, aware that some, if not all, of the others had disobeyed her.

Woraag Grag picked up his pace. Pohati turned Daargesin then, and screamed at the pack. Daargesin joined her, and the others retreated from them. She glared at the children a moment longer, then Daargesin turned again and sped north, Pohati clawing at his neck, desperately trying to keep her seat and praying that no harm would come to them as they drew dangerously close again to the Arakoy army.

Thyri stopped when the trail of the pack lost its regularity to sudden, chaotic confusion. She skirted the mass of directionless tracks, discovering that, ultimately, only Kuorok, Pohati, and about ten other mountless wolves had left the others to travel north as fast as they could possibly travel.

She growled and raced after them.

The trail drew within a bow-shot of the Arakoy perimeter, and as she neared it, she could hear Aralak nearby. She slowed, torn by the need to follow Pohati and a burning desire to taunt the haiki nagara further. For the latter, she required only a moment's effort; she turned for the Arakoy. She would catch up to Woraag Grag soon enough.

Aralak screamed his rage, stamping along behind his defensive perimeter, waking the sleepers, battering several of them senseless.

The night would not defeat him. He glared defiantly into the mist. "Demoness," he screamed. "Come to me! Face me here! Face my wrath!"

He paused; he sensed her nearby. He screamed for her again, then one of his warriors shouted, pointing at a nearby ridge.

Aralak looked up. There, on that ridge, she stood, a white ghost with those same red eyes bearing into his own. He charged her, drew closer, and threw his spear. It flew true, but she disappeared and it clattered against the rocks behind where she'd stood. A moment later he reached the spot and stooped, eyeing the tracks there, reassuring himself that he fought a physical, mortal foe. Then he picked up his spear, stood, and began to scream for her anew.

Daargesin ran until he collapsed to the forest floor, panting rapidly. Pohati fell with him, then scrambled to his side. She looked down into his eyes and began to cry. He licked her face and struggled to his feet, still looking ahead. Pohati followed his gaze and saw Kuorok standing in a glade ahead. Gripping Daargesin's fur, she continued forward. At the glade's edge, she stopped and looked on:

Kuorok stood next to Woraag Grag, but it was another there who filled Pohati's eyes: a tall, incredibly beautiful woman whose skin glowed green under the moonlight. She was naked but for a silver staff clenched in her right fist. She stood facing off Woraag Grag, who growled at her deeply.

"You aid his enemies," the woman said to the wolf. "You cannot stand before me. You cannot deny my right to gain his side."

Woraag Grag growled again. Pohati sensed other wolves gathering behind her—the few who had followed against Daargesin's wishes. She looked around and saw all eyes fixed on the confrontation. She wished she could speak to them, learn what Kuorok's wolf had to say to the green woman.

"We will battle then," the woman said, "alone." She waved a hand, and Pohati watched Kuorok fall to the ground; then her own vision clouded over and her knees buckled. She slept before her head met the earth.

Thyri reached them and stopped over Pohati's body. In the glade, she saw Woraag Grag and the Earth Mother facing each other, motionless. She snarled and dove for them but a force threw her back.

When she gained her feet, she saw the goddess fading, then Woraag Grag stood there alone. Again she attempted the glade; this time she succeeded.

Woraag Grag turned to her before she reached him. *"You should not be here,"* he told her.

"Who was she?" Thyri asked, still consumed by anger.

"One who would have been your death had I not stopped her. You are very powerful, akiya toyn," he said, *"but you are yet mortal."*

She looked at him silently, seeing him now for what he was, her realization banishing her fear of his threat.

"I involved myself in your battle tonight to save the life of a child," he said, indicating the still form of Kuorok. *"My action invited her to join her own champion. So the wheel turns."*

Kuorok stirred, and the wolf turned for him. Thyri heard Pohati and the rest of the wolves beginning to return to life behind her. *"Why are you here then, old one?"*

"These are truly my children," he said. *"You have only adopted them."* He looked at her again. *"You are chaos, woman. You have come, but you will go, and I will remain. Think on that when the blood flows tomorrow."*

Kuorok groggily gained his feet and, as if in a trance, climbed upon Woraag Grag's back. The ancient wolf set off with his burden toward Hagara Bod.

Thyri watched him go, then motioned the other wolves and Pohati to follow. After they'd left, she shook off the echoes of the encounter and cast about herself for the scent of prey so that the wolf could sate its hunger a final time before sunrise.

She chose a secluded spot at the north edge of Hagara Bod for the transformation. Becoming woman again, she rose and stood at the lip of a short ridge alongside a mountain stream. Nearby, she heard the bubbling of a small waterfall. There she went to swim. The chill waters braced and invigorated her.

She thought again on the night. With Aralak, she had accomplished all she'd desired and more. With Woraag Grag, she felt less certain. The images of those moments in the glade where a god had faced a goddess began to fade from Thyri's memory like dreams; she fought to retain them. She had involved herself in things that she realized she knew nothing of. Not only with Woraag Grag, but with Hagara as well: that experience yet haunted her when she felt the rock of Hagara Bod surrounding her. She was glad he had granted her wish—at least, thus far no harm had come to her people inside the caverns—but she decided then that she didn't wish to understand any of it. The Bear slept, enduring her fleeting presence; Woraag Grag posed no threat to her own life or her control of the upcoming battle; nothing else mattered.

Aralak would enter the pass within an hour. Or would he wait? Try to retreat?

No, Eiriksdattir. He will come after you. He will come whether an army marches behind him or a thousand demons block his path.

Her thoughts turned to relish their upcoming confrontation. He would fall by no other hand. She wouldn't have to order it; she doubted any in her command could stand against him. The thought of the test warmed her, fueling her longing for it. The darkness inside her was a treacherous, spectral foe. Today, she had something real, something she *knew* how to handle. She smiled at the feeling. *Let it build*.

Within an hour. For all her efforts, the warlord's host yet outnumbered her own forces. In the end, she had gained the allegiance of a mere fifteen tribes—less than a fourth of the original Arakoy number. And all her guerrilla tactics had done little to equalize the overall imbalance. The wolves cut her disadvantage in half, but she was still the weaker commander.

In numbers, the caverns gave her advantage. Once in the pass, the bulk of Aralak's forces would be caught in the middle, unable to aid their comrades at either end. There, a direct confrontation would be even, and drastically in her favor due to the state of the Arakoy warriors. And the maze of passages her wolves had mapped out gave her many openings: many small, concealed strongholds from whence brief, terrible assaults could be launched. Force placement had been relatively easy. A command of two tribes would emerge from the caverns behind the Arakoy, joining with a legion of wolves under Daargesin and Pohati. Tribes under Togarin's command would man the caverns and their openings, and Thyri herself would lead the Habnakys and the remainder of her warriors against the point of Aralak's army and the warlord himself. But what if he would not meet her? What if he turned to face the weaker forces to his rear or to his flanks? What if he had surprises of his own?

Thyri realized that she feared not for her plan. She feared for Pohati and the other children. Should Aralak turn on them, he could well wipe them out. But she could not bring herself to suggest safer, less deadly tasks—especially to Pohati, an amazi at heart now. At the time of the formulation of her strategy, Thyri had still considered her overall chances slim at best. Over the nights of the full moon, things had suddenly changed. Now she felt victory within her grasp. She felt a need to avoid risk. She felt as if she could defeat Aralak and all his forces alone.

Too many people, ones she cared deeply about, had died. She feared the thought of adding Pohati to the list. She wanted her safe, waiting for her at battle's end. The back of a front-line hunt-master in a battle with men and arrows was not a safe place. But even then, Thyri could not think of ordering Pohati from the fray.

Even if she loved her...

Like Akan? Like Meg? Astrid?

Aralak will come to me, Thyri thought. *I will scream for his blood until he stands before me. He will not face the children. He will not ignore my call.*

"Our forces are placed and ready, akiya toyn."

Pohati stood at the entrance of Thyri's command tent. She smiled at Thyri, and scratched Daargesin behind the ears. He growled softly in approval.

"And mine," said Togarin from his seat as Thyri entered.

A group of lore-masters huddled tightly in one recess, bickering and speaking in frantic half-whispers. They debated the nature of their threat: the sorceror who had laid his curses upon akiya toyn from afar.

Thyri nodded to Pohati and Togarin. So easy, she thought. "Go then," she said softly, looking squarely at Pohati. "Go and stop them. We must do it here. Today."

Thyri went to a cavern at the end of a short series of winding, upward passages. It afforded the perfect view: from the bottle-neck Aralak would enter to the gauntlet in which she would squeeze him. Warriors under her direct command lay hidden in farther caverns and the crags and splashes of wood at the southern end of the pass. Awaiting her command to seal it. But she had plenty of time to get there. Plenty of time to watch. She watched and she braided—forty-one knots.

She wondered again if Aralak would simply march into an obviously indefensible position. He had to be a canny leader. No fool could have achieved his conquests. But he was enraged, and he hadn't slept, Thyri supposed, in days. He would enter her trap. He had no other way to go.

Akiya Nagara

Aralak, indeed, attempted the pass. Thyri watched, meditatively working the knots of her war-braid, until he was nearly beneath her, then she raced to her command post to give messengers last-minute instructions for her lieutenants. When she heard Daargesin's howl, signaling that the last of the Arakoy had entered the pass, she led the front line of her defenses onto the field. Aralak stopped a hundred paces from her.

She smiled. He towered over his warriors, and even at the distance she could see the great muscles banding his chest ripple and tense. He held up his staff and stared at her. Her hand rested on the hilt of her sword.

"Stand aside," he bellowed. "I am Aralak, haiki nagara of all children of the Earth. Stand aside or you will die." His words came from a cross section of the Habnakys and Arakoy tongues. The mix sounded stranger than either tongue alone.

She laughed. Bloodshed already consumed her thoughts, though none had yet spilled under the morning sun. Her sword whispered from its scabbard. A short battle-ax appeared in her other hand.

"I am your nightmare, haiki nagara," she returned. "Do you not recognize me?" She raised the needle of her sword over her head. "I am akiya nagara. I am mistress of the moon. I have led the mountains against you, and I deny you the valleys of my people. Turn now and take your men back to their women. You will not get another chance."

For a moment he simply stared at her, his body rigid, only his eyes betraying his mounting rage. And from where she stood, Thyri actually *felt* those waves of fury. The part of her that was woman fell away. Her awareness expanded in all directions, noting everything from the scents of flowers to the positions of her men and the angles of their weapons.

Aralak's bellow of rage split the air and echoed off the walls of the pass. Thyri responded with a war cry of her own, a howl to call her forces to the attack. A shower of arrows fell on the Ara-

175

koy host as archers rained death from concealed positions along the cavernous sides of the pass. Daargesin returned Thyri's battle cry from afar, signing that he had sealed all escape routes.

The distance closed slowly as the commanders stalked toward each other. Turmoil raged behind Aralak, his warriors panicking under the sudden fire and new screams of death and a howling of wolves from the rear.

Under the sun, amid mounting cries both of bloodlust and death, they met. Metal crashed into wood, but the wood did not shatter. It had been blessed by the Earth Mother who, though far away, did still exert at least that much influence over her champion.

Thyri's attack had been deflected, but between her sword and ax she remained ready to block any of Aralak's possible counterblows or offensive combinations. He, as well, left no immediate opening. Thus did they join. Thyri's forces quickly pushed the remaining Arakoy back, stranding Aralak behind her lines. Though he surely must have been aware of this, he did not seem to care. The combat between them, they both knew, was all that mattered.

They fought—Aralak with amazing speed for his bulk, but Thyri with more. It hardly aided her. Aralak's greater reach and longer weapon neutralized her slight advantage in quickness. And, blow for blow, he was stronger. Thyri's thoughts began to turn to certain martial attack sequences, lessons learned in the very last of her seven years under Scacath, methods she had scarcely kept honed through experience. They were of a mystical nature, and they carried within them dangers to the user. Those dangers included death, if too much strength were tapped too quickly. She had never had actual cause to tempt fate.

She found herself shifting instinctively into what Scacath had called mind-of-the-tyger, a series of stances from which the warrior could begin combinations leading to the death strike. She retreated, fighting defensively, observing the patterns in Aralak's style. One of them even surprised her. Feigning an overhand blow, he shifted grip on his staff and swung wide, catching her in the side. She rolled with the blow, getting out of range before closing her guard again quickly to protect her cracked ribs.

She fought on, amazed at the feeling in her side. The pain she could shut out easily, but she'd never before faced an opponent as deadly as Astrid or Scacath. And them she had fought only in mock battles, tests of skill. With Aralak, she fought to the death.

She gritted her teeth and allowed him a seductive smile.

"Come to me, haiki nagara," she whispered from the mind-of-the-tyger.

He lunged, and she turned his attack into one of her own. The sequence ended in an overhand death strike. Her blade met Aralak's staff at the point in front of his left hand. It sheared through the wood, and a demoniac wail pierced the air of the battlefield as whatever power the staff had contained was suddenly released. Fingers of pain fired up Thyri's arm and stabbed at her through the flaws of her gauntlet. The blade continued on, splitting Aralak's hand between the two middle fingers and traveling through hand, wrist, and forearm before exiting through his elbow.

Aralak's other hand dropped the shards of his staff and grabbed at her, catching her hair. He lunged forward, nothing in his eyes revealing any awareness of the mortal wound she had dealt him. Blood poured from his rent arm like heavy, crimson rain.

He threw Thyri back, though she got the point of her sword between them. As he fell on her, he fell on the sword. Still, his good hand struck her solidly on the side of her head, momentarily clouding her vision and blurring her thoughts. When she could see again, she looked into dead eyes.

"May Odin see you this day," she whispered, staring up into those eyes, "and find you worthy of Valhalla. He might hold at bay forever the forces of Ragnarok with warriors such as you, haiki nagara."

She rolled him off herself and looked to the field. Her warriors had gained much ground. Arakoy dead covered the space between them. Shifting her sword in her grasp, she closed the gap.

Pohati

Pohati loved Thyri. If that is possible to say—if it is ever truly possible to say that one loves another—it is true. As she was light and laughter to Thyri, so was Thyri mother, lover, and mentor to her. Her fears for her mentor during the battle were actually as deep as Thyri's own for her. Pohati had seen Aralak. She had seen the man Thyri had to face. She wished they could battle him side by side.

When she joined the battle, those fears shifted to the back of her mind but they never left her. She had tasks at hand, and she worked with Daargesin, and Kuorok and his wolf, to coordinate all the activities of the families with those of the human warriors at their sides. For a time, all went well. The Arakoy were confused, and most were hardly in any condition to fight. The number of allied casualties remained remarkably low. They had smashed the Arakoy rear guard and had turned on the trapped masses within.

And then the cry went up: Thyri had slain the Arakoy warlord. Her armies cheered, rejoining the battle with joyous fervor, victory seeming imminent. The Arakoy panicked: they panicked in Pohati's direction.

For several minutes, the wolves kept them contained. The fear of Aralak, though, was suddenly lifted from the Arakoy; their fear of his killer grew. They lost all sense of reason, and fingers of them broke through Daargesin's lines. The fingers quickly became arms, the attack formations suddenly bursting apart like dams under the onslaught of rivers fed by mountain storms. The Arakoy had tapped their last reserves of strength, and they were using it to retreat.

Daargesin's howled orders might yet have contained them, drawing in further lines of defense from his reserves, had not a stray arrow caught him in the neck. It came amid a shower of arrows, ironically from his allies above, who were wildly directing their fire in a useless effort to stop Aralak's stampeding forces. Another arrow bit deeply into Pohati's side. They fell together. Pohati scrambled, as best she could, away from the fray.

Danger, however, drew ever near. A band of fifteen Arakoy charged straight at her. Just when she thought she would die, Kuorok flashed to her side upon Woraag Grag and yanked her to her feet; the pain she felt then nearly overcame her. Out of immediate danger, he helped her onto the wolf's back. She was only vaguely aware that it was not possible that the wolf could carry them both. And then the lines before them truly shattered.

Woraag Grag dashed across the battlefield, seeking the sanctity of Hagara Bod. He reached it, but not before several Arakoy noted his flight. He took Pohati and Kuorok into the caverns, still followed by the enemy.

Once far in, Kuorok halted the ancient wolf. He listened (or Pohati saw him listen—I could see only through her eyes), and he heard the sounds of pursuit. He and Pohati counted footfalls. Five, maybe six warriors. Kuorok had seven arrows—Pohati had none; her quiver had emptied during her fall.

She collapsed against the wall of the cavern. She was dying. Her blood spurted out along the arrow's shaft in ever-increasing amounts. Kuorok tried to pull it from her side, but the pain of his touch sent flares of agony into her mind.

"Tell Thyri," she gasped, "not to mourn." Her eyes closed, and her breathing grew shallow.

I viewed this event twice. I departed here the first time, then I thought on the presence of Woraag Grag. I returned to Pohati. She never actually died. After her eyes closed, I felt a rough wetness on her cheek—the ancient one's tongue. Then I felt Pohati drawing away. But she wasn't dying. She was entering the body of the wolf. Try as I might, I could not follow.

Departures

Near dusk they brought Thyri Pohati's body. She had been ready to call off the families—they had been tracking down the surviving Arakoy all afternoon. Seeing yet another lover, her skin flushed white by the absence of life—seeing Pohati with, of all things, an allied arrow in her side—changed her mind. Let them fear the shadows forever, she thought. *Arakoy! Your blind allegiance to him whose ambition caused this—I am your doom!*

Near the end, Thyri had lost much. Countless among the families had fallen by Arakoy spears during the retreat. Thinking that, Thyri doubted she could command the wolves to desist at all. Not those who had lost mothers, fathers, sisters. And Thyri estimated a full third of her human warriors dead after those last moments of fighting. After fighting to maintain her own spirits all afternoon, Pohati's thin, silent lips finally turned Thyri's victory sour.

She lifted the girl from her fur bed and held her to her breast. Thus did she sit, motionless, her eyes staring off into the sky.

Togarin, behind her, shifted nervously. "She was in the darkness, deep. Kun, with his wolf-friend who humbles my best trackers, found her. There was a battle there, akiya toyn. I saw it myself. Six Arakoy laying lifeless, four wearing Habnakys arrows, two with torn throats. Beyond them, Kun found her. She was truly amazi."

Slowly, Thyri shook her head. No, she thought. She looked at Togarin, her rage filling her eyes with tears. "*Your* archers killed her, haiki! Can't you tell the feathering of your own arrows!"

Togarin, his face full of sadness, stepped back. He tried to speak, then turned from Thyri and walked away.

She glared about her, and the others left as well. She was suddenly, for the first time since that morning, alone. The cold, lifeless girl in her arms could not comfort her.

It was an accident, little one. Togarin mourns for you as well. You died as all true warriors do—in battle.

* * *

No one heard from Kuorok for many days after that battle. He and Woraag Grag had disappeared after their skirmish with those last Arakoy warriors.

For Thyri, the pursuit of vengeance quickly lost its edge. She slept little that night, and the next day she apologized to Togarin. She even sent word to the families to plead for the last Arakoy lives. There had been enough bloodshed.

While she rested, allowing her rib to heal, they named her again akiya nagara. She smiled weakly under the shower of presents that followed, but she moved through the festivities only barely there. I can liken her frame of mind again only to her condition following Astrid's death. Events went on around her. She would be part of them, but then she would not.

A fortnight later, the chieftains that she theoretically ruled persuaded her to take half the army through the mountains into Arakoy lands to exact tribute from the defeated. She agreed to go, but not for that reason. She had begun to see in all the Habnakys the ghost of Pohati's spirit. And the Arakoy did need her. Without some sort of strength in the North, neighboring warlords had an open door, and the entire cycle could start over again. She desperately needed a change.

She left after enduring the next moon. For the most part, she avoided the other wolves. They had lost many while under her leadership, and she told them that she must make that calm within herself, and that she could do that only alone.

She roamed that summer through the Northern lands. They saddened her; women and children were starving even as the crops began to ripen the fields. They had lost many hunters. Aralak, it seemed, had driven his people like slaves.

She found no evidence anywhere of foreign threats. If there were people further north, they were few and free. When autumn neared, she founded a new capital for the Arakoy, made a young Habnakys named Hoorantas haiki, assigned to him an army, then ordered the rest of the Southerners home with a request to give Togarin her right of leadership. She stayed to see Hoorantas test his reins of power, then left before first frost.

And so I reach that point at which I dropped this work some thirteen months ago. Some of that which you have read I have left untouched these past weeks. Other sections have exhausted me in my attempts to separate fact from my own fantasy. But you will not know what I mean.

This work demands much of me, more than I was, at one time, willing to give. It began with Akan.

He was a simple, beautiful savage; in seeing him through Thyri's eyes and feeling the things she felt, I found myself fearing, for the first time, the loss of my own identity. Thyri's lovemaking with Akan was animal in its fury. Always before, when I'd dared to enter the moments of Thyri's passions, they had been rooted in emotions, loves and fears *she* felt deeply, and I had felt like an unclean intruder, an observer unseen but nevertheless unwanted. When she first took Akan, Thyri did not love him. She later grew to care for him, but the first time she sought only release. The power of that release left me shaking and afraid, ending that day of my work and haunting me through another day, the first day my work on this task was disrupted.

My memories of that lost day are still hazy. I remember stealing through the streets of the city, somehow aware of pathways that I had never previously taken. I went into taverns. I drank heavily. Of that evening I have no memories at all. I awoke in my chambers near dawn. My sword lay unsheathed at the foot of my bed, and the rusty brown of dried blood stained its edge. I felt nauseous and became ill; the bile that rose was stained red. I do not know whether the blood in my stomach came from Satan's Chalice or from somewhere else. I have not tried to find out. But I have dared the city streets since, and none have eyed me any more curiously than usual. The guard did not attempt to arrest me.

Two other things I must mention of that night. The moon was not full. No reports surfaced in the city of wolves.

Whatever I did, I did as myself.

For a brief time then, I considered abandoning my work, to spend what years are left me away from my fellow man and my past. I felt I was losing myself to her. But I realized that I had done that long ago. My decision was never really in doubt—the past called me back then, just as it has now.

Things got worse. My talent can deceive me, for I have felt at times that I am like unto a god. Such powers this pool of blood grants me! And yet they are treacherous sorceries, denying me those I most crave to see inside: Astrid, Scacath, Megan.

Aralak's was perhaps the strongest mind besides Thyri's I have managed thus far to enter. His tongue was not too unlike that of the Habnakys and the other Southern tribes. Even his gods were similar. Earth Mother—akiya toyn. Like Aphrodite/Venus and Ares/Mars of the first and second great Southern empires. But there were differences. Akiya toyn was, by legend, one with the land of her children. The Earth Mother was thus also, but she desired more. And in desiring more, she lost a part of the beauty at her roots. Her people were never truly happy, never at one with themselves.

Once I dared to look into those dream-walks with Aralak's goddess. His thoughts turned to them often enough, and the idea that she appeared to him as a woman in need of physical pleasure and comfort intrigued me. Not, I think, because the idea was unique—far from it. But I wondered just to what extent she exerted her will over his. In truth, I wondered if she existed at all. And if she did, I wondered if she possessed power enough to release Thyri from her curse. Beyond that, I wondered at her motivations—what moved her to seek more? To push her followers out of her bosom, to conquer realms she seemed to desire in much the same way a child desires the stars? So many other gods have taken such paths—I sought for myself an insight into their ways.

I didn't gain it. I learned, in fact, very little except that she did exist—as Pohati saw her: tall, with large eyes, a long face, and a sad beauty that paled the splendor of life around her. And she *did* wield power. I saw her for but a moment; then a force more ravaging than the sea against a cliffside struck into my mind. I am not a cliffside that might prevail against such a force. I am made of flesh, bone, and blood—not rock. The impact hurled me from the side of my pool and smashed me against the wall of my room. I think for a time I lost consciousness; I do not remember (unconsciousness seldom carries lasting visions).

I have not since attempted my art upon a deity unless one counts Thyri herself among the grouping. I have little desire to do so in the future, but I cannot write that I'll never try again.

I felt some trepidation the morning I arose to research that battle in *Hagara Kohn*. I was gazing already into a phase of Thyri's life about which I knew nothing, about which I scarcely had clues. I *had* been with her in battle before, but not when she had been so in tune with her brethren of the wood, and not when I had no idea of the battle's outcome and the nature of the events that would immediately follow. For instance, I've assumed, all along, that Thyri will survive—all events thus far covered precede my initial encounter with her. But where I knew for a fact that Kaerglen Isle would not sink during Thyri's battle with Pye, my *personal* experience of details in the new land extends out of ignorance at only one point, that being my acquaintance with Kuorok, another being closed to me, and another like Thyri to whom past reflections do not come easy.

Seated by my pool, thinking these things, and preparing to partake of the blood that would give me vision, I dwelt again on the episode with Akan and how I had nearly lost myself and the strength of my purpose in those brief, fantastically intense moments. A full year still separated my researches from that day I would meet Thyri in a Danish port far from the new land. The Thyri I met resembled little the *akiya toyn* of the new land, and whatever her memories of these events I now relate, they were not such that she wished to speak freely of them. To my present knowledge, she never spoke of them openly to anyone—and only to Megan, in any way at all. Deep within me, I feared for her.

I sensed that the battle in *Hagara Kohn* contained within it the seeds of her future misery and anarchistic fury. If a great tragedy had befallen her that day (and I imagined I might see her entire army perish and Thyri reduced to slavery or worse by Aralak's wrath), I did not want to be within her when it happened. I feared what that might do to my own sanity.

So I took extra precautions that morning. I quaffed two full cups of blood, hoping I would thereby acquire strength far exceeding my usual. I observed Thyri after the change, then sought a perspective that would grant me safety as well as a view of the battle. I chose a bird—one of the bright red ones that are alien, as far as I know, to other shores. Its thoughts were extremely simple, and I found that, to some degree, I could exert my will over it by suggesting, for instance, that wherever I wanted to look was where it should look for the possibility of food. I found also, however, that its visual apparatus differs greatly from mine—things are much flatter through a bird's eye, colors are far paler, and a sudden movement tends to appear as little more than a threatening or edible blur depending on its size and speed.

The bird was useful for observing the overall direction of activities, but useless for details. I found myself that day jumping my perspective into and out of Thyri, Aralak, and a few others, ready to retreat back into the bird at the slightest sign of danger. Due to the diversity of events, I was required to observe sometimes the same span of time through different eyes so that, in the end, I had lived the battle fully twice, and certain parts of it five times.

And this day, I concede, consumed me, terrified me—for Thyri knew I was there. It was just before she joined battle with Aralak: no sound or movement escaped her; she could detect, for instance, the unnatural breathing of a nearby bird.

I had left it there, of course. I had desired to experience with Thyri the seemingly harmless moments preceding the conflict. But I hadn't dared to remove myself from it entirely. I held it still in my grip with tenuous strands of my consciousness. My meddling in this manner had somehow affected its metabolism. And Thyri felt the tang of sorcery! When her cold, deadly gaze fell upon the bird, then did my nightmares truly begin. Thyri's perceptions had exceeded, through her newfound harmony with her dual existence, any level that had previously held them, and the power that flowed through her was so heady, so intoxicating, that I feared complete loss of myself to her if I let go of the bird. But if I remained exactly where I was and she felt a need to kill it?

I retreated completely into the bird and forced it into the air. I have yet to experience death within a psychic host. I have more than passing reason to fear that Death's fingers might yet reach me through my voyeuristic endeavors.

I must write that I observed later those same moments from fully inside Thyri. The rushes of power the second time were not so intense, and I think that I might overcome in time those sensations of subjugation by practicing this art of mine on particular instances of Thyri's time line. I have yet to pursue this speculation in depth. At any rate, I stayed with her the second time through my departure the first. I wished to understand the exact extent of her awareness of sorcery. It began the same time as it did the first. It ended just when I had first left. So, once I was back fully in the bird, she couldn't sense me. Yet I still fear that somehow she *might* have. Aralak's war cry at the same moment must have distracted a significant part of her concentration. I think that she might have been capable even of sensing the subtle power in her sword. She did not, but I think the only reason for that is this: her senses extended into that blade forged by Scacath. It was a part of her then. She had not trained herself to sense sorcery *within* herself.

This past week I have completed my investigations of Thyri's involvement in matters across the Great Ocean. What I offer here, however, is slight:

Thyri spent the remainder of her time in the new land wandering, keeping to herself. Her heart was dark, and it grew darker.

Of the details of this new darkness I *cannot* write—the thought of doing so has kept me sleepless for several nights. And, I'm thinking, it has no bearing on the events I intend to relate.

But that's not precisely true. I expect I'll continue to lose much sleep dwelling on this decision. Perhaps, in time, I can find the words.

Last night my investigation took me into the new land of the present—the new land of today. I desired to see Thyri's legacy—her small empire, so long after she'd abandoned it. The empire still stands. Togarin is strong, and he has kept the legend of akiya nagara and her victory over the might of the Arakoy alive. The very pass in which they fought is now a north-south trade route, and both Habnakys and Arakoy feet tread regularly the ground upon which their fathers shed blood.

Kuorok also became legend to them. He is *haiki grag*—war-chief of the blood. It is said that Thyri has returned to him, and that he is shadowed everywhere by a huge, gray wolf. Among the Habnakys there is a new song that the children sing while in the woods. It calls out greeting to Kuorok, and it asks for his favor should a darkness arrive to harm them at play.

Of Elaine: she has become a warrior under Togarin. She thinks herself Habnakys and remembers nothing of her past on Kaerglen Island. She has not taken a husband. It is said that Kuorok loves her.

I must write one last thing—concerning Non Sai. He never truly wakened from his attempt to enter Thyri's dreams. He was found dead within the remains of Aralak's last camp.